THAT DEVIL'S

NO FRIEND

OF MINE

THAT DEVIL'S

NO FRIEND

OF MINE

J. D. MASON

ST. MARTIN'S PRESS ❧ NEW YORK

This is a work of fiction. All of the characters, organizations, and events portrayed in this novel are either products of the author's imagination or are used fictitiously.

www.stmartins.com

Book Design by Rich Arnold.

Library of Congress Cataloging-in-Publication Data

Mason, J. D.
    That devil's no friend of mine / J. D. Mason.—1st edition:.
        p.   cm.
    ISBN-13: 978-0-312-36885-2
    ISBN-10: 0-312-36885-2
  1. African Americans—Fiction.   2. African American families—
Fiction.   3. Morticians—Fiction.   4. Interpersonal relations—Fiction.
5. Family secrets —Fiction.   6. Domestic fiction.   I. Title.
    PS3613.A817T53   2009
    813'.6—dc22

                                                          2008035456

First Edition: March 2009

10   9   8   7   6   5   4   3   2   1

THAT DEVIL'S

NO FRIEND

OF MINE

PROLOGUE

The day Bishop Fontaine was buried, more than two hundred people gathered together to bid farewell and lay him to rest. Kristine Fontaine, his only child, was cloaked in black as she sat in the front row, her eyes fixed on her father's body surrounded by white satin in his silver coffin. She blinked through tears, half-expecting the mighty Bishop Fontaine to surprise everyone, and sit straight up in that coffin like he'd just been sleeping, all the while praying silently to herself that he was gone for good.

"The Bible says that there is a friend who is closer than a brother," his best friend and business partner Lamar Brown said at the end of his eulogy. "Bishop Lee Fontaine was my friend. He was my best friend, and I know that I speak for us all when I say that he will be missed."

Amens filled the church as Lamar stepped down from the podium, and on the massive stage the choir, dressed in white, rose to their feet to begin a soulful rendition of "Amazing Grace." Bishop was regal and elegant, and most people often mistook his first name for his profession. His mother had been a spirit-filled woman who believed her son was ordained for greatness when he was born, so she named him Bishop. But he ended up becoming a mortician instead.

Bishop Fontaine had been a handsome man: strong, tall, dark, with unnaturally light eyes. Out of all his siblings, he had been the darkest, but he had light eyes like the rest of them, making him look strangely haunting, as if he was from another world. Kristine had his eyes, but that was the only physical trait she inherited from him. Before her mother died, the memories she had of her father were that of a happier man, one who laughed all the time and loved openly and freely. But he had changed after her mother became ill and as her mother died, so had the joy in her father.

Growing up, she was the fat girl, the ugly girl whose father was a mortician. Needless to say, she wasn't very popular. Looking back, she'd seen the transition in photographs of her father, the long dark shadow he had cast over her. In later pictures, it was painfully obvious that he wasn't the same man he'd once been and the dark brooding that had replaced his personality had soon filled that house he refused to move from, and had even washed over Kristine. She had become a prisoner of his grief and it wasn't until he died that she was finally set free.

Maybe it would've been different had she been allowed to be more like other kids, if she'd been allowed to wear the same kinds of clothes, or to participate in school activities and dances. Bishop wouldn't let her exhale without permission, let alone live a so-called "normal" life. Kristine never asked why, and she never argued. His will was her will and whatever burden he bore, she bore it, too. Losing her mother had left him devastated, and the thing he feared most of all was losing her again in Kristine.

"You look so much like your momma," he would often say.

As much as she relished the fact, she hated it, too, because maybe if she'd looked like someone else, perhaps he would've given her room to breathe.

Kristine couldn't take her eyes off of him. She stared at her father's lifeless body as if she was in a trance, as everyone in the room showered her with sympathy and concern. That's not what she needed. Kristine needed to close that casket, lock him in it, and to run as fast as she could from that church and her father.

She had been sixteen when her mother died from ovarian cancer, and ever since then, it had only been her and her father living in that big house in Woodbridge, Virginia. Kristine was now twenty-nine years old, and she'd never lived away from home. She'd never even given it much thought. Her place had always been by his side and the two of them settled into that fact a long time ago.

Every once in a while, growing up, Kristine would test Bishop's mighty waters. She was nineteen and pushed the limits of her curfew to eleven o'clock. When she walked in the front door, with her Uncle Lamar in tow, Bishop was waiting in the parlor. He met her at the door, and the look on his face made her hang her head in shame.

"Thank you, Lamar," he said, solemnly, "for helping my child to finally find her way home."

"I went to the movies, Daddy," she muttered. "I asked you if I could go."

"As long as it was over before ten," he said sternly.

"I stopped to eat afterwards," she argued, quietly.

"You have food here, Kristine."

Finally, she found the courage to look at him. "Daddy, I'm nineteen." She nearly raised her voice, but didn't. "It's eleven o'clock on a Saturday night. I don't see why I have to be home so early, when other kids my age. . . ."

Bishop would never lower himself to argue with her, or anyone else for that matter. He didn't have to. Her father pulled back his shoulders, gazed down his nose at her, and dismissed her to her room, with nothing more than a look.

"Bishop," Larmar said, "I found her in a coffee shop eating pie. She wasn't doing anything wrong," he argued in her defense.

Bishop walked past him to the door, and held it open for him to leave. "What she did wrong, Brown," he explained calmly, "was to worry her father because he had no idea where she was. She's a good girl. Nobody knows that better than me. But I can't speak for everybody else and things they're capable of. Kristine is naïve, and it wouldn't be hard for the wrong person to take advantage of her and hurt her. As long as I'm here, I can't let that happen."

Kristine shuddered at the memory and blinked away tears. She would miss him, but not for long.

"It's just God's will, sweetheart," a woman said, gathering her in her arms. "We all have our time to go, and Bishop knew that better than anybody."

"Be strong, sister," a man told her, pressing her hand between his.

"Don't close yourself up in that house, now. We're all here for you and we'll check up on you from time to time."

Everybody believed her heart was broken, They all believed she was too shocked to speak or to cry, or too proud to break down in front of so many people. Kristine was going to miss her father more than anyone would ever understand and after they all disappeared and she was alone in her house, she'd probably finally let herself cry. But for now, she was overwhelmed, speechless, and awed by the fact that for the first time in her life, she was finally and absolutely free.

Lamar had been ashamed of his thoughts when he'd heard that Bishop, a few months shy of his sixtieth birthday, had died suddenly of a heart attack. An older man than Lamar, Bishop had mentored him and in his own quiet way, had embraced Lamar like he was a younger brother.

When he met Bishop, Lamar was struggling to support his young family, Rhonda and their two small children, working full time during the day as a janitor at a local high school, and finding whatever odd job he could in the evenings. At the time, Bishop was a mortician at Beekman's Funeral Home in Alexandria, Virginia. He hired Lamar to keep the floors and toilets cleaned.

Gradually, the two men developed a friendship, and Bishop began to teach Lamar the skills of his trade.

"Never thought I'd find myself embalming anybody," Lamar said as he carefully followed Bishop's direction, and prepared an elderly woman for burial.

Bishop laughed. "Well, not too many people come into this line of work on purpose. But there is a need. There's always a need, son."

"Money's pretty good, too, from what I hear."

Bishop nodded. "Indeed. It most certainly can be."

Lamar became Bishop's assistant until the day Fred Beekman retired, and Bishop decided to buy the business.

"I'm a better mortician than you, Lamar." Bishop smiled. "But I think you've got a better head for business than I do. I could use a partner."

"You serious?" Lamar asked, holding back his excitement.

"Dead," Bishop said dryly, and then burst out laughing.

They bought it and changed the name to F&B Funeral Services. That had been nearly twenty-five years ago.

While the choir sang, Lamar took his seat next to his wife Rhonda, sitting in the front pew. He stared at Bishop's regal form, knowing that he was going to miss this man more than anyone he'd ever known. But in the midst of his grief and heartache, Lamar was appalled at himself. Bishop's death had been a tragedy, but in it he also saw a doorway open. Lamar held his wife's hand in his lap, but his thoughts lingered on Kristine and the very real possibility that with Bishop gone, he could finally have the one thing he coveted most in this world.

Cole Burkette came to Bishop's funeral without his usual entourage of personal assistants, publicists, or bodyguards. Bishop was family. Before Cole left Philadelphia to move to DC to begin his training as a boxer in the professional ranks, his Aunt Irene had made him swear to look up Bishop Fontaine as soon as he got there.

"He's my second cousin, which probably don't make him much kin to you, but that don't matter to Bishop. If you get there and you need food to eat or a place to sleep, Bishop will surely make room for you."

Cole had never needed Bishop's hospitality, but he sure appreciated it when he could get to it. After his career took off, and Cole suddenly found himself sitting on the edge of his first title fight, he had driven down to Woodbridge the night before, and sat with Bishop and Kristine, who had pretty much stared and grinned at him whenever he was around. She was cute. But she was family, which definitely made her off limits.

Cole sat on the porch next to Bishop; neither of them

saying much for a while. But that was Bishop's way, unhurried and calming. "That boy got a mean right hook," he eventually said to Cole. "If he tags you with it, that'll be all she wrote."

Cole smiled. "I think mine is meaner, Bishop."

Bishop nodded, and then inhaled deeply on his pipe. "Yeah," he slowly let the smoke seep from his nostrils, "I know. But do me a favor, son," he turned to Cole. "Do me a favor and duck when you see it coming—for me."

The old man was big on family, which for Cole, was a wake-up call coming from his home environment in South Philadelphia. Cole had never known a steadier role model in his life than Bishop. His own father was a sorry mothafucka, and the men he knew growing up as a kid were flawed and always finished their sentences with the same testament, "I'm doing the best I can." For Bishop, he never had to say it. All you ever had to do was watch him, and you could see him doing the best he could, which was pretty damn good as far as Cole was concerned.

He was solid, and Cole aspired to be the same kind of man when it came to his own family. He wanted kids someday, but that day seemed to stretch further into the future every time he broached the subject with his wife Nora, who'd never spent more than ten minutes talking to Bishop.

"He's a mortician, Cole," she said, packing for another impromptu trip to Europe for a cover shoot of Italian *Vogue*. Cole had to accept the fact that international fashion models and morticians just didn't have much to say to each other.

"He gives me the creeps, baby. I know he's your family, but—"

But Nora always did what Nora wanted to do. Bishop made that observation the moment he met her. Cole worked overtime not to let it get to him, but he was slowly but surely learning a tough lesson about marriage. Love, sometimes, was just not enough. Cole had invited Bishop to a dinner party not long after he and Nora had gotten married. Nora did what she did best—be Nora James, international supermodel—and while everyone else in the room flitted around her like moths to a flame, Bishop kept his distance and watched it happen. Cole was used to it, of course, but he knew that Bishop wasn't, so he went to try and help Bishop understand the kind of woman Nora was, and the world she'd grown up in. Bishop listened, while Cole tried to explain that all the attention and accolades was normal for Nora.

Bishop nodded, understandingly, but he never took his eyes off of her. "'Normal' and 'Nora' are two words that don't even belong in the same sentence, son," Bishop responded, and smiled. "You got your hands full with that one." With that, Bishop took a sip of his martini, and turned and walked away.

Sugar daddies came in all shapes and sizes, but Bishop had been exceptional because the only thing he wanted from Rayne Fitzgerald was what she wanted for herself—a second chance.

None of these people knew her or the impact Bishop had on her life. No one knew how far he'd gone to save her from herself. Rayne was a different woman because of him. She was clean and sober, and still breathing thanks to Bishop, so yes, she had every right to cry right alongside the rest of them.

He'd buried her husband, J. T., four years ago. Only Bishop and Rayne had attended J. T.'s wake.

"Today we're putting your husband in the ground, sweetheart," he'd consoled her, placing his arm around her shoulder. "How long do you think it's going to be before I'm here burying you if you don't change your ways?"

He wasn't a minister or anything, but Rayne had opened up to him as if he was ordained. J. T. had been her life, her love, he'd meant everything to her, but what had killed him, was killing her, too, and Bishop was there to catch her before her final fall. She had wanted to die with J. T., but Bishop wouldn't let her give up so easily. Rayne squeezed her eyes shut, and silently thanked God.

"I can't do it alone, Bishop," she sobbed that day. "I'm not strong enough to do this by myself."

Bishop chuckled. "Oh, I think you might be stronger than you think, but I wouldn't dream of letting you take something like that on all by yourself, darlin'."

He took her to rehab that same day they buried her husband and stayed with her until visiting hours were over. Bishop found her a small apartment to live in, and paid her rent, bought her food, even got her some cable TV. He never gave her cash, but Rayne didn't have to worry about anything, except recovering, and finding that lost person inside herself that she'd drowned in heroin through the years.

How many times had she called him, on the verge of hopelessness or disaster? Bishop never failed to answer. He never told her to call him back in the morning, or that this was a bad time and he'd have to talk to her later.

"I can't seem to bring myself to get out of bed today, Bishop," she'd told him once over the phone. "What's going to happen to me today if I walk out that door? And what if I have to make a choice, and it's the wrong one?" Rayne sobbed like a child.

He sighed deeply before finally responding. "Where's your faith, girl?" he asked, tenderly. "You need to believe in *you*, Rayne, the way I believe in you. You need to know that you can do the right thing, because you did it yesterday, and the day before that."

"But I might not do it today," she whispered. "I might not be strong enough."

He laughed. "You're strong enough, Rayne. When are you going to figure that out?"

She found dreams, courage, and hope because of him. She found her voice again, but now that he was gone, Rayne had to make a conscious effort to swallow her fear all on her own. Bishop had been the one to keep it at bay. Who was going to do that now?

• • •

Every culture needed a firm foundation to build upon. Until Bishop's death, Rhonda Brown had no idea the impact losing him would have on hers. It was an unsettling feeling that she'd been unable to shake ever since she'd gotten the news that he'd passed away. Every day for the last twenty-five years, Bishop had had some sort of influence in her life, on her husband, and on her marriage. Bishop and Lamar saw or spoke to each other every single day. Rhonda had stepped in and became somewhat of a surrogate mother to his daughter Kristine after her mother, Violet, died of cancer. All of their lives had been interwoven together by the thread that was Bishop Fontaine, and now that he was gone, Rhonda couldn't shake the dreadful feeling that, somehow, it was all going to unravel right before her eyes.

Lamar could hardly keep his eyes off of that girl. No one else seemed to notice, but Rhonda certainly couldn't help but to pay attention. He was her husband and the father of her two children, and they were both about to become grandparents. He was a fifty-year-old man, and had practically helped raise that girl—woman. She swallowed her disgust, and shifted uncomfortably next to her husband, squeezed his hand in hers, and prayed silently that it was only her imagination working overtime, and not some horrible truth held in check by the man lying dead in that casket.

WHO DO

YOU

LOVE?

HE'D CHAIN-SMOKE HER IF HE COULD

Tauris Diggs sat in the back of the room, cloaked in darkness, sipping on gin and tonic, taking her in an inch at a time. Rayne was built like rhythms, with flowing lines curving into hips, thighs, and ass. She didn't have much on top, but it didn't matter. Tauris glanced around the room wondering if anyone in that audience could see his fingerprints on her skin. Could they see the impression his lips had left on hers? No. And it was all well and good, too, because these people weren't grown enough to bear witness to the kind of shit he and Rayne did in private.

Sweet comic valentine
You make me smile with my heart

Addictions were dangerous. Addictions to a woman like Rayne Fitzgerald were lethal and he figured out months ago that he was a lost cause beyond salvation, destined to go belly up at her feet when the time came. Her shit was that good. Rayne was hell to deal with sometimes, but that bad-ass attitude of hers just seemed too much like right paired with the rest of her. She was a walking, talking, blues ballad. The kind that made you cry and left you wanting more just so you could cry again. Tauris was a fool over her, and she knew it. And that was the worst part.

Your lips are laughable
Unphotographable

She was breathtaking in white. White against her blue-black skin looked sacred and mystic. Rayne worked the hell out of it, too, swaying her hips slowly back and forth, as the light bounced off each and every sequin on that gown, hypnotizing and lulling people into the spell that was her. Rayne's long locks were piled high on her head like a crown, and full, moist lips circled every syllable that came from her mouth.

"People want magic when you get up on that stage," she'd explained to him. "They listen for it and look for it. Sequins, a sick-ass melody, some soul coming up from your gut and out of your mouth—throw in some booze and the whole scene unfolds like a dream right in front of their eyes," she winked and smiled. "That's what I do for a living, baby. I make dreams come true."

She sure was making his come true when she wasn't treating him like a reject. Hot one minute, cold the next, Rayne dismissed him when she was through, then snapped her fingers and whistled when she needed him. Tauris swore he wasn't going to keep putting up with her, but of course he did. And he would keep on until she decided to stop snapping fingers and whistling for him. They both knew that.

He wouldn't have taken that kind of behavior from any other woman, but then, Rayne wasn't just any woman. Standing back watching the crowd, he caught more than one man salivating at the sight of her. Hell, even a few women in the room stared at her like she was a meal.

"I want you to wait for me after the show," she'd told him earlier. Rayne's gritty and worn voice was deep and Southern, even when she wasn't singing, and it comforted him and seduced him, drawing him in like a lullaby.

He didn't respond, thinking he could outplay her in this game between them where she made up the rules as she went along. *Play it hard, man,* he told himself. *Don't be a punk and give in so easily. Make her sweat. Tell her you've got something to do.*

She seemed to sense this small internal war he waged inside himself, and she turned from her reflection in the mirror, walked over to where he stood, and ran her finger lightly across his lower lip, then kissed the corner of his mouth. "Come on, Tauris," she whispered. Rayne took his lip between her teeth, and bit down slightly. "I need you tonight, baby. What? You gonna make me beg for it?"

Women like her were a luxury. The best most men could ever do was to jack off to the fantasy of her. Rayne was that rare exotic jewel that few would ever get to put their hands on, and here she was, practically begging for him. He didn't need to bother saying yes. She saw his answer in his eyes and felt it in his pants. Rayne laughed mockingly, patted his cheek, and left him sitting in her dressing room.

"This next little number is dedicated to a good friend of mine," she spoke to the crowd, and then winked in his direction. "It's off my last CD, a song written by Joel Lewis and Tammy Jacobs, and it's called, 'Too Much Woman for You.'"

The audience howled and clapped. Tauris shifted uneasily in his seat.

"But don't worry, baby," she smiled at him, making it obvious to anyone who was paying attention that he was on her radar. "I promise to take it easy on you."

Everyone in the room laughed. Rayne laughed the loudest. Tauris didn't laugh at all. He just took another sip from his glass, and tried not to look offended.

THE CONTENDER

Rage was sexy. Nora James got off on pissing him off. She pushed his buttons when she needed her husband to do what he did best—fight. She started shit with him because he'd never dream of starting it with her, and sometimes, that's exactly what she needed from him.

The imperfection of routine drove her crazy sometimes, and Cole drove her mad with his ideas for order and his need for everything to be just right. He had notions about marriage she could never fully buy into, and ideals about her that she could never live up to. Hell, she didn't even want to. Despite what he thought he wanted whenever he looked at her, Nora wasn't the perfect little wife he believed her to be. She knew exactly which buttons to push to get him going, and when she did, the fight inside their palatial Prince George's County home was on, and Nora was exhilarated.

He had a handful of her hair, and had pushed her down to her knees. Nora could taste the blood in her mouth. "You push me too damn far, Nora! And your ass isn't happy until I put my fist in your fuckin' mouth!"

Cole was barefoot, and wearing only a pair of white pajama bottoms. Her blood smeared on one pant leg. Every muscle on his body tensed and squared as he held her head back.

"Go ahead, mothafucka!" she said, commanding him to do it, daring him to do it. Nora's voice strained in her throat. "Hit me, Cole! But you'd better make sure you knock my ass out this time, because if you don't, as soon as I get up from here, I swear I'll kill you!"

He'd knocked out men in the ring with a single blow. He could've shut her up with one. She didn't understand how powerful he was, and if he didn't love her, Cole easily could have killed her.

In her bare feet, she stood six feet tall. Nora's mother was Scandanavian, her father black. Her golden complexion and exotic features had graced the covers of fashion magazines around the world when she was younger. She strutted run-ways with the best of them: Tyra Banks, Naomi Campbell, Heidi Klum. Nora left the catwalk for him.

Breathtaking and gorgeous, he could hardly keep his eyes off her one minute; the next, all he could think about was beating her to a bloody pulp. It took every ounce of restraint he had not to follow through and break her fuck-ing face, but if he went too far, he knew he could shut her up forever and lose everything he'd worked so hard for his whole life, including her. In disgust, he pushed her down hard onto the floor, and started to walk away.

"It's not worth it!"

She watched him leave the room, and slam the door shut

behind him. Nora managed to crawl over to the bed, pull herself up, and sit on the edge. She spit blood from her mouth from where he'd hit her.

"Don't worry about where I've been," she'd told him smugly as soon as he walked through the front door. He called her while he was out of town, but Nora never answered her phone. He'd left messages, and she never returned any of them. If anything, he was concerned about her and questioned her for that reason when he returned home. It was Nora who'd taken his concern and twisted it into accusations, and she used it as a means to an end. Nora had been with another man, and it wasn't the first time. It certainly wouldn't be the last time. She squeezed her eyes shut, appalled by things she'd done. She stifled a sob, tormented in her own twisted emotions for loving him with her heart and soul, and needing something from him so badly, it nearly killed her to pull it out of him.

"They've got a name for people like you," her lover told her once. "Sadomasochist. If it doesn't hurt, then it doesn't feel good." He had laughed, and then smacked her hard across the face.

"Not the face, lover," she scolded him softly. "You know better."

Cole would never understand. Cole would never give in to her needs that way. And Nora hated herself for needing him to. Her imagination reeled with images of what she wanted him to do to her. Those thoughts pooled warm and moist in her panties, and before she realized what she was doing, Nora followed her husband downstairs and found him sitting defeated and exhausted in the dark in their living room, staring at the fire burning in the fireplace. Cole never even heard her come into the room, and he never saw what she hit him with.

He fell to the floor, clutching his head, then looked at his hand and saw that it was covered in blood. Nora pounced on him, screaming and scratching at him like a wild animal.

"Do it! Be a man, Cole!" she screamed over and over again.

He grabbed her by the wrists, then rolled her over and pinned her underneath him. "What the hell—Stop it, Nora! Fuckin' stop . . ."

Cole could never understand that Nora could never stop. She wanted him, needed him too badly to stop. And no matter what it cost either of them, Nora was determined to get him to do what she needed most.

She wrapped her long legs around his midsection, and thrust her hips up to his. Nora had peeled off her panties and left them somewhere on the stairs. Blood dripped down the side of his face, and the more she struggled to get free of his grasp, the more turned on she became.

"Come on, Cole," she whispered, breathless. Nora used the strength in her legs to pull him toward her. She ground herself against him. "Be a man," she said, gritting her teeth, and glaring at him, daring him not to fuck her. "Be a gotdamned man, Cole."

The look on his face broke her heart, but if she needed to

break his heart to get this from him, then it would be worth it. "You're insane."

"Yeah, and you're a fuckin' pussy," she rolled her hips against him, and Cole's body responded the only way it could. "Put it in, Cole. You know you want to. You know you want to, fucker!" Nora raised her head, met his lips with her own, and pushed her tongue into his mouth.

She managed to break free of his grasp, and then reached down and pulled out his rigid penis. Nora guided it into her, and moaned her satisfaction as he pushed inside her. "Hard, Cole!" she commanded. Nora wrapped her arms around him, bit down hard on his ear lobe, and ordered him again. "I said, hard . . . harder, baby! Give it to me, Cole! Give it all to me!"

They were one of the world's most stunning couples: Nora James, supermodel, the face of Opulence cosmetics and a runway consultant, and Cole Burkette, making his run for the middleweight championship of the world for the second time. Their faces were on the covers of magazines, they walked down Hollywood red carpets, and at international fashion events, and had even done a spread in *Vogue* magazine as a featured couple showcasing Karl Lagerfeld's newest collection, while discussing the challenges of being married and holding it together in a world that wouldn't give them an inch of privacy.

But if the world knew the lengths to which she had to go, to get sexual satisfaction from her man, the world would turn on its ear.

GRITS AND BISCUITS

There were some things in life that were just breathtaking to behold, like a handsome black man lying bare-assed naked in her bed. Rayne stood in the doorway of her bedroom for several minutes just taking him all in, relishing the long, exhaustive, fulfilling night they'd shared together. After the bout of good loving Tauris had given her, the least she could do was to repay him with a good, decent home-cooked meal.

Some of her memories growing up were good ones. Like the ones of Nana, her grandmother, who rose before dawn to fry thick strips of peppered bacon and mix a batch of dough for those homemade biscuits of hers. That smell of breakfast cooking sweetened her dreams and made her stomach growl long before she opened her eyes in the morning. Rayne smiled warmly at the memories.

"Wake your ass up, T. Diggs," Rayne said seductively, pressing soft, warm lips against his. "You know you can't sleep through all that Southern, home-cooked deliciousness."

"What can't I sleep through?" he asked groggily.

"Inhale," she said seductively. "Anything that smells that good will drag you out of bed by your ear, if you ain't careful."

Tauris wrapped his arms around her, and rolled her underneath him.

Rayne laughed, and turned her face from his. "Ewww, nah!" she grimaced. "I ain't giving up no sugar to that bad-ass breath you got." She playfully slapped his behind.

Tauris Diggs was handsome, and knew it. Six feet tall, muscular, cinnamon brown complexion. He had a movie-star smile, with teeth bright enough to blind a sister if the sun hit them just right. He could have his choice of just about any woman he wanted. And the one he wanted most lay pinned beneath him, wearing a forest-green apron that read "Kiss the cook" on the bib, a champagne-lace teddy beneath that, with pink and purple fuzzy socks on her feet.

"What's for breakfast, baby?" he asked, inhaling deep enough to almost taste it.

"Let's see," she cleared her throat. "Ham steak, grits, scrambled cheese-eggs, and my grandmomma's famous homemade buttermilk biscuits just waiting to sop up some thick, sweet country molasses."

He looked surprised. "Damn! What time did you wake up?"

Rayne smiled sensuously, and ran a manicured finger along the side of his face. "I woke up with the sun, lover. Rayne Fitzgerald is phenomenal. I thought you knew."

"Oh, I know now, sugar." He kissed the mounds of her small breasts. "How about another go round before we eat?"

Rayne sucked her teeth and pushed him off her. She scooted off the bed and headed out the room. "I'll be damned if I'm fucking before breakfast." She swished her entire ass, wiggling like Jell-O out of the room. "Wash your hands and brush your teeth before you sit down at my table."

You can take the girl out of the South, but she'll damn sure bring it with her no matter where she goes. Rayne didn't cook much these days, and she missed it.

Tauris smacked his lips, licked his fingers, and never raised his head more than two inches from his plate. She cringed when he doused hot sauce on her eggs. "Why the hell you messing up my cheese-eggs like that, fool?"

Rayne snatched the bottle from him, and he smiled like a mischievous kid. "You put your foot in this meal, baby. And I don't even like grits." He heaped a fork full in his mouth. "Mmmm."

There were moments, like this, when she appreciated Tauris Diggs. Moments when she felt almost normal and free to be like any other woman having breakfast with her man. Moments when she wasn't afraid, or defensive, or tormented by her past, and it was okay to care, maybe even to love, a man like him.

As she watched him enjoy every bite of the meal she'd

made, Rayne couldn't help but to smile inside. Tauris called himself being in love. Every time he said it, it pissed her off. And it hurt her down to the core because she was too fucked up to let herself say it back, let alone feel it.

"Love is reserved for people who don't have as much to lose as I do, T. Diggs," she'd told him once. He stared at her like she was crazy when she said it. Maybe it didn't make sense at first, but it would make perfect sense if he'd been through what she'd been through.

"Who the hell doesn't have a lot to lose, Rayne?" he'd asked. "Shit, we've all been hurt. We've all been burned. So, you've been burned by drugs and a husband who didn't give a shit—"

"Don't go there!" She wouldn't let him talk like that about J. T. Rayne wouldn't let anybody talk about him that way. "Be careful, Tauris. I swear to God—"

He never brought up J. T.'s name again.

In another life, she could see herself letting go, and falling for Tauris Diggs. The sex was good. The man was good. Tauris was that dependable type. The kind a woman could count on to make the money and pay the bills. The kind who would do his best to be supportive and generous to a fault. He might even be a tad bit bossy, though, the take-charge type who thought he could fix everything and take care of everybody in the house. It all sounded good in theory, but in real life, Rayne knew that just wasn't for her. Or maybe, she just felt that she didn't deserve it, but that was a conversation for the *Dr. Phil* show.

Of course, after breakfast, Rayne found herself straddling him on the living room floor, riding that big, black pony for all he was worth. Dick in the morning was the breakfast of champions, and Tauris was the man to beat.

"Mmmmmm, baby," she said breathless, her head thrown back, hips rolling wide circles on top of him. Tauris held on tight to her hips and stared up at her, afraid that if he said a word, he'd break the spell. "Ooooh, you got it, T. Diggs," she moaned. "Damn! Damn, baby! Shiii . . ."

Her long, beautiful locks brushed against his face and chest. Beautiful, blue-black Rayne hovered over him like a spirit, her juices sweeter than the molasses he still tasted on his lips.

She leaned down as if to kiss him, but instead she licked the outline of his lips with the tip of her tongue. Rayne stared deep into his eyes, her plump behind rising and falling against his palms.

"You do me good, Daddy," she whispered. "You do me so damn good."

Rayne sat back up, hissed like a snake, closed her eyes, and bucked wildly until she made the mistake of pulling his orgasm from him first, but thankfully, hers wasn't far behind.

They lay collapsed together on the floor, next to each other. Tauris spooned behind Rayne, draping his arm across her waist.

"You ought to do us both a favor and let me get used to this," he said quietly.

He played his role in this game the way he always did, trying to convince her to see the situation his way, and to let go of all her reservations so that the two of them could finally be together for real. Rayne treated him like a king one minute, and then turned a cold shoulder to him the next whenever he broached the subject of anything permanent happening between them.

"We could do this, baby." He kissed the side of her face. "I know we could."

Rayne tensed up, and jerked away from him. "Please," she said, annoyed. She sat up, and ran her hands through her hair. "Why you got to ruin it, Tauris?"

"Since when would the two of us together ruin anything?" he asked, offended.

He wanted something and she wouldn't give it to him, and all it did was make him want to work harder. Rayne was a challenge and damn if he didn't get off on rising to challenges.

"We were together a few minutes ago all over my living room floor. How much more together do you need to be?" Rayne got up and went into the bathroom. She knew he'd bring it up. He always did. And she always let her agitation show through, enough to wound his ego and to make him take a step back.

She turned on the shower and stepped into it before the water had a chance to heat up. Tauris was worse than a woman, sometimes, always feeling shit he had no business feeling, and worse, wanting to tell her about it.

He wore his feelings like ugly clothes, and insisted on trying to share them like she wanted anything to do with it. The water slowly warmed and Rayne stood still while it washed over her from the top of her head down to her toes. She felt sorry for him. She felt annoyed by him, but dammit if she couldn't get him out of her system.

Tauris stepped into the shower behind her, wrapped both arms around her, and held her. Rayne closed her eyes and let him. If she'd met him first, she'd have fallen head over heels in love with him. If she'd loved him first, so many things in her life would've been different. Rayne might not be up all night singing in clubs and dives. Maybe she could've been happy without the drama of a good high. The water blended the two of them together until she couldn't tell them apart anymore. He had no business trying to force himself into her world, or trying to make her fit into his. Life had been hard on her. Rayne had lived the blues, and Tauris only thought he had. She'd died and gone to hell, then come back to do it all over again, and love had no place in the mess that had been her life. She knew it. If he wasn't so full of himself, he'd know it, too.

By the time she opened her eyes again, the water was starting to get cold, and Tauris was gone.

UNCLE LAMAR

Bishop had no idea what he'd done. He'd died and left Lamar Brown alone with his thoughts, his desire, and most important, his daughter. He was a fifty-year-old man being driven insane by obsession and until now, Lamar had been a dog on a leash held tight by Bishop. With him gone, Lamar was dangerously free to do whatever he wanted. Every moment of the day he thought about Kristine, and every time he closed his eyes to sleep he saw her in his dreams. And now, who was there to stop him from completely crossing the line?

F&B Funeral Services was a multimillion-dollar operation, but like Bishop Fontaine, Lamar lived comfortably, yet well below his means. There was no need for extravagances in his lifestyle. His children were grown, and all that was left in the house was Lamar and Rhonda. She'd even mentioned a desire to downsize and to find something smaller for the two of them to grow old in.

The office assistant poked her head into his office. "Mr. Brown, you have a meeting with Martin Schultz first thing in the morning to discuss pricing for the line of limos he'd like to customize for you, and Brent Dobbs wants to know if you can meet him for drinks tomorrow afternoon to go over some outstanding invoices."

The new assistant was a bright, efficient young woman, hired to replace Kristine, who'd quit working right after Bishop passed away. Lamar had to admit he was glad she no longer worked for the company. Legally, however, she was still his business partner because Bishop had willed his share of the business to his daughter. Kristine had no interest in the company, though, and Lamar knew that the time would have to come for the two of them to sit down and discuss her options. He wasn't in a hurry to end their alliance; as her business partner, he still had a place in her life, and as thin as that relationship was these days, at least it was something.

Bishop had been a mentor to him. Nine years older than Lamar, he'd been the older brother Lamar never had, but secretly wished for growing up as a child in Alexandria, Virginia. Lamar had been a handful back then, a troubled kid, in and out of juvenile hall, and eventually adult prison for burglary. He was locked up for three years, until he was twenty-two, when Bishop hired him.

Lamar stood on the deck in back of his house, looking out past the open space. His wife, Rhonda, was upstairs asleep. He married Rhonda because back then, he loved her. But Lamar hadn't been in love with his wife in years. They'd grown into the dullness and routine of marriage until there was no longer the spark between them that excited him. Time, children, the day-to-day living with the same woman for the last thirty years had made his desire for her stale. Till death was a mighty long time to spend living like this.

Bishop was only nine years older than Lamar, but he seemed older than that, morose and burdened, cursed by his wife's death long ago.

"We should go out and get a drink, Bishop," Lamar remembered urging him. "Find a pool hall and shoot pool like we used to. Come on, man. Let's go have a good time."

Bishop's dull, gray eyes died long before the rest of him did, and he stared back at Lamar as if he'd said something in a foreign language.

"I've been up since before the sun, Brown." Even his voice sounded old. "I think I'll turn in early tonight. Maybe we can do something another time."

Bishop had never complained when Violet became ill. Through all of the chemotherapy treatments and surgeries, he doted on her hand and foot. Little by little, Lamar watched Bishop waste away with his wife, and after she passed away, he wasn't the same man he'd once been. At her funeral, Bishop didn't shed a tear, but Lamar knew that inside, the man was destroyed.

"Half of me is gone, Lamar," Bishop said, quietly watching them lower her casket into the ground on that rainy day. "The other half—my daughter—is all I have left."

The devil refused to let him sleep tonight. Lamar could stand here trying to deny and ignore the feelings churning deep inside of him, but they were never far from the surface, especially since the death of his best friend. Kristine was alone now, living in that house by herself. She'd never known what it was like to take care of herself. Bishop had been too protective, had sheltered her too much, and had depended on her being there. She'd obliged and in doing so, she'd denied herself the experience of being a grown woman, independent of her father's approval and guidance. Kristine was a child, despite her age, and she still needed someone to take care of her. Lamar had practically helped raise that girl. He and Rhonda had been there for her even before Violet's death, and instinctively he knew that she needed him now. With Bishop gone, who else did she have?

His erection swelled underneath his bathrobe. Lamar had stopped denying what he felt for her years ago. Lust. Love. Both. She'd always been a beautiful child, the most beautiful he'd ever laid eyes on, and she'd grown into a woman, even more beautiful. Her sweet face, golden-brown skin, and hypnotic green eyes lingered in his mind constantly. Kristine's petite frame—curved, round, and soft— tortured his thoughts, and excited him to the point that it was all he could do to maintain control of the urges that threatened to take him over.

To this day, she still called him Uncle Lamar and he hated it. "I'm not your uncle, baby," he told her the older she became. Kristine needed to know that he wasn't really family and that he thought of her as more than just a child. Bishop wouldn't let her grow up, but Lamar watched her blossom despite his friend's efforts to keep his baby girl, a girl.

He groaned low and deep at the image of her. He wanted her so badly he could taste her. When Bishop had been here, Lamar fought the private battle to stay away from that man's daughter. But Bishop was gone now, and Kristine was by herself. Lamar was married to a woman he didn't love, and obsessed with a woman he couldn't have—until now.

There was nothing stopping him now. Not Bishop. Not even Rhonda. Kristine knew how he felt. She had no choice but to know. He sat down in a chair on his deck, freed himself from his robe, and slowly massaged himself.

"Lamar?" Rhonda called his name softly from the doorway behind him. "You all right? It's late. You should come to bed, honey."

He rolled his eyes, annoyed. "Go back to bed, Rhonda."

"You're going to have a hard time getting up in the morning," she reminded him.

Lamar never responded, and Rhonda quietly went back to bed.

A DAY IN THE LIFE

The Brothers Johnson's "Strawberry Letter 23" played softly from Tauris's record player. He prided himself on his album collection and, despite the lure of technology, refused to upgrade to CDs or MP3 players or anything digital. Tauris was in the kitchen stacking crisp bacon strips, fried eggs, and cheese on hamburger buns he'd slathered with grape jelly. He pulled a cold beer from the refrigerator and carried his meal back into the living room to eat. Tauris owned a small bungalow duplex he'd bought years ago with the intent of renovating and then selling it as soon as he could. He owned both sides. The other one was empty. And he'd never done much work on either. His place looked almost like it wasn't even lived in, with a secondhand couch in the living room, a box for a coffee table, and a forty-two-inch plasma hanging on the wall. In the bedroom, he had a bed, and that was it. The bare white walls held no pictures or paintings of any kind, and boxes stacked in the corner were filled with junk he didn't need.

These days he preferred the notion of having his own woman, and the idea of finally settling down. At thirty-seven years old, he'd been married twice. The first time he was nineteen and in love with Tina, the high school valedictorian. Tauris never even graduated from high school, which made the whole thing even more absurd. He worked as an apprentice at her father's construction company, so when the old man found out Tauris had been stepping out with his pride and joy, he nearly twisted Tauris's neck right off of his shoulders. But Tina loved him, and cried and threw enough of a fit to convince her daddy that they should be married. The old man even gave them a place to live over his garage, which meant that Tauris was under thumb twenty-four hours of the day.

Eventually, the old man convinced his baby girl that she was way too good for Tauris, and shipped her off to Penn State in her sophomore year. Six months later, Tauris got his divorce papers in a Dear John letter, and the old bastard fired him.

A few years after that, he met and married Doreen. Doreen was five years older than Tauris, and had a kid, a six-year-old boy named Derrick. Six months after they were married, Tauris's daughter Tyanna was born, and Tauris found himself right where he wanted to be—married with kids, and content, at least for a while. Everything was cool until she found out he was stepping out on her. Doreen was pissed when she found out, but they worked through it. And then he found out she was cheating on him. But instead of begging for forgiveness as he'd done when he cheated and giving Tauris a chance to forgive her, she packed up the kids, all of her shit, and some of his, too, and moved to California with the mothafucka. And just like that, eleven years of wedded bliss went up in smoke.

His relationship with his daughter had gone from full-time father to a weekly phone call and child support check. Every now and then, Doreen would let her visit him for the summer, but gradually other things tended to get in the way: ballet lessons, cheerleader camps, and shit like that.

About the best thing he had going for him at the moment was business. He'd started his contractor service five years ago, and jobs had been coming in steady ever since. The other good thing in his life was also his curse.

Tauris walked outside and sat on his back porch, staring out into a yard that needed to be dug up and completely landscaped from the ground up.

Rayne was the ache in his side. She was that hunger pain that made his stomach growl, and that buffet he could never seem to get full off of. But she didn't want him. Not the way he wanted her. No other woman had ever been so indifferent with him before and the notion perplexed the hell out of him. He'd called her earlier, thinking that today would be a good day to go to breakfast and maybe spend the day together. Rayne shot him down without missing a beat.

"Breakfast?" she asked, groggily.

Tauris had made the mistake of calling before nine in the morning. Deep down, he thought maybe she'd be so glad to hear from him, that she'd bolt up in bed, and be ready to roll.

"What time do you want me to stop by?" he asked, grinning.

"I'm about to hang up, Tauris," she sighed. "You come by here if you want to, but don't expect to get in."

"But baby," was all he could get out before he heard the dial tone. He should've been smart enough to leave her ass alone, but he was too far gone to do that.

"You got access to all kinds of women, playa," his boy Larry reminded him the other day while playing pool. "Why you had to mess it up and fall for just one in the first place is beyond me. Get it. Hit it. Quit it. That's my motto. Especially if I could pull 'em like you."

"Can't help what I feel, man," he responded, taking his shot. "I got caught up. Can't help that."

"Sure you can. Cut her loose and move on to something else. It ain't hard. We're men. That's what we do."

"I'm guilty of wanting something I can't have, Larry, man," he said matter-of-factly. "It happens to all of us from time to time."

"So, that's it? That's what's got your nose so wide open you sucking up tanks and shit? The thing is, brotha, it's been my experience that the things I ain't supposed to have, I'm better off without. But if by some chance you do manage to get it—all I'm saying, is don't believe the hype."

Tauris grinned. "You've seen her on stage. Don't sit there and try to tell me she can't live up to the hype."

"Your ass is starstruck, mothafucka. Yeah, she's fine and all, but fine comes with a price—always. And that one right there, comes with a serious price tag from what I heard. She might dress it up on stage and cover it up with a nice voice, but that don't mean she still ain't got that monkey on her back."

Tauris was offended, and he didn't bother trying to hide it. "That was a long time ago, man. She's past all that now." He took his next shot, and missed.

"A smack-head ain't never truly over nothing, Tauris. Wave that shit in front of her face, and I guarantee she'll turn flips for it. My cousin is caught up in that mess. He's crazy."

"Yeah, well, Rayne ain't your crazy cousin."

Larry smirked. "All I got to say is that the pussy must be potent, brotha, 'cause your ass is damn dizzy over it."

Tauris resisted the urge to swing that pool stick into the side of Larry's head. Instead, he threw it on the table. "I'm out," he said, leaving.

Driving home, Tauris flashed back to a conversation he had with Rayne about her past.

"Every day is a new day," she explained quietly over coffee. "It's a new chance for me to get it right. But it's also another chance to screw up, so I have to walk the straight and narrow, probably for the rest of my life."

"When's the last time you used?"

"Three years, four months, two weeks, and two days ago." She smiled. "But who's counting?"

"Sounds like you are."

"Because every second of every day matters, Tauris. I have come within inches of losing my life, and I have lost my dignity too many times to count. It's taken a whole lot of determination on my part, and the help of some good people to get me to where I am right this second, sitting here having coffee with you, as sober as a nun. And if I decide to take you home with me tonight and give you some of the best sex you've ever had, it'll be because I want to, and not because I'm hoping you'll get me to my next fix." Rayne smiled mischievously. "Makes choice a whole lot more appealing."

"Damn right."

Tauris finished eating his bacon, jelly, and egg sandwiches and spent the better part of the day with his mind on her and nothing else, bent over a shovel in his backyard digging up weeds taller than him. Later, he showered, got dressed, and then climbed into his car on a quest to go see her regardless of whether or not she wanted to see him. That's what obsession does to a man. It makes him stupid.

Tauris parked across the street from Jackson's, a jazz club on the waterfront in southwest DC. Rayne was performing tonight with her band. It wasn't a bad crowd for a Thursday night, but then again, she had a nice little following. Tauris spotted her sitting at a small table in the back of the club with a man he didn't recognize. Tauris made his way through the crowd to where she sat, and kissed her cheek. "Hey, baby." He glared at the brother sitting across from her, making sure he knew that she had a man.

"Excuse me," she told the man at the table, then stood up and pushed Tauris back out of earshot of the table. Immediately, he knew he'd pissed her off. "I'm busy, T. Diggs," she said, annoyed.

"I can see that. You auditioning for new band members?"

"No, but I need you to leave so that I can get back to my business meeting."

"Why can't I stay and wait for you to finish your business meeting?" he asked sarcastically.

"Because I don't have time for you tonight," she snapped. "If I didn't know better, I'd think you like making me hurt your feelings." She glared at him.

He stared at her like she was crazy.

"I'm having a conversation here, Tauris, that don't have shit to do with you. I'm handling my business," she said indignantly, propping her hand on her hip. "Now, being a businessman yourself, I would think you'd know what that means." She didn't hold back on the sarcasm. "What you see here is me working, Tauris. I'm doing my job whether I'm up on that stage or sitting at the bar. You pick up a hammer and knock down some walls; I don't bother you, because I respect that. You see what I'm saying?"

Tauris scratched his head.

Rayne rolled her eyes and turned to leave. "Go home,"

she commanded over her shoulder, before making her way back to the dude at the table.

"Is that how it is?" he muttered, offended.

"Yeah. That's how it is." Rayne muttered back, and sat back down at the table.

He was getting tired of her shit. Pure and simple, it was getting old.

WHAT HE DOESN'T KNOW

Nora James stood on the balcony of her Manhattan apartment, overlooking the magnificent views of the city and Central Park. The warm glow of the setting sun washed over her, and Nora embraced herself and sighed. She and Cole owned homes all over the world, but this one was hers. He hated New York, but the energy of the city was intoxicating to Nora, and she escaped there to renew her soul and to remind her that she was living the dream she'd spent a lifetime pursuing. He could be stifling at times with his old-fashioned ideas of what marriage should be. He wanted the kind of family life he never had growing up as a child and she couldn't give him that because Nora's view of happiness looked nothing like her husband's.

Taylor Donahue took the liberty of letting himself in. Like her husband, Taylor was a contender in his own right—as one of Hollywood's most sought-after leading men, he was a box-office gold mine. The action-adventure flick ruling god was stunning, with a head full of thick, jet-black wavy hair, sapphire-blue eyes, and olive-toned skin.

They'd met at an after party for a movie premiere in Los Angeles almost a year ago.

He'd backed her into a corner of the room, and kept her there most of the night. Nora was filled with booze and venom, and she was prime for him that night. "You're even more beautiful in person," he told her.

"You sound like a fan," she responded.

"Your number one fan." He smirked.

Taylor followed his introduction with the most seductive and tantalizing come-on she'd ever received from a man. He ran his fingers lightly up the inside of her thigh, slid her panties over to one side, and massaged her clit until she whimpered with her orgasm.

Nora was insulted and intrigued. "Fuck you," she whispered angrily.

He took her drink from her hand, and finished it in one gulp. "I'm looking forward to it," he said, then took her cell phone from her other hand and pressed his number into its memory.

She snatched it back and pushed past him and left him standing there. Moments later, she called him from the back of her limousine. "I'm a happily married woman, I don't do dick in public," she told him. "So bring it to my hotel room, and maybe I'll see what I can do."

He was there in twenty minutes.

She slapped him viciously across the face, when he entered her room, before he'd even had a chance to say hello. "Don't you ever disrespect me like that in public again!"

Without hesitation, he grabbed a handful of her hair, forced her to her knees, unzipped his pants, and glared down at her. "Let's see what we can do," he growled. That was almost a year ago.

They were a match made in hell, and she couldn't get enough of him. To her relief, Taylor lived and breathed for California, and Nora's heart belonged with her husband. The thought of the two of them having unlimited access to each other, with no real estate between them, overwhelmed her, and she was thankful for the distance.

Taylor followed her out to the balcony, wrapped his arms around her waist, and kissed the side of her neck.

Nora smiled. "How was your flight?"

"Long," he said, simply, pressing against her. "I've missed you."

"I can tell," she said seductively.

He'd had the nerve to profess his love for her once, but the blank stare she gave him in return was enough to keep him from saying it again. She knew he still felt it, but Nora couldn't bring herself to utter those words to anyone else because every bit of her belonged to Cole. It probably always would.

"I've got one hell of an appetite, love," he said, huskily. "Flying always makes me hungry." He raised the back of her silk gown, and then pushed her forward, penetrating her from behind. He pushed into her slowly, deeply, becoming more and more rigid with each thrust. Nora bit down on her bottom lip and moaned, meeting him somewhere in the middle. He reached around her and freed one of her breasts. The breeze kissed her nipple, and he pinched it hard between his fingers, twisting it until she squealed.

Nora stared out across the park, twenty-four stories below them, while he fucked her into a dream state. Taylor was just getting warmed up. He was just getting her warmed up, and surely, it was going to be a nice, long weekend.

As lovers, the two men were as different as night and day. Taylor never minded inflicting pain, whereas Cole needed to be coaxed. He never wanted to hurt her the way Taylor relished it—the way she needed it. But Nora had pushed and pushed until Cole's worst fears threatened to send him toppling over the edge, angry and out of control. He didn't understand. She wanted him over the edge and out of control.

"C'mon, love," he whispered, biting hard on her earlobe. "I need to eat."

He led her inside, pushed her down onto the sofa, spread her legs and buried his face between them, scraping his teeth against her swollen clit, and tugging on it, until she quivered. The pain was excruciating and lovely and she hated herself for the way she needed him, loathing and savoring every sensation of tongue and teeth.

Cole should've been the one making her come like this. He should've been the one she held in her arms every night, and kissed to sleep. Taylor brought her to ecstasy in a matter of minutes, then hovered over her, and wrapped both hands around her neck, squeezing tightly, until she couldn't breathe. Nora clawed at him, pleading him with tear-filled eyes to let her go. It wasn't until she was nearly unconscious that he did. He leaned down and kissed her passionately. Nora wrapped both legs around him, desperately needing to feel him inside her.

Taylor broke her embrace, and then roughly flipped her over onto her stomach. "Showtime," he said, freeing himself from his pants, spreading her cheeks, then forcing himself into her anus.

Nora screamed in agony.

Taylor screamed his satisfaction, and pumped mercilessly until he came. Nora's blood was all over his shaft.

She glanced at him over her shoulder with tears in her eyes, and gritted her teeth. "You can do better than that, Taylor." Nora raised her ass in the air. "Now fuck me like you mean it!" she demanded, meeting every painful thrust from Taylor, with thrusts of her own.

He slapped her bare ass hard with an open hand.

Nora groaned. "Again!" her voice cracked, and he knew she'd started to cry. But crying was a turn-on for Nora. Crying and pain was what got her off. He slapped her again, hard enough to see the imprint of his hand on her skin.

She yelped in pain. "I'm coming, Taylor! Oh, fuck! I'm coming so hard!"

She pushed hard enough against him to almost knock

him backward, but Taylor held on tight to her hips, and mercilessly pounded her until, shit! "Awww ffffff . . . !" He grimaced, and he came, too.

To say she had issues was an understatement. Her shrink wanted to blame it on an unstable upbringing, being tossed back and forth between parents and countries like a volley-ball, complicated by an identity crisis of being neither black nor white, or of being both black and white. Nora had an overwhelming fear and need to be loved and accepted, but was as afraid of those things as much as she wanted them. Whatever. It was all bullshit. Her father or mother had never sexually abused her. She'd never been beaten as a child, though sometimes she felt that maybe she should've gotten a good ass-whooping from at least one of her parents. Nora had been a beautiful baby who had grown into a beautiful child, then into a beautiful young woman, and people overindulged her because of it. She overindulged herself, as well, and gradually her hunger for stimuli in her world became more intense. It wasn't enough just to be loved. She needed to be hated and loathed, then loved in a way that was so over the top it was scary.

Cole hated her sometimes, but he loved her more. She knew the drill when she got home. Two dozen long-stemmed roses would be waiting for her on the dining room table. She'd follow a trail of rose petals up the stairs and into the bedroom. The lights would be dimmed and the room lit by

candles. Her favorite strawberries dipped in white chocolate would be placed meticulously in a silver tray centered
on the bed. Her husband would be waiting for her in the
bathroom, having run a warm bath filled with scented oils.
He'd undress her slowly, then himself, kiss her lightly on
the neck and shoulders, and help her into the tub. Cole
would climb in, too, and pour handfuls of warm water over
her aching body.

"I can't stand it when I hurt you," he'd whisper, brushing
hair back from her face. "I can't stand it when we fight,
Nora."

He would apologize first even though she'd been the
one who started it. And he'd be as remorseful as if he'd
struck the first blow.

"Can you forgive me, baby?" he'd plead.

She wouldn't answer at first. Nora would turn her head
to one side and let one passionate tear fall from her eye and
slide down the side of her face.

"Please, Nora," he'd beg.

She'd take a deep, dramatic breath, bite down sensuously on her lower lip, and nod reluctantly. And then, they'd
make love: in the tub, on the bedroom floor, and finally, in
bed. He'd never know she'd taken out all her anger on another man, in another bed. Afterward, they'd doze in and
out of a luxurious sleep, nibbling on strawberries and champagne for two days, then go on with life as if nothing had
ever happened.

She knew all this because it was routine. A beautiful,

lovely routine that she lived for each and every time she took a swing at him, or a blow to the mouth from him. While Taylor slept next to her, Nora picked up her cell phone off the nightstand and called Cole.

"It's me," she said softly.

He sounded so happy to hear from her, and seemed so concerned.

"I'll be in tomorrow," she explained, quietly. "No, Cole. I'll have a car waiting, so . . . I'd just rather you didn't."

He sounded hurt, but she said good-bye, and hung up. This was the theater that was their life and she played her part the same way she always played it. Cole played his, too, and was probably on the phone at this very moment, calling his assistant and telling her to order flowers first thing in the morning.

"Anybody ever tell you," Taylor once said, "that you ought to be in show business?" He laughed.

WHO IN THE HELL LEFT THE GATE OPEN?

Dwayne "Cash Money Man" Johnson laughed heartily when he saw Rayne sitting in that coffee shop. And for a moment, he would've bet money that she looked almost as glad to see him too.

She shook her head at the sight of him, tall, skinny, ugly . . . some things never changed, and he was one of them. He'd had the nerve to come wearing what looked like his Sunday best.

"Well, look what the cat dragged in," she said sarcastically.

"I'm happy to see you, too, lovely." He leaned across the table and kissed her cheek. "Looks like you've put on a little weight." He nodded. "And it looks good on you."

Rayne took a sip of coffee. "Yeah, weight gain is a side effect of being drug-free."

He stared at her intently. "I wouldn't know."

He still had that same look in his eyes she'd always seen in them; pleading, hungry, wistful. On more than one occasion he'd called it love. Rayne never really knew what to make of it, but it came in handy when she was desperate, and admittedly, she had used it to her advantage.

She'd married J. T. and she'd loved J. T., but it was Cash who had controlled her life. Every instinct warned her to steer clear of him, to turn down this invitation for coffee and conversation. Call it curiosity or stupidity, being with him was testing dangerous waters and when it was all said and done, Rayne would ultimately either sink or swim. She scolded herself internally because only a drug addict could make sense of that kind of flawed logic. He'd done things with her with her man's permission, and of her own free will, all in the name of addiction, and Cash had reaped the benefits of that in ways he had dreamed of since the first time he laid eyes on her. She'd been his whore back then. Smack had turned her into that.

The two of them had grown up together. As kids living up in Gainesville, Florida, they did everything from play kickball in the streets to playing doctor and checking out each other's privates before either of them really knew how to work their little bits and pieces. He'd been her best friend sometimes, and her worst nightmare as time went on. Cash Man, Dwayne, had been the one who introduced her to horse. He'd been her dealer, the one she could count on when money was tight and she was weak. It all came with a price, though: pussy, maybe a blow job, and they'd be right

as rain, debt paid in full. Rayne never wanted to be that
desperate again.

"Saw you sing in that club over there off Fourteenth," he
nodded approvingly. "Still got a set of pipes on you, girl.
Sounded damn good."

"Thanks, Dwayne. I try."

"You ain't never had to try too hard, darlin'. The Lord
blessed you with a gift. I'm glad to see you still using it."

Rayne managed to smile back. "So, what brings you to
town, Cash? And why aren't you in prison." She winked.
"Or dead?"

"That's my Rayne Bow," he chuckled. "No bullshit, cut
straight to the chase. How's big-ass Papa Bear doing? Still
married to Mavis?"

She nodded. "And still willing to drink her bathwater,
too, if that's what she wanted. They've got six kids now."

He looked shocked. "Six?"

"All of them bad, and looking like him. But you can't tell
him he's not happy. Bear is the only person I know . . . just
look into his eyes when he talks about Mavis and those
kids, and for him, it just doesn't get any better than that."

Cash slid his hand across the table and touched his fin-
gertips to hers. Rayne pulled her hands away and folded
them in her lap.

"What about you, lovely? You happy?"

"Happy is a concept reserved for people like Bear and
cartoon characters, Cash. So, why'd you ask to see me?"

He leaned back and sighed. "I don't know anybody out

here. Found out you were here and thought I'd just touch base, baby. That's all."

Rayne stared at him, then shrugged. "What? Like it's the good old days or some shit like that?"

"Yeah, some shit like that," he said sarcastically.

"I don't remember many good old days between me and you, Cash," she said solemnly. "Either I was high, or you were high, or both. Neither one of us knew how to function unless we were shooting smack in our veins and I honestly can't remember much about us when we did."

"C'mon, baby. It wasn't all bad. We had some good times."

"Not good enough, Cash," she said dismissively. "Junkies don't know how to have good times—just high times." She leaned forward and stared into his eyes. "Anything we did when we had that crap in our bodies didn't count, Cash. If you came here expecting to see that dumb broad sitting across from you, hoping and praying that you had the good stuff and the two of you would party the night away, you're going to be disappointed, because when J. T. died, he took her with him."

"I never thought you were dumb," he laughed nervously. "I always cared about you, Rayne, and you know that."

She leaned back, sighed, and shook her head. "You don't know a damn thing about caring for somebody, Dwayne. I never needed the kind of love you had to offer, and I came here today to show you that. I'm ten times better off without that shit you're holding in your pockets, and that fool you're looking for that looks like me, she ain't here no more, and you need to go back to Chicago or wherever the hell you pulled in from and forget you ever knew her."

He couldn't help but look offended. "Once a junkie, always a junkie."

"Nobody knows that better than me, Dwayne." Rayne picked up her purse to leave. "Stay the hell away from me, Cash. Papa Bear still owes you an ass-whooping. Fuck with me, and I'll be sure you get it."

Rayne walked out of the shop without looking back, but his gaze burned a hole through her, and she knew Cash Money Man wouldn't disappear so easily. She shuddered as she headed for her car. Just being near him brought back so many memories and unhealthy desires. Urges surged through her veins, begging her to turn around, to go back into that coffee shop and ask him to fix her up just one last time. Rayne stopped dead in her tracks, resisting the need to turn around. "Don't let me do this," she muttered under her breath to that Higher Power she'd come to depend on. "Don't let me . . ."

But she turned anyway, in time to see Cash leaving the coffee shop and climbing into his own car, then pulling away from the curb.

Rayne took a deep breath and unlocked her car door. "Thanks," she muttered again. "Big ups for that one." She hadn't been to a meeting in months, but damn if she didn't need to go now. She pulled out her cell phone and hit speed dial. "Hey, Anna," she said, taking a deep breath. "I need to talk, girl. I need to talk bad."

HANDY MAN

The house was old, dark, and ancient. She'd grown up in it, feeling as if she lived in a tomb. In the three months since her father passed away, Kristine had hired contractors to remove the old carpet and to refinish the original hardwood floors, to replace all the windows and doors, paint each and every room in colors her father would've never approved of, and to get rid of the old heavy velvet drapes and replace them with fresh new window treatments.

Kristine stood in front of the full-length mirror in her bedroom, relieved that she'd finally found the right outfit. She'd been through just about everything she'd owned searching for something she knew he'd never seen her in before and that would get his attention. She settled on a pink-and-white floral wrap dress that accentuated every curve on her short, shapely frame.

Little things as simple as being able to choose an outfit to wear these days were causes for celebration. Her father would never have approved of her wearing a dress like this. He wasn't the kind of man who would raise his voice—he never cursed, and he never hit—but he had a way of looking at Kristine when he didn't approve of something she said or did, which left her feeling small and disappointing.

"Do I need to buy you more pretty dresses?" his calm voice echoed through the rooms of their quiet home. "Put it away, darling. I'll have Agnes take it to the Goodwill." Agnes had been their housekeeper.

Her mother had been the obedient and dutiful wife to Bishop. "We need to take care of Daddy, Kristine," Violet would tell her daughter quietly. "He takes good care of us, so we need to take care of him. You be a good girl, and that'll make him happy."

Her past seemed so surreal now. Her parents reminded her of people living in a gothic and forbidden novel, but they had been real. And her life with them had been real. She had never known anyone to argue or disagree with her father. He had a way about him that intimidated people on levels that even they couldn't dispute. It was his tone, his mannerisms, his eyes. The tenderness in his eyes reflected your own ugly shamefulness until you quietly relinquished who you really were, for whom he believed you to be, which was always better than the truth.

He had adored Kristine. And she loved him for it. She worshipped him because of it.

At five-foot two, what she lacked in height, Kristine more than made up for in curves. Like this old house, they'd spent years covered up by the rules of her father, but Kristine had been born again in the last few months. *It ought to be a crime to cover up something that looks this good,* she thought, smiling and admiring her reflection. She tousled her thick head of hair, worn natural most of the time. Every now and then she'd splurge on a press and curl, but she liked it wild, and suspected that he did, too.

She slipped into a pair of pink sandals, wiggled her freshly pedicured toes, and adjusted her full breasts in her bra, fluffing her cleavage to mouthwatering heights. Her green eyes sparkled, her freckles flirted back at her, and her glossed lips couldn't help but to be enticing. She looked good, but not overly good, like she'd been primping for the last four hours—which she had been—but not in that obvious way. Her heart palpitated in her chest, and she had to make a conscious effort to slow her breathing and calm down before leaving that room. The sound of his truck pulling up into the driveway let her know that he'd arrived.

Tauris Diggs was so handsome. Kristine met him at the door, smiling and waving like a fool before she caught herself and managed to lasso in her composure. All six feet of him climbed out of that truck looking like a bald, black Adonis. The muscles flexed in his forearms, and he smiled at her and winked, his head glistening in the sun. Tool belt in hand, he took long strides in her direction.

"Morning, Miss," he said, brushing past her as he entered the house. She'd been so fixed on him, that Kristine let the door slam shut on his helper, Reggie, coming in behind him.

"Kristine," she said, grinning way too hard. "How many times do I have to tell you to call me Kristine?" On a subconscious level, she batted her eyes and hated herself for it when she realized it.

"Tell me again," he said in a voice so deep she swore it had to come from somewhere underground. "And I'll make sure to fix that, too, before I leave."

Tauris had been working on updating her house for two months, since she fired her last contractor for charging her for time and materials she never received. Kristine had been her father's bookkeeper, so she good and damn well knew how to decipher an invoice, but the man had thought she was an idiot, which infuriated her even more than the fact that he was trying to rob her blind.

"I'll be expecting a credit memo along with my refund," she told him before throwing him out. "Or else you'll be hearing from my lawyer."

Tauris and Reggie immediately began working on remodeling the mantel around her fireplace. Kristine stayed out of the way, but she took advantage of the time she had with Tauris and talked, wishing long and hard that his assistant would suddenly be caught up in the rapture and leave the two of them alone, but no such luck. Every now and then, she noticed Reggie getting a glimpse of her legs, behind, and chest. Tauris kept his eyes on the job, though, and when he did look at her, his eyes never dropped lower than hers. Kristine's knees weakened every time.

"I keep thinking that maybe after I get this place fixed

up, I might sell it, and get me a little apartment somewhere," she explained, sitting on the sofa behind them, admiring the spread of Tauris's shoulders.

"It's a beautiful home, Miss," he told her. "Got all your history here. You sure you want to sell that?" He glanced over his shoulder at her, and smiled. He had dimples! How could she have missed that? Kristine's heart skipped.

"I, uh . . . ," she swallowed, and quickly composed herself again. "Well, it's just too much house for me. I could probably sell this place to a big family, and I move into a smaller place."

"What about your own family? I'm sure your father would've liked knowing that you kept this place. You could pass it down to your own kids one day."

He mentioned family—didn't he? She breathed a silent sigh of relief, knowing that he thought of things like that. "Do you have a family?" she asked hesitantly, hoping she wasn't prying too much.

Tauris helped Reggie lift a piece of drywall up off the floor and position it around the fireplace covering up the ugly rock foundation surrounding it. "Had one," was all he said.

Tauris watched her walk out of the room and disappear into the kitchen to get them something to drink. Kristine was a luscious melon of a woman, compact and shapely, and delicious to look at. And she was sweet. So sweet, she'd probably give a man cavities. A woman like her deserved the kind of man who worshipped her sweet ass, and who didn't mind propping her up on that pedestal she'd been perched on her whole life.

"Damn, she gives me a hard-on," Reggie muttered low enough for Tauris to hear.

Tauris shook his head. "You and me both, man. You and me both."

"I think she's got it bad for you, though. You gonna hit that?"

"Nah. She ain't that kind. You love that one or leave it alone. Know what I mean?"

Reggie shrugged. "I could love her. Love her all day and night," he laughed.

Reggie was young and clueless. He had no idea that there were some women out there whose hearts shouldn't be broken like that. They had a special place in heaven or something and if you messed with them, you'd get it back eventually, and it wouldn't be nothing nice.

She swished her savory self back into the room carrying two chilled glasses of ice water. Kristine leaned over in front of both of them just enough to make them want to bury their faces between the soft folds of her breasts and die there. "Drink up, fellas," she smiled and batted those dynamite eyes of hers again. "I made some sandwiches, too. When you get hungry, just let me know." She stared into Tauris's eyes when she said it.

SHINING BRIGHT TO SEE

"You should spend more time with her, Janet." Jean Moss blew gently across her cup of tea to cool it. She and her daughter Janet had finally managed to coax Kristine out of the house, to meet them at the restaurant for lunch. The last time they'd seen her had been a few weeks after Bishop's funeral and the girl had looked like a lost and clueless puppy. Janet was a year older than Kristine, and growing up, they'd been "play" cousins. "I'm sure she could use a friend. You know how shy that girl is. Kristine ain't never been one to make friends easily."

"I've called her, Momma," Janet said exasperated. "We speak every now and then, but hello," she said sarcastically, rolling her eyes and her patting her swollen stomach.

"I'm not asking you to babysit," her mother reasoned. "Just get her involved with the kinds of things you do with your other friends. Take her shopping," she said excitedly. "Kristine dresses like an old woman. You could help her learn what to wear. Poor thing has always been heavyset, and she just makes it worse by covering herself up from her neck to her ankles. She's got such a pretty face."

Janet sighed. "Kristine could have friends if she wanted. If anything, she's stuck up, more than she is shy."

"She's shy and insecure," Jean corrected her daughter. "The poor thing's absolutely pitiful."

"Momma, look at me. I'm married, and pregnant, and tired. I ain't got time, or patience, or the energy to be giving pep talks."

"Watch your tone with me, Janet. I'm still your momma and it ain't nothing for me to reach across this table and thump you right in the mouth, married or not. You can tell your little husband I said it, too, and if he wants some I'll thump him in his lips, too."

"You know," Janet grabbed her purse to leave, "I didn't want to come, Momma, and if you feel you've got to talk to me that way—"

"What way? I've been talking to you like this all your life, Janet, and you ain't never—"

"Whatever!" Janet threw up her hand to shush her mother.

Jean Moss slapped it away. "Don't you be—"

She was interrupted by the sound of screeching tires outside the restaurant. Both women stared out of the window from the booth they were sitting in.

"Is that—?" Jean adjusted her eyeglasses.

"—Kristine?" Jean Moss asked, stunned.

"Damn!" Kristine heard the man behind the wheel of that car say when she walked in front of him.

"Can I get your number?" he called out to her.

Kristine glanced at him, then slipped on her Christian Dior shades, and smiled.

"You looking good, girl!" the man said as he drove off.

She'd come out of her shell and it was about time, too. She felt like a million bucks wearing skin-tight jeans, Loriblu Swarovski Crystal T-strap gold leather sandals, a sexy, sleek, black knit top with a plunging V neckline trimmed in blue, and empire waist that flattered Kristine's hourglass figure. Her hair was pulled away from her face, exploding into a huge puff in the back of her head, and her makeup was flawless.

Kristine entered the restaurant and approached the women. "Hello, Mrs. Moss," she said, leaning down to kiss Jean on the cheek. She slid into the booth next to Jean, then reached across and patted Janet on the hand. "Girl! You look beautiful! When is that baby due? This is your second one, right?"

Janet nodded, unable to take her eyes off of Kristine's ample cleavage practically spilling onto the table. She wasn't gay, but Kristine's boobs were mesmerizing.

"And how've you been, Mrs. Moss?"

The waiter interrupted them. "C-c-can I get you something?" The young man was nearly speechless, caught up in the spell of Kristine, as was almost everyone else in the room.

She thought for a moment, and then smiled brilliantly at him. "Small Chai with soy, please."

He smiled back, and didn't move.

"Did you hear her?" Janet said, indignantly.

"Oh. Oh yes. Yes. One small Chai with soy."

"Thank you," Kristine said graciously.

Janet cleared her throat. "You look, uh . . . you look good, Kris. You look great, as a matter of fact."

"Thank you, Janet. I got highlights." She turned her head to the side. "Can you see them?"

"Yeah, girl. They look good. Really." All of a sudden, Janet felt pregnant. Extremely pregnant. "So, you're doing all right then? Momma and me have been worried about you since your daddy passed."

Jean stared at Kristine with her mouth hanging open, unable to say a word.

"Ain't that right, Momma?" Janet kicked her underneath the table.

"Huh? What? Oh! Yes. Yes," she said, meekly. "We have been worried—about you."

Kristine sighed. "Well, I miss him," she said, thoughtfully. "I mean, you know how much of a daddy's girl I've always been." She pressed her hand gently against her breast. Jean fought the urge to say something—she wasn't sure what exactly, but something. "But he's always with me, Mrs. Moss. I believe he's watching over me now the way he always did, and knowing that has helped me to cope with losing him."

"Oh, yes," Jean said, distractedly. "I'm sure it has."

"Have you decided what you're going to do about the house, Kris?" Janet recalled the last time she saw her and how distraught Kristine was over how big the house was and that she was thinking of selling it.

The young waiter came back with Kristine's tea and sat it gently on the table. "Is there anything else I can get you?" he asked nervously.

Kristine needed to stop smiling at that boy and cover up them titties of hers. Janet was starting to worry about him.

"No, thank you," Kristine told him.

He reluctantly left the women alone.

"I haven't decided," Kristine explained. "But whenever I think about selling it, Janet, it makes me sad. It's the only home I've ever known and leaving it just wouldn't feel right. But I've hired a contractor to fix it up for me," she said, excitedly. "That place is trapped in the 1800s, and it needs to be brought up to the twenty-first century."

"Really?" Jean finally managed to say. "You're having it remodeled?"

Bishop died a rich man and left his only child millions. If she wanted to remodel that house, or tear it down and build it again from the ground up, she could certainly afford it.

"I'm having the kitchen remodeled, Mrs. Moss," she explained. "Got new granite countertops, stainless-steel appliances, and tile floors. It's going to be beautiful. I'm having all the fireplace mantels redone, the hardwood floors refinished . . . oh, and I took down all of those old velvet curtains and had custom blinds put in all the windows." She smiled. "Daddy had this thing about leaving the house the way it was when Momma passed, but that house was filled with death," she said, sincerely. "I want my house to be filled with life." She looked first to Jean, and then to Janet, who both nodded their agreements. "It feels brand new. And as for that old guest house in the back, I'm gutting the whole thing and having the contractor add a small kitchenette, a bathroom, and put in all new windows. It'll be like a little cottage."

"Sounds nice," Janet said, trying not to sound as envious as she felt. Growing up, Kristine had always been the shy, frumpy, fat girl that nobody liked. Janet had felt sorry for her more than anything. But now, Kristine seemed to have it all: money, a mansion, hot clothes—and she looked like a million bucks. Janet hated this woman.

"Well, Janet and I were just talking before you came in about the two of you spending more time together," Jean interjected. Janet glared at her, but Jean ignored her. "Maybe you two could go shopping or something." Jean smiled sweetly, and gently patted Kristine's arm.

"That could be fun," Kristine said, much too enthusiastically. "There is a fantastic boutique over on—" Before she could finish she was interrupted by her cell phone. "Excuse me," she said before answering. "Yes?"

Both Janet and Jean noticed Kristine suddenly blush.

"Is there a problem? But you can fix it, right?" She

breathed a sigh of relief. "Oh, good. You are wonderful. Yes. Of course. I'll be right there." Kristine hung up, then looked apologetically at both women. "I need to go meet my contractor, ladies. I'm so sorry to have to cut this short." She gathered her purse, put down a few dollars for her tea, and stood up to leave, kissing both women on the cheek. "We definitely need to do this again and soon. And Janet? Call me and I'll take you to that little boutique I was telling you about. You'll love it, girl. I swear." Kristine waved at both of them as she left.

Jean and Janet didn't speak for several minutes afterward. Both women sipped quietly on their teas, and Janet ate small pieces of her pound cake, which had suddenly lost its flavor.

"She looks wonderful," Jean finally said, quietly.

"Yeah, she looks good. Sounds like she's got a really good handyman, too."

"I'll say." Jean and Janet both watched as Kristine swished her wide hips across the street, balancing in the tiny high heels of her shoes and climbed into her black Cadillac CTS. "Yeah A damn good handyman."

GOT ME TWISTED

He'd once been the International Boxing Association's Middleweight Champion of the World, and in less than six months, Cole "The Hammer" Burkette would be facing his toughest opponent yet to win back his coveted title from London, England's most popular transplant originally born in the heart of Savannah, Georgia, Hector B. Dalton, aka "Stone Mountain."

Cole had been in the gym since dawn, and was winding down from his last sparring session of the day. A few more left hooks, uppercuts, and a right hand that seemed to have a mind of its own, and he was through. An assistant trainer met him at the edge of the ring to cut the strings off his gloves.

"We really appreciate you coming in, Nora," his cornerman R. J. McNair said sarcastically. "But we've got a bout with a killer coming up and I really think it would be a good idea for your husband to start showing up to spar instead of you."

Cole shook his head at the sarcasm. "What the hell is that supposed to mean?" he grunted, frustrated.

"It means I don't know if I've got you here stumbling

around in the ring, or your wife. You're looking like a limp dick up there, Hammer. And I don't mind telling you." That was R. J's problem. He didn't mind telling Cole anything that popped into his cryptic brain. But McNair was the cornerman of champions: John Daly, Reggie Roberts, Felix Windham. He'd learned under the best, though, right alongside Angelo Dundee when he was training Sugar Ray Leonard, Carmen Basilio, and Jimmy Ellis.

Cole headed to the locker room, ignoring McNair's ranting about how sorry he looked in that ring. It wasn't as if he didn't already know. Nora had his mind all messed up, and the rest of his shit was way off balance because of it.

"Can I shower by myself, R. J., man, or do you want to wash my back?" he said with some sarcasm of his own, grabbing a towel.

"Don't waste my time, son." McNair stood toe to toe with Cole. In another part of his life, this man was a father, a grandfather, and probably even a great-grandfather. His mahogany skin looked weathered and worn, and that wide-ass nose of his took up too much real estate on his face, but the brotha was a genius, and Cole knew better than to take a genius for granted. "If you don't want this, then tell me now, and I'll gladly step aside and head quietly into my retirement." His breath smelled like cigars and beer.

"I do want it."

"Then fuckin' act like it. You ain't got no heart, Hammer. And if you ain't got the heart for this, then you ain't got a chance on getting that belt back. You hear me?"

Cole nodded.

"What's that mean?"

"Yes," he said, agitated. "I hear you, man."

"Next time you set foot in my ring, you'd better bring it, or keep on stepping." With that said, R. J. McNair turned and left Cole standing in his own frustration. As usual, the old man was right. Cole looked like a punk in that ring today, and if he didn't get his act together, Hector Dalton was going to stand his ass straight up with that right hook of his in fucking Las Vegas and on cable television for the world to see.

Cole lost track of time in the shower. The water was starting to get cold, but he barely even noticed. Images of the fight with Nora kept coming to mind. He ran his hand over the knot on his head from where she'd hit him with that damn skillet. The shit was still tender. He shook his head and sighed deeply, letting the water stream into his face. They were cool now, but three days ago they were ready to kill each other. He'd done his part, apologizing profusely for laying his hands on her like that, and giving her a bouquet of her favorite flowers. They made love and poof! Like magic, it was as if the incident never happened. Only it had happened, and both of them had the bruises to show it.

Before Nora, Cole had never laid his hands on a woman like that. He'd been brought up by his mother, and he'd been taught to respect women. But Nora had a way of triggering the part inside him that rose up like a dark cloud and confused his lovely wife for some mothafucka in the ring. Cole balled up his fists in anger, just thinking about how much he could hurt her if she pushed him too far. Nora pushed all the time, though, almost as if she liked the shit.

"Hit me, pussy! You think you're man enough? Hit me and see what you get!"

In the beginning he'd turn and walk away, but when he did, she'd push him hard in the back. Instinct almost took over a couple of times, but he managed to maintain control.

"I married a fuckin' woman, Cole! You're a bitch! A weak sissy bitch!"

The first time she lunged at him with all her weight, she took him by surprise and he nearly fell backward after he caught her in midair. Nora scratched and clawed at him like a wild animal, spitting obscenities at him, daring him to stand up to her and be a man. All he remembered feeling was rage. Then he remembered her long, lean body flying across the room and into the wall.

Instead of fear, Nora had another kind of expression on her face that, to this day, scared the shit out of him. She looked like she'd gotten exactly what she wanted from him. For a split second, he could've sworn he saw her smile. Before he realized what was happening, he had Nora on all fours on the floor, pumping her from behind like a madman, while she screamed at the top of her lungs for him to fuck her harder. The next two days were a blur, but he did know that he'd had some of the best sex he'd ever had in his life, and that's how it was between them.

Cole dried off, got dressed, and headed out to his car. He sat behind the steering wheel trying to think of someplace else he could go. He missed the good old days of being able to go to a bar and get a drink without the burden of someone recognizing him. But hell, he was in training and R. J. would kill him if he knew he'd been drinking. Cole didn't want to go home, though. Nora would be there, waiting on him, happy to see him, cooing like a dove about how much she loved him. She'd had her shot of venom and from experience, he knew that it would last for another week or two before the cycle would start all over and somebody would fuck up enough to piss the other one off, and the fight would be on.

Sadness crept over him. Cole fought for a living. He shouldn't have to fight at home, too. "This shit is getting old," he muttered as he started the car. He'd lost count how many times he'd swore he'd never hit her again, no matter what she did or said. But more and more, it was becoming too easy to break that promise, and Cole hated the kind of man he was turning into. The twisted part of this whole thing was, Nora really seemed to dig the dude.

RAYNE FALL

Her mood was bluer tonight. Music bellowed up from the sad, dark part of her that recalled memories she'd just as soon forget. She shouldn't have agreed to see Cash. You don't exercise your demons by drinking coffee with them.

> *. . . Just to think I'd find someone new*
> *One who'd love me better than you . . .*

Any song by Anita Baker was an ode to J. T. Fitzgerald. He'd been her love, her life, her next breath. Six years ago, he was her drowning man, and they struggled together to stay afloat. In a seedy apartment in southeast DC, Rayne and J. T. lived off love, heroin, and desperation. They had a band then, too, and played when and where they could. But in between gigs, Rayne and J. T. did whatever they had to do to survive and to keep the dope stream flowing.

He loved her first. Maybe that's why he was so hard to shake. J. T. saw a little nappy-headed black teenager, and thought she was the most beautiful thing he'd ever laid eyes on.

"You were a different kind of pretty," he told her.

"Ain't but one kind of pretty, J. T.," she argued back. "Anything else is a distorted view of reality."

"Nah, now I have to disagree. There's pretty that the whole world sees, and then there's pretty like one man in particular is supposed to see. And don't nobody see it but him, because it wasn't meant for anyone else to see."

Damn if she didn't blush. "And you were meant to see me?"

"You are all I see, lovely. My God! You are everything I see."

Words like that were music to a seventeen-year-old girl's ears. J. T. was ten years older, but nobody cared. A tall, caramel-skinned man with brown wavy hair, and penetrating eyes, women swooned over him, plucking the strings on his bass. But she was the object of his affection for the first three years of their marriage. J. T. was a recovering addict, kicking crack cocaine like a champ. Early in their marriage, he was good. Never touched the shit, or even alcohol, until they ran into an old friend of hers from back home. Seeing Cash Man in DC was nothing short of a miracle.

"Whatchu doing here, boy?" she asked, squeezing him. J. T. stood back and watched the reunion.

"You know me." He smirked. "I'm doing what I do, baby. Making it my way."

She sucked her teeth. "Still selling that shit. Boy, please. When you gonna get a real job?"

Cash came by for dinner, and he brought some of his real

job with him, and from that moment on, J. T. and Rayne were hooked like fish, slaves to that shit and to Cash. He was their savior when they needed one and their devil when they didn't. She did things back then for horse that killed her off piece by piece. J. T. did what he had to do, too. Love between all of them became an ugly threesome.

"Wait for me, J. T.," she'd called him from the pay phone on her way home from her job working as a waitress. "I'll be there in fifteen minutes, baby." Damn, she was feenin.

"Hurry up," he snapped. "Get here, baby girl. I mean it."

J. T. couldn't wait, though. By the time she got home, he was convulsing on the floor, foaming at the mouth, his eyes rolled back in his head.

"Come on, baby," she sobbed, cradling his head in her lap. "Stop it, J. T.! Wake up! Wake up, baby! Please!"

The phone receiver was off the hook and on the floor next to her by the time the ambulance arrived. She'd called them, but she didn't remember. He died in her arms, but she didn't remember that, either. It's just what they told her and she believed it because the next day, he never came home again.

Cash was too close for comfort and he'd dredged up some bad memories, almost as if he'd brought them with him in his luggage. He came with temptation and, she knew, with drugs, even though he hadn't come right out and said it. Rayne was an addict, a junkie on the verge of falling off the wagon at any given second of any given day. The dumbest thing she could've done was spend a minute of her time with him. He had her back in his sights, and that was a dangerous and worrisome place to be.

"Seems like clubs are the only way I can catch up to you. Why is that?" Tauris came up behind her, standing at the bar. "You can't return a phone call?" He eased his hand around her waist and kissed her softly on the neck.

Rayne was sitting on the edge of her worst nightmare and Tauris was giving her attitude about not returning a phone call? Rayne rolled her eyes. "Club soda, Tony," she said to the bartender. "Two limes."

Tauris sighed. "You can't return the favor, Rayne? I mean, I'm doing all the chasing here. Can't you at least act like you want to be caught?"

Rayne sipped on her drink, before finally deciding to answer him. "Is life really that simple for you?" She turned and looked at him. "Because mine has got me way off balance, T. Diggs. I'm swinging high in the air from left to right, good and bad, trying to keep from falling too far to either side, and all you have to think about is whether or not I want you to catch me?"

"There you go again, talking in code. Why don't you just say what you need to say, and make it plain?"

"All right, I will. I have a lot going on right now and it's all I can do to keep it together."

"Like what?" he challenged. "What do you have going on, exactly?"

She resented his intrusive tone, but damn, maybe by telling him, he'd back the hell up off of her, long enough for her to get her bearings. "I might be getting a record deal," she said quietly. "The dude you saw me talking to the other night is a producer from All Talk Records, and he's interested in working with me."

Tauris's face lit up. "That's great, baby! I mean—damn! That's fantastic, girl!"

She nodded. "It is," she whispered, despondent.

"So, what's the problem?"

"Me. I'm the problem, Tauris. I've let some shit come back into my life, and if I'm not careful, everything I've ever wanted could blow up in my face, and I'll be the reason it did."

"What shit?" he asked, hesitantly.

"A blast from the past," she said coolly. "And all the drama that went with it."

"You using again?"

She shook her head. "I just think about it, or think about not using, all damn day. And then I think about this opportunity and how badly I want it, how much I need it, and that it's practically sitting in the palm of my hand, and how much I'd hate myself if I blow it."

"Then don't blow it," he said casually.

Rayne looked at him and shook her head. "Anybody ever tell you how brilliant you are?"

He ignored her sarcasm. "You've made the decision not to use that mess every day for a lot of years, Rayne.

Why you want to go around feeling like you're weak and out of control is beyond me, because it's obvious that's not the case. So, handle your business, and walk away from that shit to get yours. You've been doing it all along."

She almost smiled. "I haven't had a pep talk since before Bishop died."

"Yeah, well, that old man kept you on the straight and narrow, but he's not here, and what you can't do for yourself, you come to me, baby." He grinned. "I'll pep talk your ass all day and night if you want me to."

Rayne sighed, finished her drink, and got up to start her next set. "I've got to get back to work, T. Diggs."

"Your place or mine tonight? I say mine. It's closer."

"Neither," she said, kissing him on the cheek. "I'll call you."

She missed the old man. He had taken care of her the way a father takes care of his daughter, sometimes sitting up with her at all hours of the night in her tiny apartment, while she cried over a cup of hot tea, trying not to crave a fix, trying not to feel sorry for herself or to miss J. T., and scared to death of what she might be doing had Bishop not crawled out of his bed that particular night, driven for nearly an hour to get to her place, and talked to her until dawn and he was hoarse, trying to convince her that she was strong enough to beat this.

"You called me, didn't you?" he asked, smiling. "And this old man came running like I said I would if you ever needed me."

"I almost didn't call, Bishop," she whispered, shamefully.

"But you did, Rayne. And if you can get up the courage to pick up the phone and dial my number, then I can meet you halfway, and be here when you need me."

EVERY WOMAN

There was only one reason Lamar would come to see her. He'd been calling, and she'd been making excuses as to why she couldn't see him. Today, he didn't bother to call. He couldn't accept that she didn't need him anymore; that she had moved on, and that the relationship she'd had with him was never meant to last forever.

He tried to hug her when he let him in. Kristine slipped away from him before he could. "Kristine," he sounded disappointed as she turned and walked away.

"I've got coffee, if you want some," she said over her shoulder. He could come in, and have coffee, and then he could leave, and he would leave without touching her.

When she was a child, Lamar frightened her. She didn't like the way he looked at her, or the way he spoke to her, or touched her. He'd never touched her in the way she'd heard about abused children being fondled and molested, but his approach was a more subtle one that often left her wondering if she were just imagining things or if he were, in fact, flirting with her. Grown men didn't flirt with children, but then what else could she call it?

As an adolescent, she became curious and romantic, practicing kissing on the back of her hand, dressing up in her mother's clothes when her father was working late in his study, and touching herself. She wanted a boyfriend, but boys didn't want her. She wanted to be held, caressed, and kissed. She wanted someone to tell her he wanted her, but most boys still crossed to the other side of the hallway when they passed her in school.

Lamar seemed to notice changes in her and to appreciate them. She was uncomfortable about it at first, but as time went on, Kristine began to realize the power of a gaze, the influence of a smile, the seduction of a touch, and she experienced these things through Lamar.

Boys her own age never seemed to notice she was even alive. But Lamar noticed something. It wasn't until after her mother's funeral that she truly understood what was happening between them. And she let it happen because, at the time, there was no one who understood how lonely, brokenhearted, and vulnerable she was. Lamar kissed her on the lips, and he told her that she was beautiful, and he held her in his arms. Bishop barely let her out of his sight, but he trusted Lamar. And it was her father's trust that set the stage for their relationship.

In the last three months she'd transformed from a caterpillar to a butterfly, gradually, quietly. Lamar didn't know what to think of her transformation. She was radiant, sitting across from him with hair wild and free on her head, wearing a pink tank top that fit snugly against her breasts, baggy sweatpants, and thick white socks on her feet. Confident and sensual in an open, unapologetic way threw him off-balance mentally and emotionally, and Lamar couldn't help but feel a bit intimidated.

"How's the new office assistant working out, Lamar?" She stopped calling him "Uncle" after her father died, and when he was alive, she only referred to him in that manner when her father was in the room. But between the two of them, he was simply "Lamar."

He sat in the antique Victorian chair across from her in her parlor. "She's learning." He smiled. "I wish you would've stayed on, though, Kristine. No one ran the office better than you."

She rolled her eyes. "I only worked there because Daddy wanted me to."

"Well, it was your first job, and he wanted you to have the experience."

"He wanted to keep an eye on me, Lamar," she said, with a surprising tone of resentment in her voice. "I think both of you did."

He squirmed uncomfortably, not quite sure what to make of her attitude. She'd been avoiding him. There was a time when she curled up in his arms and purred like a kitten, but now, she seemed repulsed by him, aggravated by his being here. "Why are you doing this to me, Kristine?" he asked pitifully. He waited a few moments for her to respond, but she only stared back at him. "I've been there for you, baby. I'm still here for you. I will always be."

"I don't need you like that anymore, Lamar," she blurted out.

Lamar looked wounded.

And she felt bad for hurting him. He *had* always been patient toward her. Lamar's tenderness, and patience, and understanding filled in the blanks Bishop left empty. "We can't do that anymore, Lamar," she said sympathetically. "I'm— I don't have to live like that."

"Live like what? What? I thought you loved being with me, sweetheart."

"I was young, and I was confused, and I was vulnerable, Lamar. What we did wasn't right. You should know that. I shouldn't have to tell you that."

"I know it wasn't . . . right, Kristine, but it meant something—to me, and to you."

"Even if it did," she said defensively, "I need to move on, Lamar. I'm twenty-nine years old, and it's time for me to grow up and get a life, and that means meeting new people . . . maybe men, Lamar. Men my own age. Men who aren't married to someone I love. It hurts me to know I'm hurting her."

"She has no idea!"

"But *I* know! And you know, too, Lamar, and we don't need to do it anymore. Why can't you understand that?"

"Because I love you!"

"I love you, too, but not like—"

"You can't do this to me," his voice cracked.

"No! You can't keep doing this to me!" Kristine bolted to her feet. "I was sixteen when you first touched me, Lamar. I was a child."

He stood up, too. "I know, baby. I know, and I'm sorry for that." But she'd never turned him away. She never told him to stop. Kristine was young, but she knew that she wanted him, and she wanted him to make love to her, and that's exactly what he'd done. Lamar was careful, and he made love to her like he'd never made love to another woman in his life. How dare she stand and accuse him of doing something vile when there was nothing vile about it.

"You need to get on inside, Kristine," he'd told her one day after picking her up from school. Bishop couldn't get away, and he'd asked Lamar if he could. He pulled up in the driveway of her house, and waited for her to get out, but Kristine sat there.

Lamar ached in his gut at being so close to that girl. He ached, and all he wanted to do was hold her. But he'd come to his senses. He blamed himself for taking advantage of her, and he loathed himself for it. "Go on now. I need to get back to work."

"Can you come inside?" She said it so softly, he almost wasn't sure he heard her. He looked at her. "Please?"

There wasn't enough strength in him to deny that girl. It

was her idea to sit on his lap, her idea to raise her skirt and slide her panties to the side. He covered her mouth with kisses so intoxicating that they made them both drunk. In her inexperience, she pressed against him, rubbing herself against the swell in his pants, but she wasn't quite sure what to do. He unzipped his pants, and as wrong as he knew it was, Lamar couldn't help himself.

She gasped when she felt his skin against hers. She stared bewildered into his eyes, and if she would've just stopped right there, he was convinced to this day that he'd have gotten up to leave. But she didn't stop. Kristine rocked her hips against him only once, and that was all it took.

The confident young woman standing in front of him now was so far removed from the one that had so desperately needed him years ago. "I've missed you, baby," he said in a low, husky tone. Lamar nervously wrung his hands together, working hard to maintain his composure. "You know that . . . don't you?"

He was pleading. Lamar had left his dignity outside her front door, and yes, if he had to get down on his knees for her, he would. "Please, Kris, don't—"

She jerked away from him, and Lamar stared woefully at her.

"I told you not to touch me like that," she said coldly. "If Daddy was here he'd—"

"But he's not here, baby. Bishop's gone," he reached out his hand to her, "and I'm all that's left, Kris. I'm here for you, sweetheart. Don't you know that by now?"

Kristine stared back at him in disbelief. "And what about your wife, Lamar? You there for her, too?"

"Since when have you ever given a damn about my wife, Kristine?" he yelled, regretting it the moment he did. "I'm sorry. I shouldn't have said that." He started to approach her, but she backed away.

"You need to leave," she said quietly.

Tears glistened in his eyes. "I love you, sweetheart. I need you."

He slipped his arms around her waist again, and gently pulled her close. He wasn't much taller than she was, and Kristine rested her head on his shoulder. Sometimes, it really was simple. Lamar was just a man, and she was just a woman. Kristine felt sorry for him, and she felt sorry for herself, too, for giving in to her needs, when she knew better. Lamar wasn't a stranger. He knew her, and she knew, like always, he'd take good care of her. "We are a mess, Lamar," she whispered.

"Can't we go upstairs?" he asked, praying she'd say what he wanted to hear most.

She thought back to the last time they were together, before her father died. Lamar wasn't the man she wanted, but he was the only man she had ever had, and being close to him like this reminded her that she had needs, too. If he were Tauris, she'd have said yes the moment he'd asked.

But that's not who he was, and he wasn't the man she wanted.

She shook her head. "No. You need to leave, Lam—"

Before she had a chance to finish, he kissed her passionately, the way he knew she loved to be kissed.

"Please, Kristine," he whispered between kisses.

Every time was supposed to be the last time, because even though there was no blood shared between them, there was the pact of brotherhood he shared with her father. There was his wife, a woman who'd treated Kristine like her own daughter. But there was the very real fact that she needed Lamar and he had become very skilled at fulfilling those needs.

"Will you kiss me," she whispered. "The way you did the last time?"

A nervous and anxious smile spread across his lips. "Until you tell me to stop, sugar."

She took him by the hand, and led him upstairs to her room.

Tonight he was a blessed man. And he'd make sure to bless her, too, before he left.

She showered after he left, changed the sheets, and crawled back into bed.

"I'll leave her, Kris," he had said several times. "But only for you, baby. Just say the word."

If he ever left Rhonda, it wouldn't be because she said

anything. The idea of the two of them together was ridiculous. Tears pooled in her eyes, as she pulled the comforter close underneath her chin. This was the last time, she swore to herself. Lamar had left her satisfied, her knees weak, her skin tingling, the way he had since she was sixteen. But he was never touching her again. It was long past the time for the insecure girl to move on.

She might as well have been in prison growing up, and even when she was old enough to know better and move out on her own, or defy her father, she never could because Bishop made it clear that she was his little girl, and always would be. After her mother passed away, Bishop reminded her constantly of how much he needed her at home with him, and how his heart would break if he lost her, too, in a way that he never quite expressed out loud, but it was loud and clear, and a pact sealed in blood. However, adulthood has a way of coming whether you want it to or not. Kristine learned to be a woman in the place where Bishop least expected it—from his best friend, the only man he'd ever trusted with his daughter.

Kristine shook her head at the irony. "Daddy was a fool," she muttered, before turning off the light.

FIGHT THE FEELING

Johnny "Bear" Williams was more than just a keyboard player, her producer, and the band's music director. He was more than just her friend. He was like a brother to Rayne, and he'd been her saving grace right alongside Bishop after J. T. died of that overdose.

"You must wanna see some mothafucka dead!" His voice shook the ground. Bear matched his name: big, and scary as hell when he wanted to be. "Either Cash with my hands wrapped around his skinny neck, or me sitting in the electric chair for killing his ass! Which one is it?"

Rayne sat across the room from him and waited patiently for this tirade to end. Bear's basement was soundproof and great for rehearsing, but she doubted seriously that it could withstand his temper. She'd casually mentioned that Cash Money Man was in town, and he went off.

"What the hell is wrong witchu, girl?" He looked at her like she was crazy. "You fuckin' wanna get back in that shit? Is that what you want?"

"No!" she said, exasperated. "You know I don't."

"Then why in the hell would you talk to him?"

She shrugged. "I don't know, Bear. I just—I don't know." She knew it sounded ridiculous as soon as she said it, and Bear's expression confirmed it. "I don't know."

He pointed a thick finger at her. "Don't fuck up, Rayne," he threatened.

"I'm not!"

"You fuck up and it's your ass. You hear me? I swear I will—you know I don't hurt women, but if you get back into that shit again I'll put my foot up your ass!"

She rolled her eyes.

"Roll 'em if you want to, girl. I mean what I say."

"I know you do."

"Then stay the fuck away from him."

"I don't have any plans to see Cash again."

"Lemme find out you did," he said sternly.

She sucked her teeth. He mockingly sucked his, too.

She was quiet for a long time, waiting for him to finally calm down. "Thanks for loving me so much, Bear," she said quietly. "Thanks for being there even if it is to put your foot up my ass. That's a big-ass foot."

"Yeah, well, it's a big ass."

She took off her shoe and threw it at him, barely missing his head.

Bear laughed. "You know I'm playing." Bear stared at her intensely. "You too close, Rayne. Too damn close to rising like cream to the top, girl. Don't let cowshit like Cash come in here and mess it all up."

Rayne blinked innocently at him. "Do you really believe

it's going to happen, Bear?" she asked quietly. "I'm afraid to even think about it."

"Hell, it's happening, girl. All Talk Records has been sniffing around too long for it not to. They're coming back with a deal. I'd bet one of my own kids on it. But you fuck around with Cash—you mess this up and you can forget it, Rayne. He's a temptation you don't need and one you have a hard time resisting. Play with that kind of fire long enough and you sure as hell will burn."

She swallowed hard, knowing he was telling her the truth. "I won't see him again, Bear."

He nodded. "You do, and you can kiss your dream good-bye, girl."

Bear fussed like a woman sometimes, but he cared about her, maybe more than she cared about herself. Jazz filtered through her apartment, and Rayne sat by candlelight in her favorite chair, wrapped in her favorite shawl. Her phone rang, but she didn't answer it. She checked the caller ID and saw Tauris's number. Lord! She wasn't in the mood for him. He was a good time. That's all he was to her, and that's all she should've been to him. She sighed and ran her hand through her locks.

Rayne's current CD was doing well considering that she and Bear had put it together in his basement. She and her band had more gigs than they knew what to do with. For the first time in her life, she had money in the bank and wasn't dodging the bill collectors to keep on the lights.

Rayne sat on her sofa realizing that she was standing on the verge of something great, yet teetering on the edge of destruction at the same time. Bishop had pegged her a long time ago, and as much as she hated admitting to him that he was right, now that he was gone, she couldn't shake his version of the truth.

He never approved of her singing in nightclubs and bars. Bishop went so far as to try and tell her not to do it, but Rayne tossed his warning in the wind, and Bishop didn't approve of that, either.

"I ain't property, Bishop!" He'd shown up at her place late one night after he found out she was performing in a little jazz spot in DC. "Look," she said, trying to calm herself down. "I appreciate all the things you've done for me. I really do. I'm clean now, and I know it's because of you that I am. But I am a grown-ass woman, and you will not stand here and try and tell me how to live my life. I'm not your kid!"

The old man looked wounded, but determined. She'd never heard him raise his voice until that night.

"You have no business in a place like that! There's liquor, and drugs, and every temptation in the world right there in your face, Rayne!"

"But I'm not tempted," she reasoned. "I'm singing, Bishop. I'm doing what I love doing more than anything, and the last thing on my mind when I'm up there on that stage is alcohol and drugs. See, you need to back up, and let me do my thing. I'm not going to fall off the wagon or start shooting up again because I am living my purpose again, and loving every minute of it."

She'd never forget that look on his face, in his eyes. Bishop stared at her with such contempt. To this day, she never could understand where it came from.

"You are a gotdamned junkie." Bishop gritted his teeth and stared down his nose at her. Rayne was stunned. If he ever thought it, he never said it, but he said it now, purposefully and successfully degrading her where she stood. "You are weak, Rayne. Weak down to the core, and if you haven't been paying attention, I certainly have been. If I cut you loose, you will destroy yourself. You will fuck up everything I've worked so hard to achieve, and you will end up back in that gotdamned gutter you crawled out of before your husband died."

"What *you* worked so hard to achieve?" she asked, indignantly. "What about what *I've* worked for, Bishop? Or did you forget that it's me out here on the line every day struggling not to give in to that shit calling my name? Yeah, you come through with some money, maybe a pep talk every now and then, but this is me out here!" She started to cry. "And you have no idea what I have to go through to make this happen!"

He stared menacingly at her. "If it wasn't for me, your nasty behind would be in some back alley somewhere sucking cock from here to Main to get that shit in your veins," he said, cruelly. "You're a junkie whore, Rayne. I know it and so did your husband. And without me, you'll end up right where he is. Mark my words." Bishop never blinked. He turned to leave, but before he did, he told her, "You either quit that club, or I'm through. I swear."

The loving and patient man she'd known was nowhere to be found in that room that day. Bishop had built her up, but in a moment, he'd torn her down, leaving Rayne alone with his words slowly taking root in her soul. A week later, Bishop was dead.

Rayne made up her mind to hate him the day they had that conversation. But lately, she couldn't help but to wonder just how right he might've been after all.

She turned off the light on the end table and decided to sleep on the sofa. A quiet tap at the door startled her, and then she heard his voice. "Hey, baby girl." It was Cash. "Feel like letting a brotha in?"

Dread washed over her. Of course, it was only a matter of time before he found out where she lived. He was psychic like that and connected to her in ways that weren't natural. And in the past, to Rayne, he had been irresistible. Every instinct in her blood warned her not to open that door.

"I know you there, sugar," he said quietly. "I can hear your heart beat." Rayne cringed when she heard him chuckle. Cash was high.

Temptation made her tremble. Without warning, a tear escaped down her cheek and Rayne shuddered. Willpower had never been her strong suit where he was concerned because in his pockets was the stuff her dreams and nightmares were made of. Rayne was still a junkie. She'd always be one, and she was the worst kind. The kind who wasn't always so sure she wanted to be clean. The kind who thought about that shit too much, and craved it every second of every day.

"This ain't a good time?" he asked, through the door.

Rayne dried her tears with the collar of her robe, then wrapped her arms around herself. *No,* she thought simply, but never said a word.

Cash was quiet for several minutes and she almost thought he'd left. "Then maybe another time. Good night, baby girl."

Without thinking, she picked up the phone and started to dial Tauris's number. She needed him. She needed someone. His voice mail answered. "I uh . . . ," she cleared her throat. "Call me."

THE BEAUTIFUL PEOPLE

"Our guests this morning on *Rise & Shine America* have been called one of the most beautiful couples in the world by *People* magazine, and have graced the covers of *GQ*, *Vogue*, *Cosmo*, *Life*, *Essence*, and *Ebony* magazines, consistently for the last three years."

Donna Martin, the *Rise & Shine America* host, had a tendency to exaggerate, but in this case, she was right on the money. Cole and Nora were the black Brad and Angelina, and their faces were plastered on newsstands around the world.

"Good morning, you two," Donna said, smiling, and sitting across from them in the studio tastefully decorated to look like a living room.

"Morning, Donna," they said in unison. Nora and Cole sat close to each other on the gray suede sofa, holding hands. Both of them looked like they'd just gone up for parts in a toothpaste commercial.

"Busy, busy, busy. You two have some extremely busy schedules. How in the world do you have time to be married, let alone, *happily* married? How do you make it work so well?"

The two of them looked lovingly into each other's eyes, and smiled. "Want me to answer that?" Nora asked quietly.

Cole shrugged.

"We are very busy in our careers, but I think that what works for us is that we make time for each other. Oftentimes, Cole is on one coast and I'm on the other, but we try and make it a point to meet somewhere in the middle even if it's just for a weekend."

"Communication is major for us," he interjected. "I mean, we're on the phone with each other a dozen times a day, just to touch base and maintain that constant contact, almost as if we are in the same room with each other."

Nora laughed. "It drives everybody around us crazy, but, what can I say? I love my husband."

"Now, you've just signed a major contract for the Opulence Cosmetics' new ad campaign, and you're launching your own line of lingerie?"

"Yes. I'm working with a young French designer named Basile Morreau on a new line that we plan on previewing next fall called 'Orianne.'"

"Orianne?"

Nora smiled. "It's my middle name."

"As for the new modeling contract—couldn't stay retired long, I see," Ms. Martin's sarcasm hit a nerve with Nora, but she hid it well.

"I tried, Donna. But the offer was too good to pass up, and I definitely saw this as an opportunity to celebrate the older woman."

"How old?" Donna probed, playfully.

Nora dodged the question like a pro. "Over thirty."

Donna smiled curtly, then turned her attention to Cole, staring proudly at his wife. "And as for you, sir. If you win this title bout, it'll be the second time you've held the title of Middleweight Champion of the World. What can we expect to see? You look like you're in great shape, by the way."

Cole chuckled. "I'm in the best shape of my life, Donna, and all I can say is, I'll do my best to let him last the first five rounds. After that, I can't make any promises."

Donna laughed. "Trash talk before breakfast. Gotta love it. Any thoughts of retiring?"

"I'll retire when I get old," he quipped.

"I don't know," Donna responded, instigating. "From the look on her face, your wife might have something to say about that."

Nora laughed. Cole didn't. "My wife is my biggest supporter." He suddenly smiled. "And my toughest sparring partner." He chuckled. "She knows I'll quit boxing when boxing quits me."

Leaving the studio, riding in the limo back to the hotel, you could cut through the attitude with a knife.

"What?" Cole knew when she was pissed. What he didn't always have the answer to was, Why?

Nora stared out of the window, ignoring him.

"Whatever," he turned and stared out of his own window.

"You say some dumb shit sometimes," she muttered for his benefit.

Cole sighed in frustration. "What the hell did I say wrong this time, Nora?"

She shot him a look. "Your toughest sparring partner, Cole? What the hell is that supposed to mean?"

He looked perplexed.

"You practically told the whole world that you hit me, fool! Might as well have put that crap on a T-shirt: I BEAT MY WIFE'S ASS!"

Cole shook his head. "What the hell ever, Nora. The only person to read more into that statement is you."

"Damn right I did! Because there's plenty to be read into it! The tabloids could have a field day with it!"

He shrugged. "If they're paying that close attention to what I say, then let 'em! I don't give a damn!"

"Well, I do!"

"Then fuck you, too!"

Without warning, Nora swung her open hand and slapped him hard across the face, then kicked him in the side of his leg with the heel of her shoe. "Fuck you!" She retreated back to her side of the car as soon as she said it.

Not this time, he told himself. Nora wasn't baiting him into a fight no matter how hard she tried.

Cole made up his mind right then and there that he was going to pack his things as soon as they got back to the hotel and have the driver take him to straight to La Guardia.

"Why do we have to get into this now, Nora?" he asked, disgusted.

"We do what we do, Cole," she responded indifferently.

"That's not an answer."

"Yeah, well it's the only one I can come up with at the moment," she answered bitterly.

Cole chuckled. "My God, we sound like teenagers."

They were actors putting on a public façade of the ideal couple. Nothing could've been further from the truth. Cole woke up every day hoping things would be at least normal between them and that they really could be that happy couple who'd just left that interview. He briefly glanced at Nora, sulking and staring out of the window, wondering what happened to the perfect, ideal woman he wanted to believe he married.

Nobody back home ever thought he'd amount to much when he was growing up. Cole had been an angry, troubled kid, ready to take a swing at anything or anyone that moved. But now he was The Hammer. He rode through his neighborhood in a hundred-thousand-dollar Mercedes, wearing custom designer suits, sitting next to this breathtakingly gorgeous woman, and everybody stared at him like he was the man who literally had it all. All that glittered definitely wasn't gold, though, and Cole wondered how he could've ever been foolish enough to really believe it did.

THE GIRL NEXT DOOR

Tauris installed new ceramic-tile floors in the bathrooms upstairs and finally checked on that leaky pipe in Kristine's kitchen when he finished. Reggie left early, and Kristine had been surprisingly low-key and invisible all day. He fixed the pipe, ran some water through it just to make sure it was sealed, and was about to leave when she finally showed up.

"The floors look beautiful," she said from behind him. "A million times better than that old linoleum."

He smiled. "Welcome to the twenty-first century. Your plumbing is fixed, too."

Kristine wore a cream-colored off-the-shoulder sweater, and jeans. Her pretty bare feet patted lightly against the floor when she walked. She wore her hair pulled back, and braided. *Damn, she looked good enough to eat.* He'd never seen a woman look so good without makeup: her plump lips had a natural hue all their own that rivaled any lipstick. And she had freckles. He'd never noticed before now, but she had plenty of them across the bridge of her nose.

"I think I'm going to have to ask you not to come back, Tauris," Kristine said reluctantly. She cleared her throat, and almost looked as if she were about to cry. "I've got someone coming over in a few days to appraise the house. I want to put it on the market, sell it." She shrugged. "You've done a great job around here, but I don't want to put any more money into it than I already have," she smiled. "I'm sorry. I can write you a check for everything you've done, including today." She hurried to find her purse.

Tauris followed her into the living room. He wasn't a mind reader, but he could sense that there was definitely something going on with this woman. "Kristine," he reached out and gently grabbed her by the arm.

She turned to him with a look of panic and desperation in her eyes. "I can't do this," she blurted out. "This house is too big, and there are too many memories, and—"

Before he could make sense of what was happening, Kristine let loose the waterworks and started crying uncontrollably.

He couldn't help himself. After Tauris got over that initial feeling of shock, he pulled her into his arms and held on to her while she cried into his chest. He patted her back. "Hey, it's all right, Kristine," he said trying to comfort her. "Whatever it is, I'm sure it's going to be fine." Tauris was a big ball of confusion trying to come to this woman's aid. He had no idea what to say or how to say it. He had no idea as to why she'd burst out crying all of a sudden, but he felt downright uncomfortable and helpless in all of this.

Eventually, he managed to get her to calm down, and the two of them sat next to each other on the sofa.

"I need to get away," she started to explain. "I've grown up in this house, Tauris, and sometimes I feel like I'm living in the belly of a whale. When I was a kid, I used to daydream about leaving it, and moving far away, and starting over fresh on my own." She looked at him. "I'm almost thirty, and I should've left a long time ago."

"Why didn't you?" Tauris asked quietly.

"Family. After my mom died, Daddy needed me here. I needed him, too. I couldn't leave him alone."

Tauris listened, but none of it made sense to him. Kids grew up and moved away from home. That's what they did, and parents just understood that. So, what was up here? Obviously, something wasn't right.

"Why not?" he asked simply.

She stared back at him like he was crazy. "Because he needed me."

"To do what?" He wasn't trying to be disrespectful, but it was a natural question as far as he was concerned.

She seemed stumped by the question and stunned that he'd even had to ask. "I was all he had left," she explained quietly.

Tauris was no psychiatrist, but even he knew that that was a twisted, messed up excuse. But rather than try and make sense of it, the best he could do at the moment was to maybe try and make sense of *her*.

"So, where do you want to go? What are your plans after you sell this place?"

"I was thinking about moving closer to the city," she smiled, appreciating the fact that someone had cared enough to ask her what she wanted, instead of trying to tell her what was best for her. "Old habits die hard sometimes, Tauris, and living here, I just find myself tied to rules that don't exist anymore."

"Like what?"

She smiled sheepishly. "Like getting home by ten."

He laughed.

She did, too. "Don't laugh! I'm serious. When my father was alive, he wanted me home by ten. Otherwise he'd worry. I couldn't stand for him to worry about me."

"You were a good girl," he nodded.

"Too good."

But only sometimes. Kristine had horrible secrets too shameful to share with Tauris. Lamar knew where to find her. He knew exactly what to say and how to get to her, and it was beyond time for that relationship to end. How could she ever have another man in her life with Lamar lurking around? And how far would he go to make sure she never had anyone else? And what about her? She wasn't any better than he was. There were times when she was drawn to him, too, but he was all she knew. Leaving this house and the stifling memories of this place was what she needed for a fresh start.

"What?" Tauris asked.

He sensed that something was on her mind, and she appreciated him for that. He wouldn't understand about Lamar, and she had no intention of trying to explain it to him, either.

"Do you think I'm wrong for wanting to sell this place? You told me once that I shouldn't."

He laughed. "It's your place, Kris. You do what you want to do with it."

It *was* her place, and her decision, and she didn't need anyone's permission to do anything anymore.

"Thank you for listening, Tauris."

"I can't pretend to understand everything you're going through, but I've got two good ears to offer you if you need them."

She reached over and took his hand in hers. It felt rough and calloused, but it was warm.

It wasn't really all that hard. In fact, it was too damn easy and felt like something he should do. He put his hand under her chin, leaned in, and kissed her softly. She kissed back.

The afternoon breeze gently filled the room, and washed over both of them, taking their sweet time, making love in her bed. He went through three condoms that afternoon. There was no need to rush a thing, as far as he was concerned, and as good as she felt, the last thing he wanted was for this to end.

• • •

Tauris drove home with no regrets, and with a promise to see her again soon. He knew he'd have to make that happen, because he wanted it to happen. Tauris had been wasting his time trying to fit a square peg in a round hole where Rayne was concerned and, of course, that could never work. It was long past time for him to accept that and move on. And there was Kristine, a beautiful woman, who not only wanted him, but damn if she didn't need him as well.

COLLISION COURSE

"You must have a death wish, Cash, because if Bear knew you were here, he'd beat the hell out of your ass!"

Cash followed Rayne into her dressing room of the nightclub, closing the door behind him. He'd spent the night standing in the back of the room, out of view from Bear, but he'd had a perfect view of Rayne, who looked more beautiful than ever singing on that stage tonight.

"What the hell do you want?" She spun quickly to face him. "Why can't you just leave me alone, Cash?" Even angry, she was the most beautiful woman he'd ever seen, and Cash almost forgot what he'd come here to say.

"You sound good out there, sugar," he said, trying to calm her down. "Better than ever."

Rayne rolled her eyes, and folded her arms across her chest. "Disappear, Dwayne."

"Just listen," he said, trying to maintain his composure.

"Listen to what? What in the world could you possibly have to say to me that I need to hear, man?" Before he had a chance to respond, Rayne answered questions he didn't even ask. "No, Cash. I don't want to buy any shit, and yes, I have money, and so no, I don't need to fuck you to get it. But thanks for asking, and you can fucking drop dead in the middle of the street for all I care." She pushed past him, attempting to get to the door to open it for him to leave.

In a reflex, he caught her by the arm, then let go just as quickly once he realized what he'd done. "I'm sorry," he raised both hands in a truce. "I'm not here for all that, baby girl," he said as sincerely as he could muster. "I swear I'm not."

"Then why are you here?" she asked indignantly.

"Honestly? I just wanted to see that you were all right," he said quietly. She looked like she didn't believe him, but of course he knew she wouldn't. "You never told me—how have you been since he died, sugar?"

Rayne looked wounded. "How do you think I've been?" Her voice cracked. "You wanted to see how I was getting along after my man died in my arms from a drug overdose? You wanted to see if I needed a fix, Cash? Because now that J. T. is out of the picture, what? You wanted to see if maybe me and you could be together? Is that what you wanted?"

"Our history is a mess, girl. I know that. But it is history, and I'm here to tell you that I'm sorry, Rayne. I'm sorry for what I put you through. I'm sorry for what happened to J. T. I'm sorry we ever were the people we were back then."

Tears burned her eyes as she listened quietly to his apologies that came out so easily and freely from the walking, talking lie that was Cash Money Man. There was a time when he could've told her the sky was plaid and she'd have believed him. Cash was a liar. He was evil. He was the devil and back then, she and J. T. were his most prized possessions.

"I called Cash. He's on his way over."

Junkies have no sense of reason or logic, and if they do, it's overwhelmed by the need to feed, and nothing else matters but the drug. The lights had been turned off, but J. T. had taken what little money they had left to get them turned back on, which wouldn't happen until the next day. He thought she had money, but Rayne was broke. The only food in the house was peanut butter and bread, and they were at the lowest point they'd ever been in the three years they'd been married. He was working at a grocery store, stocking shelves, and Rayne was waitressing at a diner across town.

"What about tips, baby?" he asked desperately. "Come on, now. I know you got tips."

"Not a lot." Rayne pulled a wad of dollar bills and change from her coat pocket, and spread it out on the coffee table in front of them. Together they counted twelve dollars and seventeen cents.

"Shit! Shit! Shit!" He pounded the table angrily with his fist, sending the money bouncing onto the floor. He leaned back on the sofa, rubbed his hands over his head and stared at nothing across the room.

Cash knocked on the door. "Y'all there?" he asked.

J. T. reluctantly let him in. They all considered them-selves friends. Cash had come over to dinner and Rayne had cooked some hellified meals for all of them. They'd spent hours staying up late and talking, laughing, watch-ing football games together. And sometimes they all got high together, on Cash's dime.

Cash came in and noticed the lights were off. "Yo, man. You pay the bill?" he joked.

"Yeah. Lights will be on in the morning."

A candle flickered on the table, casting a glow on Rayne's face.

"Who died, man?" Cash asked, half joking.

J. T. cleared his throat. "Say . . . uh . . . you think you could hook us up, Cash, man? We come up a little short this time."

Cash stared at J. T., then at Rayne, both trembling and trying not to scratch or look desperate. They were always coming up short, and from time to time, he hooked them up, but Cash's goodwill was starting to wear thin. "Sorry, J. T., man. I can't keep giving you something for nothing, bro. I wish I could, but—you starting to put a dent in my pocket. You understand."

J. T. nodded. "I ain't trying to put no hardship on you, Cash, but—you know how it is." He laughed bitterly. "I know you know how it is."

"I do know. I understand, J. T., but I can't do it. Not this time. I need payment, man. I need something."

Rayne's voice came out of the darkness. "I have something I can give you, Cash," she said quietly. She stared at J. T. who knew instinctively what she was talking about. The side of him that was her husband would've lost his mind, but the side that needed to get high stared sadly at his wife, knowing the sacrifice she would make would break both their hearts, but neither of them had the will-power to deny their drug-addicted needs.

She stood slowly, and pulled off her coat. Deep down, she wanted J. T. to be strong enough to tell her not to do this. She wanted him to step up and throw Cash out, and to make both of them the people they were before he came into their lives.

Cash stared at Rayne, then at J. T., who took his coat off the hook on the wall, quietly opened the door behind Cash, and left.

A bitter lump swelled in her throat as she unzipped the front of her uniform, then let it drop to the floor at her feet. She needed to get high. To this day, the rest of what happened was a blur to Rayne. But that point was crystal clear. She needed to get high, and she fucked Cash many, many times, to do it.

"You ruined my life," Rayne sobbed angrily. "You turned me into a monster, and you took advantage of me, Cash! J. T. died because of you!"

He shook his head. "J. T. died because he was a junkie,

Rayne. He got ahold of some bad shit, and he took too much!"

"You took too much!" she screamed, pointing at him. "And now you want to stand here and tell me you're sorry? Sorry, Cash?" Her face twisted in anger. "Not enough sorrys in the world can make up for the shit you did to me!" She held open the door for him. "Get the hell out!"

"I'm not the same man I was back then, Rayne," he tried to reason. "I did some terrible, terrible things to you, baby girl, but I—" He reached out to try and touch her face, but Rayne jerked away.

"I'm different, too, Dwayne. We don't have horse between us. We don't have J. T. in common anymore, either."

"We've got history, girl."

"We've got hell, D. Every time I look into your eyes, or even say your name, that's what I'm reminded of, and personally, I don't want to have to keep reliving that shit over and over again."

She held open the door for him to leave.

ALL GOOD THINGS

She looked so much like her mother. Kristine had her father's light eyes, but every other quality was a mirror image of her mother.

Rhonda wasn't surprised when the young woman answered the door looking breathtakingly beautiful and out from under the weight of Bishop's burdensome overprotectiveness. He'd been ridiculously overbearing and brooding, and Rhonda had told him as much when he was alive, but he never listened. Bishop had always been a stubborn, close-minded man, and Rhonda never liked him. Violet was a stunning woman before she took sick. But she was alive and well in her daughter, and all Rhonda could do was stare and smile.

"Aunt Rhonda," Kristine exclaimed. "What are you doing here?" She kissed Rhonda on the cheek.

"My goodness!" Rhonda's eyes lit up at the transformation of that old house that was once dark and weighted like Bishop's personality. Now it was bright, inviting, and soft like Kristine. Rhonda loved it. "This doesn't even look like the same house, Kristine," she said in awe.

Kristine trailed behind her. "I know, Auntie. Isn't it wonderful?"

"Like something straight out of a magazine." She turned to Kristine and smiled. "You have really outdone yourself, sweetheart."

Kristine blushed. "Thank you, Auntie."

Kristine Fontaine was like one of her own children. Rhonda sipped the hot tea Kris had made for them, quietly reflecting on the young woman she'd grown into. She'd been such a sad little girl after her mother died. Bishop was a doting father, but he knew nothing about the sensitivities of girls, and even though he cared for his little girl, he neglected the tender side of Kristine, the sweet side that needed her father's hugs and kindness more than regimen and rules. Naturally, she'd blossom after he died. Shine a little sun on a flower, and what else is it supposed to do?

Kristine had been doing most of the talking, going on and on like women do about shopping, hair, and the latest fashions, but she hadn't mentioned friends, dating, going out like other single people her age, dancing, and partying.

"Are you dating, Kris?" Rhonda asked, smiling. "Do you have a boyfriend?"

Kristine blushed.

"Come on," she coaxed. "Woman to woman, you can tell me."

"Woman to woman, huh?" She stared admiringly at Rhonda. "There is someone."

Rhonda's face lit up with anticipation. "Really? Just one someone or several?"

It was barely noticeable, but Rhonda picked up on a hint of something uncomfortable in Kristine's expression. But it disappeared just as quickly.

Kristine talked excitedly about the man she'd met who happened to be the contractor she'd hired to remodel the house. He was tall, handsome, kind, and patient. In a nutshell, the girl was obviously smitten and Rhonda couldn't have been happier for her.

Rhonda studied her while she spoke, quietly realizing that they'd all succumbed to Bishop's ideals, especially when it came to Kristine. He treated her like a child and so had the rest of them, blind to the fact that she hadn't been one in years. Lamar never wanted to hear it, but the truth was, Bishop was an abusive man. Not physically, or even verbally, but his kind of abuse happened on more subtle levels that didn't leave physical scars, and most of the time, didn't even register to the person on the receiving end. He manipulated people, especially his family, and even Rhonda and Lamar on some level. Rhonda had convinced herself that maybe she was just crazy, because there was nothing bad to be said about Bishop. She couldn't point to one thing he'd ever done wrong and say, "See! See what he did?" because every action, every word or intention from the man was blanketed in sentiment, consideration, even love.

Kristine had been trained from birth how to live in that house, and it wasn't Bishop who'd trained her. It was her mother. Violet was obedient to a fault. She adored her hus-band more than her own life, her own child, and she had raised Kristine to practically worship her father.

"You and I should go to lunch one afternoon, Violet," Rhonda would suggest from time to time, knowing what Violet's response would be, but still hopeful that the day would come when she'd say something to surprise her.

"It sounds lovely, Rhonda. I'll have to check with Bishop, and get back to you."

One day, Rhonda stopped being polite and decided it was time to say what had been on her mind ever since she'd met the woman. "I don't understand, Violet. You can't make a decision about something as simple as lunch without ask-ing Bishop?"

Of course, Violet was offended. "That's how things are done in our household, Rhonda," she said defensively. "I don't expect you to understand."

"And what if you were to go without checking with Bishop, Violet?" Rhonda probed. "Would he get angry?"

"My husband doesn't get angry, and I'd never go with-out checking with him first," she said curtly.

"Are you afraid of him?"

It was several minutes before Violet finally responded. "I can't believe you would ask me something like that," she said, quietly. "I love my husband. I love him in a way that is unbelievable, but I don't expect you to understand that, ei-ther, and no, Rhonda, I don't think I want to go to lunch with you."

It was the last conversation they shared outside the presence of husbands or children.

"Aunt Rhonda?" Kristine held the pot of tea in her hands. "I said, do you want more tea?"

Rhonda held out her cup. "Lamar said he was going to stop by and check on you."

Kristine filled her cup, too, but didn't respond.

"You know he worries about you like you were still a child."

"Well," she sipped her tea, "I'm not a child anymore, Auntie. And I can take care of myself just fine."

"You know we're here for you, Kris. Lamar and I are your family now."

She nodded. "Of course, I know that, Auntie. You've always been there for me."

"When was the last time you saw your uncle?"

Kristine shrugged. "I don't even remember," she said indifferently. "I've got pound cake. Would you like a piece?"

Rhonda smiled. "No, thank you."

Kristine stood up. "I think I'll have a slice. I haven't eaten all day."

"He mentioned that he'd stopped by the other day," Rhonda said.

Kristine shrugged, cutting into the cake. "He stopped by for a few minutes."

"I know you think we're worrisome, Kristine, but bear with us, sweetie. We mean no harm," she chuckled.

Kristine turned to look at her. "I know."

Rhonda's glassy-eyed expression never left Kristine's. She'd seen the way he stared at that girl when he thought no one was paying attention. It started long before the funeral. Lamar's gaze lingered too long, and he had a look in his eyes when he did. He looked like a man longing for something. It's a look that a wife recognizes instinctively.

Kristine laughed. "But as you can both see, I'm doing just fine."

"Yes, dear." Rhonda sipped from her cup. "You certainly are."

An hour after she'd arrived, Rhonda decided that it was time to leave. She stopped inside the doorway on her way out and inhaled the fresh air. Kristine put her hand on her shoulder, and Rhonda turned to face her.

"We should go to lunch or something," Kristine said quietly. "I've really missed seeing you."

If Lamar ever thought of laying a hand on this girl, then shame on him. Shame on him!

She smiled and hugged Kristine tight. "I'll call you," she said before leaving.

Rhonda watched Lamar as he sat across the table from her eating. As usual, he didn't seem to care if she was there or not. Lamar stared down at his plate shoveling food into his mouth.

"I visited Kristine today," she said, breaking the silence between them.

Lamar hesitated—just barely—then continued eating. "Good," was all he said.

She worried sometimes that maybe she was looking too hard to find something that wasn't there. Rhonda had learned in her forty-nine years and after raising two boys that if you looked hard enough, you could always find something be it real or imagined. Intuition rose to the surface of her skin and when it did, she found herself scrutinizing everything Lamar said or did, and even what he didn't say or didn't do.

"She's having a lot of work done on the house," she mentioned casually. Lamar nodded. "It looks wonderful." Moments passed between them before she spoke again. "She looks incredible, like she's finally come into her own."

Again, he hesitated—briefly.

"Doesn't she look like her mother more and more?" Rhonda inquired eagerly.

He nodded, and shrugged. "Spitting image. Doing good, too."

"Kristine has always been lovely. I'm glad she's finally starting to realize that for herself."

He didn't say anything. In fact, Lamar had just about cleaned his plate and was about to get up to leave the table.

"Did you know she's seeing someone?" Rhonda blurted out before he could.

Lamar slowly raised his eyes to hers, and dread filled her and took away her appetite. Rhonda and Lamar had been married a long time. Two people can't be together as long as they'd been together and not know some things about the other. Instinctive and innate things that maybe the other person wasn't even aware of himself. Whatever Lamar felt for Kristine now made Rhonda uncomfortable.

"A young man, the one she hired to work on the house. Apparently, they've just started dating, and she seems very happy with him. Happier than I've ever seen her."

His reaction was controlled, subtle, but it was obvious. "What's his name?" He tried to sound casual, but Rhonda heard an inflection of something else in his voice.

"She didn't say." She swallowed. "But she's definitely attracted to him."

"Good. Good for her." Lamar excused himself, and left the table.

Rhonda pushed away her plate. She closed her eyes and searched her memories for one, just one memory to let her know that she wasn't overreacting, or crazy for what she suspected he was feeling. Rhonda sat at that table searching for some past incident that raised her suspicions. One kept coming to mind, but through the years, she'd just dismissed it as a misunderstanding and hidden it under shame and guilt for giving it entirely too much thought.

Kristine was a senior in high school and she'd been home sick for a few days with the flu. Bishop had called her from his office and asked Rhonda to check up on Kristine if she had time, because he'd called the house and she hadn't answered. Rhonda agreed, but she felt silly about going to check on that girl.

"She's probably sleeping, Bishop," she'd told him. But of course, he was insistent, so she drove over. Rhonda pulled into the driveway of Bishop's house, and as she got out of her car, she happened to look up and see what looked like Lamar's car turning the corner.

She knocked for several minutes and was just about to leave when Kristine finally answered the door.

Rhonda smiled. "I see your uncle's already been here to see about you."

Kristine stared at her blankly. "Uncle Lamar? He hasn't been here."

Later that evening, Rhonda mentioned seeing his car leaving Bishop's and like Kristine, he denied ever having been there that afternoon. But Rhonda wasn't blind, and she knew full well what her husband's car looked like.

Of course, Rhonda let her imagination run a little wild after that, but not for long. She was just thinking over things, and obviously, she didn't have enough to do to keep her busy if she let her imagination run away with her like that. She let it go. She dismissed her suspicions altogether and she felt so silly afterward. The thing was, Rhonda couldn't help but wonder, thinking about it now, if maybe she shouldn't have felt so silly after all.

BLIND STITCH

"You know I can't stand it when you don't talk to me." Nora had been holding conversations with Cole's voice mail for days now. He'd text her with some excuse about training for his upcoming fight and promised to call her back, but of course, she knew he wouldn't. She had arrived in Paris this morning. Nora stood at the window of her hotel suite at the Le Meurice staring down into Tuileries Garden. "You're being childish, Cole." She hated being apart from him. They fought like cats and dogs when they were together, but apart, she felt like only half of her was alive. "Call me. I mean it, baby."

She soaked in the tub until the water turned cold. The bottle of Bourgogne Pinot Noir was nearly empty, and Nora had washed down a few sleeping pills, along with antidepressants. Nora had come to Paris to do a photo shoot for Opulence Cosmetics, and to meet with her designer, Basile, to go over some prototypes for her new lingerie line.

"Qu'est-ce qu'est cette merde? What the hell is this shit, Basile?" Garbage. The whole line looked like crap you

could pick up at Wal-Mart, and Nora was livid. She threw lavender panties in his angelic face, and dared him to do anything besides catch them.

He glared at her, disgusted, looking her up and down like he was the one paying her ass to design this trash. "It's exactly what you wanted, your highness." His accent was so thick, she could hardly understand him sometimes. He'd have been better off speaking to her in French, but Basile was hardheaded, and thought enough of himself to believe he could actually go toe to toe with her in English.

"*Point caché!*" Nora held up a thong to him and pushed it into his face. "Blind stitch! Does this look blind to you? I can see it from a kilometer away!" She rolled her eyes.

"*Je vous veux mort,*" he muttered, storming out of the room.

"What?" she screamed out to him. "What did you say to me?"

"I want you dead! I hate you!"

Nora surprised herself and laughed at the recollection. She sat in front of the vanity, staring at her reflection, running her fingers through long strands of hair. Basile was a genius, and she admired his work more than any other designer in the industry, but he was as much of a diva as she was, and both of them knew a long time ago that working together wouldn't be easy.

She dialed Cole's number again. "I wish you could be here with me, Cole," she said softly. "Paris does things to us. You know where I'm staying, baby. Can't you fly here to be with me—just for a few days, Cole? I swear, it'll be worth your time. We need this. You know we do."

He was the only man in the world she was willing to eat crow for. Cole could drive her to her knees begging for his forgiveness, pleading for him to give her just one more chance, and he always did. What was it about her that he loved so much? To this day, she couldn't put her finger on it, but she knew it was more than just about the way she looked. Gorgeous women fell at Cole's feet and he could've had any one of them, but he wanted Nora, and despite all the things she put him through, he still wanted her. Sometimes she knew that he hated himself for it, and sometimes she couldn't blame him.

Nora's phone rang and she smiled. "Leave it to my man to still know how to surprise me after all this time."

Cole sighed. "Yeah, well, you know how I feel about Paris," he said coolly.

Nora pouted. "Hey! What about *me* in Paris? That's what's supposed to make you turn flips, handsome."

"You know I'm training."

"I know, but what's a few days between husband and wife, Cole?"

"You must want me to lose this fight? I'm supposed to fly to Paris, France, fuck myself silly, and then come back here and act like it never happened? Is that it?"

She laughed. "Pretty much."

Cole was silent for several minutes until he finally responded. "There's a flight leaving at midnight," he said, against his better judgment.

"I'll be waiting."

If she wanted to keep her husband, Nora had to concede sometimes and make love on his terms. No temper tantrums on this trip. She wasn't in the mood for all that drama anyway. She missed him, and she wanted him and she wanted him to touch her and love her in his own special way. Nora throbbed just thinking about it, and she hated that Paris, France, was so damn far away from Washington, DC.

SINCE I FELL FOR YOU

Rayne hadn't seen or heard from Tauris in weeks. She found it funny that when he was around, she didn't want to be bothered, and the minute he stopped coming around, she realized she actually missed him.

That old piece of shit car of hers wasn't running again, so Rayne decided to use the opportunity to get him to make an appearance.

"My car ain't running, T. Diggs," she said to his voice mail. "I'm at home and I need to get to rehearsal. Call me. I really need a ride."

She counted on the fact that Tauris liked being her savior, and she'd been right. Five minutes later, he called her back, and half an hour later, she was sitting in his car on her way to Bear's house.

"I haven't seen or heard from you too much lately," she mentioned. "Is everything all right?"

He shrugged. "Been busy."

She expected him to elaborate, but he didn't. "Too busy to return a phone call?"

She'd left a message or two. It was unlike him not to return a call.

"Like I said, I've been busy."

Eventually, even doormats wear thin, and Rayne suspected she'd about worn out her welcome with this man. She'd known what she was doing, but despite an occasional guilty conscience, she did it anyway, half expecting that the time would come when he'd get sick of her attitude. It looked like that time had finally arrived.

"I suppose I haven't been the easiest person to get along with," she said, staring out of the window of his black Dodge Ram pickup truck.

He glanced at her. "What's that supposed to mean?"

"It means that I don't blame you for finally getting tired of my shit, T. Diggs. I haven't been the best girlfriend a man could have."

Tauris laughed. "You were my girlfriend?"

Rayne laughed, too. "I kind of thought I was, but maybe that was just my wishful thinking," she teased.

He shook his head. "Shit, Rayne. To tell the truth, I don't even know what in the hell you are thinking. You want me here, you don't want me here. I feel like a fucking yo-yo."

"I told you what was up. I told you why."

"Yeah, and I told you we could work through all that. Apparently, you were't digging that *we* part, so, I took that as my cue to back off."

"Yeah, well what if I didn't want you to back off, Tauris?" she blurted out the question before she realized it.

Tauris stared back at her, perplexed. "I don't read minds, Rayne. You tell me to leave you alone, and then I'm going to leave your ass alone. You want to work through some things on your own, then have a go at it. But don't expect me to know when you really mean it and when you're just bullshitting. I ain't psychic."

"I never expected you to be psychic, just patient."

"For how long? We've been seeing each other what? Almost a year? You were straight-arming me back then and you straight-arm me now. So, how long am I supposed to be patient?"

"You act like we should be married by now or something."

"Or something. But the way it is now, we ain't even made it to the 'or something' part, baby. Ain't even close."

Rayne laughed. "And what is the 'or something' part, T. Diggs?"

"It's—hell, it's not you whistling for me like a dog, then putting me in the backyard when you get tired of me. That's what it's not."

"That's not what I do."

"That's exactly what you do, have been doing since I met you. But it's cool, baby. I got the message."

"Is that why you came to pick me up?" she teased. "Because you got the message?"

"You needed a ride."

"If you were really through with me, Tauris, you'd have told me to catch my ass a cab instead of driving all the way up from Virginia just to take me back to Bear's house in Virginia."

Tauris didn't have a comeback for that one. He sat there, stewing in his own frustration. Despite her best efforts to ignore it, he was one hell of a good man, and he'd been good to her. Rayne's problem was Rayne. It was never Tauris, sitting and brooding behind that steering wheel.

"Pull over," she told him.

"Nah, I'm not stopping till I get your ass to Bear's and you get the hell out of my car."

Rayne leaned over to him, put her hand on his thigh, and rubbed his dick until it swelled underneath her hand. "Pull over, T. Diggs, or I swear, I'll do you while you're driving."

He looked at her. Rayne started unbuttoning her blouse and exposed two petite breasts with erect nipples pointed in his direction. "I just want you to know how much I appreciate you, baby," she purred, "and this ride you've been so gracious enough to give me."

She unbuckled his belt, then unzipped his pants, leaned down, and engulfed his swollen penis in her mouth.

"Whoa! Rayne!" He swerved, then took the first off-ramp he came upon, and drove until he found a semiprivate spot behind an office building. Thank goodness, it was dark.

Rayne got him started with her mouth, then finished him off straddling him in the front seat, rolling that plump ass of hers in his lap. Tauris sucked hungrily on grape-size nipples until she bucked on top of him hard enough to shake his truck. They didn't come together, but they came damn close together.

Neither of them said another word until he got to Bear's house. Rayne leaned over and kissed him one last time before getting out. "I know I've got issues, Tauris," she explained softly. "But not one of them has anything to do with you."

"So, what am I supposed to do?"

Rayne didn't have an answer for that. She smiled, then climbed out of the car and shut the door.

He sat in his truck and waited for her to go inside. This wasn't the first time he'd tried to pull away from her, and it wasn't the first time she seemed to figure it out, and reel him back in. But it was the first time he'd ever had an option, sitting thick and pretty in Woodbridge, and she didn't come with half the drama of Rayne Fitzgerald.

BUT U DON'T

GIVE UP

LONG LIVE THE CHAMP

"Five—six—seven—"

Nora counted under her breath, along with the crowd surrounding her and the referee inside the MGM Grand Garden Arena in Las Vegas. Oblivious to the cameraman kneeling at her feet to get a shot at her reaction, she closed her eyes and mouthed the last number—ten—before the crowd erupted around her. She opened them in time to see Cole leap into the air and hang there like Michael Jordan on his best night, with his red-gloved fist in the air.

"The new International Boxing Association's Middleweight Champion of the World," the announcer shouted over the noise of the crowd, "Cole 'The Hammer' Burkett!"

It was official. Cole had won the World Middleweight Championship belt for the second time, and tears streamed down Nora's cheeks as her husband was being hoisted up in the ring by his fight team.

He didn't know she was here. She hadn't seen him in nearly a month, ever since he'd come to Paris. Nora had stayed in

Europe, developing her lingerie line, and doing photo shoots for Opulence Cosmetics. What started out being a part-time, occasional job for her had damn near put her back on a model's schedule, and Nora was exhausted.

Cole had been busy readying for this fight at his training facility in Cumberland, Virginia, just outside Richmond. They could blame their schedules for how little time they'd been spending together lately, or they could blame the truth. Their marriage was on shaky ground and had been for a long time. The last time they were together really opened her eyes, though. She heard something in his voice that hadn't been there before and for the first time, she really believed she could lose her husband.

Paris had been what they needed to try and get their marriage back on track. They'd spent the weekend reconnecting emotionally and physically in a place that had always possessed the power to fuse them together and seal the bond they'd established years ago for each other in their hearts.

They strolled along the pathways of Place des Vosges, with her arm in his, just like any other couple in any other city, high on each other, and the breeze swirling around them. For the first time in a long time, there was no tension between them. It almost felt as if everything that happened between them leading up to this day, never happened to them at all. Cole laughed at her stories, mostly about Basile, and squeezed her closer to him whenever he felt she might pull away. Nora even managed to coax him into try-ing escargot at a little bistro called Ma Bourgogne Café.

"Not bad," he eventually admitted. "But don't you tell nobody I ate that shit."

Nora laughed. "Your secret's safe with me, tiger."

Wrapped in Egyptian cotton sheets in their hotel room, sipping on champagne, the two of them instinctively seemed to know that they had to come to an understanding with each other or risk losing what they had. Time away from him always brought clarity for Nora. She grew too full of herself sometimes, and she pushed him to extremes to get the stimulation she needed to keep her living at the level to which she'd always craved. Sex was part of it. A big part. But she knew that it was even deeper than that. Nora wasn't spoiled. She was insensitive, numb most of the time, because she'd grown accustomed to existing at astronomical heights. Cole was the opposite. He was a superstar, an icon, but de-spite all of that, he was still that kid from South Philly, who still believed he had something to prove. He was old-fashioned, and even humble. These were the traits she loved most about him, and yet, they drove her crazy sometimes.

"Most of the time," she admitted, "I don't even feel like we're on the same page, Cole. We're so different, and it makes it hard to connect. But all I want to do is connect with you."

He ran his finger lightly up and down her shin. "I think we want the same thing, baby, but we don't always know how to get it. We want each other, and we want this marriage to work, but it's hard. If it was only one of us living in the limelight, then maybe in some ways it would be easier. But the way it is now, it's hard to focus on each other, Nora. I think frustration sets in for both of us, and we lose control."

"*I* lose control," she corrected him. "I don't mean to do that."

Cole was quiet.

Nora leaned over and kissed him. "I promise to do better," she said softly.

He rolled her over underneath him, and eased himself inside her. "Yeah," he said, gazing into her eyes. "Me, too."

After the fight, Nora hurried out of the arena before he saw her, and rushed back to her hotel room. Two hours later, she was dressed and stared at her long, lean frame in the full-length mirror of her hotel suite. She'd arranged to get the room across the hall from his. Tonight she needed to make a statement, but only to Cole. The celebration was going on in one of the ballrooms downstairs. Thousands of people were crowded around her husband, congratulating him on his victory, and Cole was basking in the glory of victory.

The sweeping, deep purple Versace gown she wore was sure to get his attention and make his mouth water: halter top, French silk cascading down to the floor. Underwear wasn't necessary. She slipped into black, Jimmy Choo suede and metal T-strap sandals, and ran her fingers through her hair, flowing down her back. She'd gained twenty pounds since her runway days, but standing six feet tall, she wore it well. He'd be surprised to see her—pleasantly, she hoped. Nora smiled at her reflection.

Nobody made an entrance the way Nora did. A hush fell over the crowd of hundreds filling the ballroom at the MGM. Even before he saw her, he felt her, and Cole turned in time to see the most beautiful sight he'd ever laid eyes on. Nora glided down the staircase to a sea of parting bodies, her eyes fixed on his, strutting like the whole room was her runway. Cole stood his ground, unable to take his eyes off her, knowing that everyone else in the room was immersed in a trance right along with him. She never hesitated, or skipped a beat, and the next thing he knew, his beautiful wife stopped in front of him, standing four inches taller in heels than he was. That shit turned him on. Nora pressed both hands against his chest, then tilted her head to the left, and grazed her luscious lips to his.

"I knew you'd come, baby," he whispered.

She smiled. "How'd you know that?"

"I needed you to be here."

Her long lashes brushed lightly against his cheek. "I need you, too, sweetie."

He grinned. "Let's get the hell out of here." Cole put down his drink, took his wife by the hand, and filtered his way through the cheering crowd.

"Way to go, champ!"

"Hammer! Don't hurt her!"

Nora would've blushed had she been the type.

He started at her toes, taking each one individually into his mouth until she squirmed. She was a long woman, and traveling the length of his wife was the task of a patient man. But they had all weekend, and if it took forty-eight hours to get the job done right, then it would take forty-eight hours.

By the time he'd made it to her sweet spot, Nora was writhing like a snake on the bed, hissing and scratching into the skin on his back.

"Bite it, Cole," she said, breathless. He tugged on her clit with his teeth. Nora moaned. "Again, baby! Please!"

He nibbled on it hard enough to make her come. Nora liked it rough. She wasn't the tender kind of woman who wanted him to make love to her. Cole pulled her hair, smacked her behind, jerked her around because it satisfied her.

"I love the passion, Cole," she confessed to him one night. "I need to know you want me and not apologize for it."

It was dawn when they finished. They slept until one o'clock in the afternoon, ordered room service, showered, and then started all over again.

WE BELONG

Cash leaned back on the sofa in the dark, with the volume turned down on the television. He was high, because it was the only way he knew how to be. Hell, he couldn't remember the last time he wasn't high. Dope was his bitch—or was it the other way around? And it was moments like this when he could feel her love for him. Drowning in euphoria, every thought that came to him was a good one. And the ones that weren't good, he made good.

Back in the day, he was a class act, sporting business suits, living in a nice house, with money burning in his pockets. Cash ate in fancy restaurants, drank high-end booze, and ran a polished operation. But that was back when he had his shit under control. Now, heroin had control of him, and he owed the wrong people a whole lot of money. Dwayne left Chicago running for his life, and everyday paranoia had him looking over his shoulder or in his rearview mirror, moving from one cheap motel to the other, just one step ahead of the kind of mess that could get his ass killed. Cash was living on borrowed time and a fucked-up liver. He'd gotten so bad with smack that he couldn't even shoot up anymore. Instead, he snorted it or smoked it, but never once had it ever crossed his mind to give it up.

Rayne thought he was here to hurt her. He let his eyes close slowly and pictured her in his mind. Thick thighs, hips, ass, smooth licorice-colored skin, he remembered every inch of that woman, and despite what she wanted to believe, he cared for her. He cared for J. T., too, but not in the way a friend—a good friend—would care for another friend.

Right after J. T. died, Cash moved to Chicago until he had no choice but to leave. She wasn't hard to find. Sweet Baby Rayne was doing her thing again, and doing it well. He followed a trail of posters and flyers to where she performed and for him, it was love at first sight all over again. He admitted to himself a long time ago that he loved her. Even when J. T. was his friend, Cash coveted the man's woman so bad, he hurt his own feelings. She only had eyes for her man, though. Back in those days she loved J. T.'s ass so deep that no man could compete with that.

But horse could, and it handed her to him on a silver platter, fulfilling every last one of his dreams. Despite what she wanted to believe, he made love to her. Rayne fucked him for dope, but he made love to her every time like she belonged to him and not that shit she was shooting up in her veins.

She kissed Cash probably imagining he was J. T., but it didn't matter. He filled his mouth with purple-black nipples, and tender pink pussy, and swore he'd died and gone to heaven.

"You got me hooked on that shit! And then you used me! You took me and used me the hell up, Cash!"

Nah, sweet baby, he thought remorsefully. *We used each other.*

He'd promised to leave her alone after her man died, to walk away and never look back. But they were soul mates on a level that she would never accept. If he could have her again, yes—he'd take all of her. But if he could ask her forgiveness and get a little bit of that, then yes. He'd take that, too.

Cash opened his eyes and stared at the television screen. Who the hell was he trying to fool? Her forgiving him was a fantasy. Rayne was easy. She was like him. She was a drug addict . . . a gotdamned junkie. If he wanted her, he could have her. They both knew that, and on some level, regardless of what she said with her mouth, the rest of her begged him to fill her up and take her back to that place and time when a fix was just a fuck away.

WHAT YOU WON'T DO

"I'm not crazy, Lamar." More and more, Lamar's wife was becoming insignificant to him. *"I don't know what's going on with you, but I know something is. You're never home, and when you tell me you're working late, I call the office, and no one answers. If I didn't know better I'd—"*

"You'd what?" He glared at her.

Rhonda swallowed her accusations, and changed her tone. *"We've been together too long to mess up now, Lamar,"* she said, gravely. *"We're at a time in our lives when we aren't responsible for anybody else but each other. Whatever is going on with you, we need to get past it, Lamar. There's too much to lose."*

Lamar sat in his car, parked on the dark street half a block from Kristine's house, recalling this recent conversation he'd had with Rhonda. Lately, all of their conversations had been sounding like this and he was getting sick of it. Rhonda was right about one thing. There was indeed too much to lose. More time, more wasted energy, more regret over not having what he really wanted out of life. He wanted Kristine. Lamar wanted a chance to live like a brand-new man, with a new love, and a new outlook for the next half of his life. As ridiculous as he sometimes felt, he couldn't help but to feel any other way.

"It's me, Kris." How many messages had he left? "Please, pick up, baby. Or call me. Please call me back."

How many times had he knocked on the door that she didn't answer. She was there. He knew she was. Lamar knocked all hours of the day and night, but she wouldn't let him in. Years ago, Bishop had given him a spare key, but Kristine changed the locks after the funeral.

She was driving him crazy keeping herself out of reach from him. Lamar watched a truck pull up in front of the house. He watched Kristine climb out of the passenger side, and moments later, a man joined her from the other side of the truck, and the two of them disappeared into the house. Lamar quickly climbed out of his car, and ran the half a block to her front door, and immediately rang the bell. She had to answer now. He took slow, deep breaths to calm himself, but it wasn't Kristine who answered.

Tauris held the door open. "Yeah?"

The knot in his stomach was hard enough to almost make Lamar double over. Gotdammit! He wanted to punch that mothafucka in the face. "Kristine," he said, trying to gather his composure.

Tauris looked at him strangely. "It's late, man."

Lamar stared back in disbelief. "I'm her uncle," he blurted out without thinking.

Reluctantly, Tauris stepped aside and let him in.

A few minutes later, Kristine came downstairs wearing a pink satin robe. "Tauris? What's taking so—" she stopped when she saw Lamar. "What are you doing here?"

Lamar stepped past Tauris, then stood at the bottom of the staircase staring up at her. Lamar put it all together quickly in his head, and it took everything he had not to give in to the rage churning in him. "I've been calling," he told her. "You haven't returned my calls, and I was worried."

She glanced at Tauris standing behind Lamar with a strange look on his face, then turned her attention back to Lamar, looking like a man possessed. "I'm fine, Uncle Lamar."

Kristine came down the staircase, and gently brushed past him and made her way to Tauris. She wrapped both arms around Tauris's waist. He put his arm around her shoulder.

"It's late," she said to Lamar. "Aunt Rhonda must be worrying sick over where you are."

"Can I talk to you, alone?" There was no mistaking the tension in his tone, but Lamar didn't care. Kristine was hesitant, but Lamar was determined. "*Now,* Kristine," he said sternly. Or so help him, he'd tell this mothafucka everything. She knew better than to refuse.

"What's going on here, man?" Tauris took a step toward Lamar. Uncle or no uncle, he didn't like the brotha's tone.

Kristine tugged on Tauris's arm to hold him back. "Let's

go into the library," she told Lamar, then turned to kiss Tauris. "It's all right, baby. This will only take a few minutes."

Lamar followed Kristine into the library, and shut the door behind them. "I have been calling," he said, clenching his teeth. "I've stopped by."

"And you need to stop calling and stop dropping by whenever you feel like it, Lamar," she said, keeping her voice down. "It's over! Oh my God! It's been over."

"Bullshit! You know how I feel about you. You know what you mean to me! It's not over! Not for me, Kristine."

"So—what? You're going to leave Rhonda and move in here with me? I don't want you like that, Lamar. I never did."

He looked enraged. "But you did, Kristine. You gave yourself to me, baby. You gave yourself to me of your own free will."

"I was a teenager."

"You weren't a teenager the last time I was here. Were you?"

Kristine turned away ashamed. "I'm not doing this, Lamar," she finally said. "I'm not letting you make up my mind for me. I'm not letting you come into my house and try to rule me. I'm not a child. I'm not Daddy's helpless little girl anymore, either."

"That's not what I'm doing," he protested.

"That's what you're trying to do!" she argued. "You can't make me want you, Lamar. You can't make me be with you.

You can't barge into my house and demand anything from me!" She crossed her arms defiantly. "I'm a grown woman, and I don't need you or anybody else telling me what I need to do. What I need to do"—she knew it would hurt him when she said it, but she needed to hurt him—"is that man standing out there in my living room."

She might as well have stabbed him in the heart. She hurt him, so Lamar struck back. "You're a fuckin' slut, Kristine," he said coldly. "Always have been."

Tears filled her eyes, but Kristine blinked them away. "Which was fine, I guess, as long as I was your slut. Right, Uncle?"

Kristine was noticeably upset after the old man left. "What's going on, Kris?" Tauris probed. It took some coaxing, but eventually she decided to open up and tell Tauris the truth.

The two of them sat on the sofa and he held her close. "I knew it was wrong, even back then." She couldn't bring herself to look him in the eyes. "I needed someone, Tauris," she explained earnestly. "No man had ever looked at me the way he did, and no one had ever held me that way."

"It's been going on ever since?" he asked quietly.

She nodded. "Off and on. More off than on."

She knew he didn't fully understand, and she didn't expect him to. "Lamar was safe," she said, shamefully. "He knows—knew—me, and I could be myself with him. I was so shy, Tauris, and I felt alone. He made me feel beautiful and cared for, but not like Daddy. Like a man cares for a woman, and I was young, so. . . ." She shrugged. "He was better than nothing, and the best I could do."

"So, what was going on tonight?"

She didn't answer.

"He doesn't want it to be over."

"No," she whispered.

Tauris stood up, and started pacing the room. Damn if he didn't just jump from the frying pan into the fire. He thought Rayne had drama, but at least her man was dead and buried. Kristine's man was practically family and the mothafucka was probably sitting outside the house at this very minute waiting for Tauris to make an exit.

"So, what the hell, Kristine?" he asked, annoyed.

"I told him to leave me alone, Tauris."

Tauris thought for a moment, then came to the only logical conclusion he could. "I need to talk to him."

"No!" She stood up.

He looked appalled. "You don't want me to talk to him. So that must mean you like being stalked by your perverted uncle."

"He's not my uncle!" she protested. "And no I don't like it, but that's not the way to handle this."

"He's probably outside," he said, heading toward the door.

She grabbed his arm. "He's married, Tauris!"

"I don't give a damn." He shrugged away from her.

"But I do! His wife has been like a mother to me. . . ."

Her voice trailed off. "If she ever found out . . ." Kristine's knees felt week, and she sat down, feeling like she was about to faint. This whole situation was just ridiculous, and telling it to someone else, only made it seem more so. "I don't want to hurt her."

He stared at her. "Yeah, well, I guess now is as good a time as any to figure that out."

She stared embarrassingly at him. "Maybe you should leave."

They'd had a nice dinner, seen a good movie, and had planned on making love until they fell exhausted into each other's arms, but after the scene with Lamar and having to confess the truth to Tauris, Kristine suddenly wanted to be alone.

"Is that what you want?" he asked, quietly.

She surprised him and shook her head. "No, but maybe you should."

Leave and do what? Think about her all night? He'd been looking forward to spending time with her all week, and all it took was that pseudo-uncle of hers to crawl out from under his rock to fuck it all up. That chump was outside. Tauris could feel it in his gut, and he wasn't about to let that fool think he'd run him off. Besides, she was gorgeous.

"I really would like to stay, Kristine."

She stood there, staring wide-eyed and confused and vulnerable all at the same time, and all of a sudden, he could see why the rest of the world felt like she needed to be taken care of. "What if I stay, but I don't say nothing. I don't touch nothing. And we don't do nothing."

She smiled. "Then what would be the point of you being here at all?"

He shrugged. "I'd just be here. You know? In case."

Tauris kept most of his promise. For the rest of the night, he didn't say another word, he didn't touch her unless she touched him first—which she did—and despite their best efforts, eventually, they did do something.

Lamar sat outside in his car until he finally saw the light go out in Kristine's bedroom window. The man in the house never left.

CAN'T TAKE MY EYES OFF OF YOU

She performed the way she always did, finding her groove, and bringing the audience along with her for the ride. Sometimes singing was like being high. It took her away to faraway places where nothing in the world mattered but the music and she regretted it when the journey ended and she had to come home.

Do know what I say is true
That I'll be loving you always

Rayne was center stage performing her rendition of Stevie Wonder's "As," scanning the room looking for Dwayne. He was there. She could feel him, lurking in the shadows like a damn ghost haunting her. Since that time she'd sat down and had a conversation with the man, Rayne had gone out of her way to avoid him. Finally, common sense had taken hold and she realized that having anything to do with Cash was a tragedy waiting to happen. He was her demise, pure and simple, and to let him take root in her life now would only serve to destroy everything she'd worked so hard to achieve.

Rx Williams from All Talk Records had been buzzing around her like a bee to honey in recent months, grooming her for what could possibly become the deal of her lifetime.

"They've listened to your CD, Rayne, and they liked what they heard. For years, the talent pool in this industry has been digitally enhanced to give the illusion of talent where there really was none, because an artist looked good or could dance. True talent is what I'm looking for. Someone who can sing, for real, and," he smiled and winked, "who ain't bad on the eyes, either."

"Just get me a contract, Rx," she told him. "And I'll do what I do best."

She'd been kicking her own ass for ever agreeing to see Cash. He'd tracked her down to the club all the way from Chicago, and had been hot on her tail ever since. The thought had crossed her mind several times lately, to leave DC. She could go someplace else, start over from scratch, and finally leave the bullshit behind her, but the possibility of this record deal coming through kept her here. Shaking things up by relocating and having to start over entirely wasn't a move she needed to make right now, if she wanted to see this thing come to fruition. And besides, All Talk Records wasn't looking for a drama queen on the run from a worn-out drug dealer. They needed to see a woman who had her shit tight and together. A woman who could handle the magnitude of a music contract with a major label.

Besides, if she was ever going to leave she missed her opportunity years ago. Rayne should've left town after her husband died, but she stayed here like her feet were glued to the ground. Staying here only served as a constant reminder that she was who she was, her old man was just as bad, and old friends and drug dealers would always know where to find her.

Dwayne finally stepped out of the darkness and into the light where she could see him. He watched her the way he'd been watching her since he'd come back to town, and Rayne uncontrollably shivered, and forgot her words. She hummed to hide the missed cue, and then turned away snapping her fingers, looking desperately to Bear.

"You all right, girl?" he asked, playing his keyboards.

Rayne shook her head no.

"Finish this set, baby girl," he told her. "You can do it. Just finish the set."

She slowly spun around and went back to the microphone in center stage. Cash stood looking up at her with red, bloodshot eyes, toying with something in his pants pocket, taunting her in that silent way he did. She knew what he had in his pockets. He wanted her to know, and all of a sudden, her veins felt like they were on fire.

• • •

The room was dark, except for the candles. Rayne was naked, lying on a bed of pillows, or a feather mattress. She couldn't tell which. Nancy Wilson's voice crooned from a distance.

"I saved the good stuff for you, darlin'." Cash knelt beside her, gently tying the rubber cord around her arm, then tapping her skin lightly to find a vein. His shirt was unbuttoned, and his sleeves rolled up to his elbows. Rayne stared up at him, terrified and afraid to move, afraid to scream or to run, but she wanted to do all of those things. She lay still and frozen, watching in horror as he pressed the tip of the needle to her arm, slid it painlessly into her skin, and emptied it.

"Shhhhh, lovely," he said pulling it out, and then stroking her hair. "I take care of you, Rayne," he said tenderly. "Don't you know that?"

That old familiar euphoria washed over her and Rayne felt heavy and weightless at the same time. Her head fell back, her arms sunk into pillows, her knees fell apart, and all that mattered was absolutely nothing.

"We gonna be together forever, baby girl," she heard his voice, and she knew he was there, but Cash might as well have been a million miles away.

He eased himself between her thighs, and kissed her shoulders. "People like us belong together. All you need to do is let me do what I do best, Rayne. Let me take care of you the way I always did. Stop pushing me away."

He kissed her, but Rayne didn't kiss back. Cash grabbed both sides of her head, and raised it to his, forcing her to give him what she didn't have the strength to give, or the desire. All that mattered was being high. Didn't he know that?

Without warning, he broke the seal of their kiss, raised his head to the sky, and screamed at the top of his lungs. Rayne floated above both of them, watching the whole scene unfold.

The shrill of his scream woke her up from a dead sleep, and Rayne bolted upright out of breath, her heart pounding a million miles a minute. She looked around her bedroom, and then rubbed sleep from her eyes. Damn! She drew her knees to her chest. The sun rays sliced through the closed blinds, and Rayne took another deep breath, relieved that she'd had a fucking nightmare. "It wasn't real," she said out loud. Rayne fell back on her pillow, and stared up at the ceiling.

She thought about calling her counselor Anna, just to talk and to hear all the reasons that Rayne should start going back to her meetings on a regular, consistent basis. And then, she missed Bishop, but not the old man's lectures, just his presence. In the past, just knowing that he was walking around someplace on this Earth, judgmental and condemning was enough to scare her straight.

"You're a big girl, now, Rayne," she said out loud. "So stop believing in the boogeyman and tighten up your game."

MON CHERI

Luxurious. Everything about Ms. Fontaine was luxurious, and comfortable, and warm. On any other Sunday, he'd be holed up at the house, eating takeout from the little soul-food joint up the street from where he lived, kicking back, and watching some game on television. She'd invited him over for supper, and of course he'd said yes. Red beans and rice, cornbread, smothered pork chops, and, for later on, peach cobbler and vanilla ice cream.

She'd been kind enough to give him another kind of dessert to tie him over in the interim. They basked in the laziness of the afternoon, in her queen-size bed, cocooned in pillows wrapped in the softest cotton sheets he'd ever felt. Tauris rested his head on the pillows of her full breasts, the rest of him cradled between her soft thighs, while she softly stroked his head. A cool breeze blew in through the open window, and the rustling of leaves from the tree outside made its own kind of quiet music, softer than a lullaby. You couldn't tell him that his ass hadn't died and gone to heaven.

"I think I need to start looking for a job," she said, introspectively.

Damn, he wished she'd be quiet and just savor the peace and quiet and the aroma of good sex. "Why is that?" he replied, not really caring one way or another as to why this rich woman would feel the need to get a nine-to-five.

"I'm getting fat sitting around all day doing nothing."

Tauris sighed, and kissed the swell of her breast. "Really?"

"Maybe I should go to college and get a degree in something."

"Maybe."

"Are you even listening to me?"

"Yep." She smelled so damn good. Tauris buried his nose in the crease between her full breasts and inhaled deeply.

She hit him playfully on his shoulder. "You're too neck-deep buried in boobs to hear a word I've said," she argued.

"I'm listening, baby." He pulled his face up out of the trenches long enough to gaze into her lovely eyes.

"I don't want to run a chain of funeral homes," she said emphatically. "And I don't want to be in business with Lamar."

"Nobody's making you do either one, Kristine. If you want to go to college, then go to college. If you don't want to run funeral homes, then don't. But all that's up to you, sweetheart, so make up your mind and make it happen."

He was absolutely right. Kristine had too much time on her hands, but it was her time and she could do whatever she wanted to do with it. "I think I'll call my attorney tomorrow, and talk to him about selling off my half of the business," she said triumphantly.

"You do that. And when you decide to go to college, let me know and I'll buy you your first book bag."

He studied her, making note of every freckle on her lovely face. She was the kind of woman he imagined men just fell in love with as she passed them on the street. What caught him off guard was the fact that he could easily see himself being one of those men.

"Why are you looking at me like that?"

"I like what I see. Anything wrong with that?"

She laughed. "Oh, no! Nothing at all wrong with that."

"You're getting to me, baby. And I'm not sure what to do about that."

"What would you like to do about it, Tauris?"

Tauris smiled. "I just want to take my time and enjoy it while I can."

"Me, too," she said softly. "But I don't know if I'm as patient as you are. I've had a crush on you for a long time," she teased.

"Yeah, I know," he said, confidently.

"Don't sound so cocky about it."

"Hell, what man wouldn't be cocky? A fine-ass woman like you, scoping a common brotha like myself—I'm pounding on my chest like a damn ape, right about now."

"You're a mess, Tauris," she laughed. "If I told you I loved you, would you be offended?" she asked shyly.

"No, baby. I wouldn't be offended," Tauris replied softly. "I'd just tell you to slow it down a bit. You don't know what I know about love, and I'd hate for you to end up disappointed."

"I don't think I have anything to worry about with you."

Tauris wasn't ready to commit and say that he loved her, but he knew that he was well on his way to getting there. He didn't want to hurt this woman. He didn't want to let her down, but loving her was a word away—Rayne.

SET IT FREE

He wouldn't apologize for love. When it was all said and done, Lamar might burn in hell for it, but he'd never apologize for it. That was a solemn fact.

She was on his mind, all day and all night long. But Kristine didn't want anything to do with him anymore. She wasn't that same cornered, lonely girl who'd needed him to show her what it was for a man to love a woman. Lamar leaned back in his leather chair behind his desk, and closed his eyes, recalling the times when they made love in his office. She was more woman than she realized she was, and enough of a woman to take possession of his soul. It was her innocence, her uncertainty about herself that entrenched him. But those traits were slowly diminishing in Kristine, and she was beginning to see what he'd seen in her all along: that she was a desirable woman with the power to win any man's heart.

The thought of her making love to that sonofabitch infuriated Lamar. He'd laid her gotdamned floors, for crying out loud! What the hell made him think that he deserved a woman like her? Kristine was worth millions. Lamar might not have been as insulted if she'd stepped over him for the CEO of some corporation, a doctor, a diplomat, someone better than the gotdamned repairman, but that alone was a sign of her true naïveté. Kristine didn't know any better. Despite her efforts and declarations about being grown, she didn't know her ass from a hole in the ground when it came to men. This one was a snake, a scavenger, who found out how much she was worth, and was slowly taking advantage of her.

She had no idea what she was doing. Lamar felt himself drowning in the disappointment that she was making a huge mistake with this man. This one would surely break her heart and probably get away with some of her money, if not all of it when the dust settled. How many more men would end up doing the same?

Lamar didn't need her money. He needed her. Just her.

"Mr. Brown," his assistant called him on the intercom. "Your wife is on the line."

Lamar sighed. "Thank you, Dahlia."

"Do you need anything else before I leave for the day?"

"No. You have a good evening."

"You, too."

She put through the call from Rhonda.

"When are you coming home?" his wife asked, uneasily.

It annoyed the hell out of him that she'd even ask him that. But then he remembered that she'd always called him up at the end of the day to ask him when he was coming home. Rhonda was a creature of long, drawn-out habits that turned her into a dull, uneventful woman. He had loved her, once. But it had been so long ago, he could hardly remember when.

"You've got a good woman in Rhonda," Bishop used to tell him all the time. "Good women are hard to find, Lamar. Pay attention to her. Keep her close and take good care of her until there's nothing she could possibly want that she doesn't already have. A good man can keep a good woman. A greedy man will lose her, every time, then hate himself for it, when she's gone."

"You've never been a greedy man, Bishop," Lamar laughed. "So you don't know anything about losing a woman. Violet would never leave you."

Bishop stared solemnly at Lamar. "Violet is not my first wife, Lamar," he confessed. "And yes. I have lost and I have regretted, but I learned my lesson. I learned it the hard way."

Bishop never elaborated on his confession, and no one was more shocked than Lamar to learn that Bishop had been married before. Like with most things, though, Bishop's words took root deep in Lamar and he kept them, even tried to live them as best he could. Rhonda had always been a good woman. She always would be. But Lamar was tired, he'd lost interest a long time ago, and Bishop was buried in the ground. Lamar saw no point in trying to keep his friend's advice anymore.

"I'll be leaving in an hour," he finally said.

"Then I won't keep dinner warm."

"That's fine."

He expected her to hang up, but Rhonda had more to say. "Oh, before I forget, I've invited Kristine over for dinner next Sunday."

Lamar's heart jumped in his chest at the mention of her name.

"She said she'd try and make it and she's going to check with a friend of hers to see if he can come, too."

He clenched the pen he'd been holding in his hand. "That's . . . nice, Rhonda."

Lamar was about to say good-bye when she continued talking. "I think he's more than a friend by the way she went on and on about him the last time I spoke to her."

"Well, that's none of our business," he said curtly.

"Of course, it is," she said flippantly. "She might as well be our daughter, Lamar. I care, even if you don't."

"I never said I didn't care. Kristine doesn't need our approval to see anybody."

"No, she doesn't. But Kristine doesn't have a lot of experience when it comes to relationships. I just don't want to see her get hurt. That's all."

"Neither do I."

"Then I think it's a good idea for us to meet her new friend."

"And if we don't approve?"

Rhonda hesitated. "Well, I don't know about that, Lamar, but we can at least make sure she is aware of what we think."

"I doubt seriously she cares what we'd think about her boyfriend, Rhonda."

"Probably not, but I'd do the same with my own children, and I have, Lamar."

"She's not your kid." His irritation was starting to show through.

"Does saying that out loud make you feel better, Lamar?" she asked quietly.

It was an odd question coming from her. Lamar suspected there was more to it than the obvious, but this wasn't the first time he sensed something strange coming from Rhonda on the subject of Kristine. He wondered if maybe she knew about their affair, and then he wondered if it wasn't just his guilty conscience condemning him.

"It's just the truth, Rhonda," he responded. "I'm sure that if she needs us, she'll let us know, but I don't think she needs us at the moment."

Rhonda didn't respond right away, and he almost thought she'd hung up on him. "I'll probably be asleep by the time you get home. Good night, Lamar."

Lamar dialed Kristine's number, knowing he'd get her voice mail. "Don't bring him to the house, Kristine. I'm begging you. Please, don't bring that man to my house."

HERE'S TO YESTERDAY

Cash was dying.

"Got a bad liver," he told her. "Bad heart. That's the price you pay, I guess," he laughed. "Gotta die to fly."

It was the only reason Rayne had agreed to meet with him again, but again, only in a public place. He sat across from her wearing a wrinkled, brown suit and a stained tie.

Watching him, Rayne wondered if she should feel pity for him, but she knew better. Disdain was the emotion she sat in at the moment, but he was a shining example of what they'd all been five years ago and she needed to stop and look long and hard at what was in her future, if she fell off the wagon.

"Time for you to let go of the past, baby girl. What's done is done, and ain't nothing gonna change that," he had the nerve to tell her.

"I'm not hanging on to the past, Cash," she argued. "I'm trying to avoid reliving it. Being around you makes that hard for me to do."

"What you see is me, right here and right now, sugar. It's

not me from back in the day. You tripping over who I—who we both were in those days. You tripping over what happened to your man."

"No, Dwayne. I'm tripping over what could've happened to me and didn't. I'm tripping over what I'm capable of with you back in my life. My man died in my arms but it could've just as easily have been the other way around."

"But it wasn't you, Rayne," he said.

"It wasn't, and it's not going to be me," she said defensively. "I've worked too hard to beat my addiction, and I'm still working hard. I can't stand the sight of you, and if you cared so much for me, the way you claim to, then you'd leave me the hell alone. But you won't do that, will you? Because you want what you want, and you think you want me. I can't give you me, Cash. You have that shit on you right now, and don't say it ain't true because I know better. I hear it calling my name. That's what you brought here to me. And you don't give a damn because dope's got you by the soul, about to carry you off to the grave, and you could care less."

He couldn't help but smile. "You got a point."

His response caught her off guard and Rayne surprised herself and laughed bitterly. "You're a fool, Dwayne."

He shrugged. "Yeah, well, some things never change, sugar." He thought better than to tell her that he was a fool for her. Cash was a man who gave up on expectations a long time ago. He didn't expect this woman to be his, but the memory of her had lured him back here, if for no other reason than to lay eyes on her again. More and more he was learning to listen to his instinct and it told him that if he didn't come see about her this time, he might not ever get another chance.

"I never meant to hurt you, Rayne," he said, sadly. "I know you don't believe that but it's true. Shit, when you made friends with me, you made friends with the devil, which is fucked up because back then I didn't know that's what I was. I know it now, though."

"I know it, too," she said quietly. "You turned me into an animal. No," she corrected herself, "I made me into an animal, and so did J. T., but we used you to do it. Sometimes I don't even know why I resent you so much," she said, introspectively. "Maybe because I resent me for not having more control. J. T. had problems with drugs when I met him, but he said he had it under control. I was young and dumb, and I believed him. I loved him so much I'd have followed him into the ocean if he'd asked me." She swallowed, blinking away tears that threatened to fall. Rayne was through crying. "I did things that I hate myself for. I did things with you that I will never forgive myself for."

Cash scratched his head and decided to take advantage of the opportunity. "Well, I don't hate you for them," he joked.

She stared at him.

"I mean, I dug being with you, Rayne. I can't lie. And however you wanted to serve it up to me, for whatever reason, I wasn't about to turn you away."

"Well, you should've. If you were my friend, if you were J. T.'s friend—"

"If he was your man, and if he cared so much for you, he should've been the one to stop you, baby girl." He knew he'd wounded her, but she needed to hear it. "Not me." Hell, it hurt, but it was the truth. "You busy blaming me and blaming you, but you never once say any of that shit was his fault. Why? Because he died? Hell, like you said, it could've just as easily been you who died that night, Rayne. J. T.'s ass got lucky, that's all."

There. He'd said it, and he meant it. She'd been so busy worshipping that junkie's ass that she forgot to see J. T. wasn't any better than either of them, and he didn't warrant the idol worship she'd given him.

"I loved you, Rayne," he confessed with tears in his eyes. "I know you don't want to hear it, and I know you don't believe it, but I did—I do. I ain't never had a damn thing in my life that I loved more than you, and if I didn't come back here for nothing else than to tell you that, well, it was worth the gas."

Cash dropped ten dollars down on the table to pay for the coffee, and left just that quickly.

Rayne had no idea how long she sat there after he left. His words had fallen on deaf ears, but they'd fallen and lay like bricks at her feet. Drug love is perverse love and all three of them had fallen victim to it in one way or another: Rayne's blind love for J. T. put him so high up on a pedestal

Jesus could've slapped him a high-five, and it had exoner-
ated him from any fault in the life the two of them had built
together. Cash's so-called love for her facilitated the destruction of the woman she'd once been. And J. T.'s love? Her
name was heroin. Enough said.

WAS IT SOMETHING I SAID?

"You have the whole world believing that you and Cole have the perfect marriage." Taylor was on location in Montreal, but she called him anyway. Nora had been driving around the city for hours with the top down on her silver Mercedes McLaren Roadster trying to clear her head or cool her desires, or both.

"How was the premiere?" she asked, trying to get him off the subject of her relationship to Cole.

"It was good. You'll probably see pictures of me on the worst-dressed list all over the Internet tomorrow, if you're curious."

"So, what else is new? You're always on that list, Taylor. Didn't some magazine name you the most handsome man in the universe or some shit like that?" she asked sarcastically.

"*People*, two years in a row. I'm shooting for a third."

"Your ass is sloppy."

"And your ass needs to be fucked properly," he said flippantly. "Why else would you be calling me this late? You must miss Daddy."

She rolled her eyes. "Cole's at home."

Taylor laughed. "I meant your real daddy, darlin'. Cole can't smack it with the same conviction as I can, and you know it."

Just talking to him, thinking about him was making her moist. Things between Nora and Cole had been tame and surreal, just the way he liked it. Nora wanted to like it that way. She wanted to be the kind of woman he always dreamed of having for a wife, who loved the missionary position, baking apple pies, and having babies every year. He never came out and said that's what he wanted, but she suspected as much was true.

It was the way he went on and on about that uncle or cousin or whatever he was to Cole, the one who died recently. Bishop was his name. Cole worshipped him, but the old man gave Nora the creeps by the way he stared at her and the even tempo of his tone that never changed, regardless of what emotion he might be feeling at the time, and the obedient disposition of his wife and daughter. Something wasn't right in that funky bunch, but Cole, for whatever reason, could never see it.

"Bishop's old school, that's all," he tried to explain to Nora. "I don't think he's ever met anyone like you, baby. Strong, independent. He just doesn't know how to take you. But he doesn't mean anything by it."

Every time Cole visited Bishop, though, the man's influence was all over her husband like cheap cologne.

"Bishop said . . ."

"Bishop did . . ."

"You should've seen Bishop . . ."

Full of admiration and awe, the man might as well have been the Messiah to Cole, and she fully expected him to come back from a meeting with Bishop one day and tell her that the man walked on water.

"When can I see you, Taylor?" she asked suddenly.

Taylor laughed. "Do you know how hard it is to be people like me and you sneaking around having an illicit affair?"

She sighed. "I can be in Montreal day after tomorrow," she said, indifferently.

"I'm busy that day."

Taylor liked to make her squirm. He liked to make himself seem unavailable to her when she needed him the most, because he was that kind of man. The kind who wanted to hear a woman beg, see her sweat, make her cry.

"What about next weekend? Mexico?"

Taylor was quiet for a while before answering. "How badly do you want it, dear?" he asked menacingly. "Tell me how bad, and maybe I'll consider Mexico."

Nora's mouth watered, and she swallowed. "Bad."

"Now, tell me how you want it, and maybe I'll consider the day after tomorrow."

She had images in her head, fantasies that she fed off of when she and Cole made love to help get her off. Things that Cole wouldn't think to do on his own, and that he'd look at her crazy for, if she brought it up. Things that Taylor did instinctively, that he came by naturally.

Nora cleared her throat. "I want you to force me to my knees."

"And?" he coaxed.

"And pull my hair," she continued quietly.

"And?"

The vision started to come into focus more clearly, and Nora pulled over to the side of the road. "Push your cock into my mouth, and shove it in so deep, that I choke."

"And what else, Nora," he asked quietly.

"Cum on my face." She squeezed her eyes shut.

Taylor sighed. "But what if I don't want to cum? What if I'm not ready to cum so quickly?"

"I want you to grab me by the throat, Cole."

"I'm not Cole," he said gruffly.

"Then hit me," she said quietly. "Hit me for calling you that."

"What else?"

"Bend me over, Taylor."

"Over what?"

"Over . . . the back of the couch, a chair—over anything."

"You like it from behind. Don't you, baby?"

"You know I do."

"You like it up the ass, Nora?"

She took a deep breath. "I do," she whispered.

Nora was so hot, she put her fingers between her legs, slid her panties to the side, and touched herself. "You can do whatever you want to me, Taylor," she said, breathless. "I just need to see you."

She waited for him to respond. Taylor took his sweet time before he finally did.

"I'll see you the day after tomorrow."

"In Montreal?" she asked.

"In Cozumel, love. You know the place."

Taylor hung up without saying good-bye, and yes, Nora knew the place well. Secluded, on the beach, intimate. First thing in the morning, she'd call her assistant and have her rearrange some things on her calendar. All Cole needed to know was that she had a photo shoot with Opulence.

NO-MAN'S LAND

"The last time I saw you we were getting busy in the front seat of that big, black, pickup truck you've got," she said, sliding into a seat at the bar next to Tauris. "If I were any other woman, I'd swear I'd been used, but I know better."

Tauris chuckled. "Thank goodness."

"So, who is she?" She motioned to Paul, the bartender. "Club soda and lime. What's her name?"

"Her name is Working My Ass Off Lately," he joked. "Know her?"

Rayne rolled her eyes. "I guess it doesn't matter what her name is. But she must be one bad-ass bitch to get your attention off me."

He glanced at her out of the corner of his eye. Rayne smirked. "You know I'm just playing."

"You got me in stitches over here, girl," he said dryly.

"I take it you wanted to see me?"

"What gave you that idea?"

"Why else would you be sitting up here in my club?"

"Your club?" He looked appalled. "Who the hell told you this was your club?"

"I'm working here, T. Diggs. Or didn't you see the sign at the front door?"

"I live less than five blocks from this spot, Rayne Fitzgerald. This is where I stop every now and then to have a drink on my way home."

"I still think you missed my ass or something. You can't miss that big old poster of me and Bear and the boys, and if you really were through with me, you'd have kept your behind on the road to your place and bypassed me altogether."

"Is that what you want to believe? That I can't get you out of my system and that I ain't got nothing better to do than to sniff around after you like a damn bloodhound?"

She leaned into him and smiled. "Hell, yes," she said seductively. "That's exactly what I want to believe."

Tauris couldn't help but laugh.

Rayne's expression suddenly turned serious, though. "You are seeing someone else. Aren't you, Tauris?"

He thought for a moment before answering. "And if I am?"

Rayne finished her drink and then got up from her seat. "Then I hope she makes you happy. I have to go make music, baby." She kissed him on his cheek and headed in the direction of the stage.

Tauris left before she'd even finished the first song. In five minutes, he was home. He showered, and had crawled into bed. There was a message from Kristine on his cell phone, but he wasn't in the mood to call her back. He stopped by the club for a drink, saw that Rayne was performing and decided to hang around long enough to get a glimpse of her. Tauris was in one hell of a predicament. On the one hand, he had the sweetest woman in the world ready to slide into position and become his everything, and on the other, he had a dull ache in his side for the one he could never have no matter how hard he tried.

Rayne was embedded deep in his system. Staying away from her helped, but it never quite cleansed him completely of her. Seeing Rayne tonight, what the hell did he expect? Did he expect for her to, all of a sudden, turn a flip in the air and shout at the top of her lungs that she was in love with him and wanted him as badly as he'd wanted her?

Absolutely, T. Diggs. I'll be your woman, and give you my mind, body, and soul and you can scoop me up with both hands, take me away from all of this, and we can live happily ever fuckin' after.

Kristine might say something like that, but Rayne never would. It was about damn time he figured that shit out and left Rayne alone once and for all.

The sound of the doorbell startled him awake. Tauris glanced at the digital clock by his bed, and saw that it was three in the morning. He rubbed sleep from his eyes, and stumbled through the darkness through the living room to the front door.

"I don't want to be by myself tonight," Rayne told him. "I can sleep on the couch," she smiled sheepishly.

She was losing him and Rayne wasn't ready for that. As many times as she'd pushed him away, solace came in knowing that he'd never really leave her. The look in his eyes lately told her otherwise, and she was starting to realize that she wasn't as strong as she thought she was. Tauris wasn't as unnecessary as she once believed he was.

He stepped aside and let her in. Tauris never said a word and he crawled back into bed, leaving her standing there in the dark. Rayne looked at the couch, and then she thought about him sleeping in that big bed by himself. She followed him to his room, quietly undressed, and crawled into bed next to him. She waited for half an hour, but Tauris never laid a hand on her and before long, she heard him snoring softly.

Eventually, she turned over and fell asleep, too.

Kristine turned the corner heading toward Tauris's house just in time to see him pull out of his driveway with a woman sitting in the passenger seat. She'd come to surprise him, and had planned on making him breakfast. Apparently, he'd already had breakfast.

"Don't jump to conclusions before you have all the facts, Kristine," her father used to tell her.

This was one conclusion she didn't want to believe was

true. Kristine hurried and dialed Tauris's cell-phone number.

"Yeah," he answered.

She took a slow deep breath to calm herself down. "Hi, it's me."

"Hey," he said, after hesitating. "What's up?"

No baby. Sweetheart. Kristine.

"I wanted to know if you were free for breakfast. I could come over or you could come here."

"Uh . . . not this morning," he sounded vague. "I'm meeting with a client. As a matter of fact, he's late."

Kristine fought back tears. "Oh. Well, maybe lunch, then, or dinner?"

"I'll call you."

Rayne stared out of the window. "I take it that was her?"

He didn't answer.

"That's what I thought," she said.

STONE COLE

"Really, Cole." Nora brushed past him and went into her closet where her stylist and assistant were busy picking out her wardrobe for the rest of the week for her trip to Cozumel. "It's not going to be a pleasure trip. Make sure to pack the silver sandals," she told them. "No, the other ones. There."

"Well, let's turn it into one." He shrugged, standing in the doorway. "I can rearrange some things, baby, and after your shoot, we can hang out for a few days and work on our tans." He grinned. "We've both been saying we need some time off together, so . . . the way I see it, the only way we're going to get it is to just make it happen. To hell with everything else."

She forced a smile, brushed past him again, and headed into the bedroom. "Easier said than done, sweetie." Nora sat down at her vanity and started brushing her hair. She'd told Cole that she was meeting her agent, Cassandra, to discuss a possible offer for her life story from a major publisher, but that wasn't the truth. The truth was that she was frustrated. Cole's sudden decision to rearrange his schedule to accommodate this trip threatened to ruin the time she'd planned on spending with Taylor. Cole's actions were smothering, and he was starting to piss her off. He thought he was being considerate and romantic, but he was being controlling in her book, and Nora didn't like it one bit. She quickly applied her makeup.

"I'm going to be super busy on this shoot, Cole," she tried explaining again.

"I understand that, baby," he said standing behind her, rubbing her shoulders.

It took everything she had in her not to shrug off his touch.

"I can entertain myself for a few days, Nora, while you work. And when you're finished, we can relax and just enjoy each other with no cameras, no reporters. Nothing but sand, sun, and us, sweetheart. We need this. You know we do."

Ideas and lies tumbled in her head. Nora couldn't let this opportunity pass. Taylor was as busy as she was, and it could be impossible for the two of them to see each other soon. If she missed this trip, Nora had no idea when the next one would come along, and she needed him. Dammit! She needed this time to scratch that itch that had been driving her mad for months now.

She was tense. Cole could feel it in her shoulders; he could see it in her face. This trip had come at the last minute, and a last-minute anything always made her anxious. "I've already made arrangements for a private house on the beach, baby," he said, soothingly. "Getting away will do us both some good." Cole leaned down and kissed the side of her neck.

Nora was disgusted with herself for what she knew she had to do. Her sanity depended on it. She loved him so much. But she needed someone else, not for long. But long enough to help her get her bearings and satisfy that primal side of her that didn't deserve this tender man.

"Lisa! Nicole!" Nora called out to her stylist and assistant. "Please leave."

The two women appeared from her closet. "Do you want us to finish packing toni—" one of them started to ask.

"Now!" she commanded. "Come back in the morning. Early."

Cole stepped back smiling, confidently believing that she told them to leave so that she could be alone with her man. Nora waited until she heard the front door close.

"I thought they'd never leave, baby," he said, stretching out across the bed. "Sugah, girl. I need some sugah."

"I told you." She stared at his reflection from her mirror. "I have to meet with Cassandra."

"Call her, and postpone. I'm sure she'll understand." He reached out his hand to her. "Come here."

She stared at him, and all Nora could see was another faked orgasm, a hunger for the kind of sex he didn't come by naturally, the dark fantasy of another man, and suddenly, she felt repulsed by him.

"Go to hell, Cole," she said icily.

The expression in his eyes darkened. "Don't start."

Angry tears flooded her eyes, but her gaze never left him. "I am not the little woman, Cole," she said, gritting her teeth. "This is not a fairy tale, and I will not have you monopolize my time."

Cole sat up. "That's not what I'm doing," he said, remaining calm.

"I have a job to do, and I will not let you fuck that up for me."

Cole sighed. "What the hell is happening, Nora? What's going on? Things have been good between us, baby. Now all of a sudden—"

"All of a sudden," she stood up and turned to face him, "you want to rule a bitch! You want to dictate my time like it's your own and I don't appreciate that shit, Cole!" Tears streamed down her face.

Cole stared at her perplexed. "Where is this coming from? I'm not trying to rule a damn thing!"

Nora walked over to him, and stood in front of him. She knew which buttons to push, and how hard to push, and when to push. She knew he loved her more than his own life, and that eventually, he could forgive her. She counted on it. "I'm going to Mexico. I'm going to do my job, and I'm going to do it without you hovering around me like some overly possessive fool!"

"What?"

"I've got enough pressure on me, Cole. I don't need you breathing down my neck like some needy bitch, watching every move I make!"

He started to stand up. "What the hell are you talking about, Nora?"

Nora's hand came hard out of nowhere and landed hard against the side of his face. "You heard me! I know you heard me!" She swung to hit him again, but this time he caught her by the wrist, twisted her arm behind her back, and threw her face down on the bed.

"I could break your fuckin' arm!" he growled, pressing his weight down on her.

Nora twisted and kicked at him. "Do it! Fuckin' do it, Cole! If you think you can!"

He let her go, then stepped back, bewildered by what just happened. "You're fuckin' crazy," he said, rubbing his face. Cole slowly backed out of the room, confused by the sudden change in her attitude. She'd flipped on him in a matter of moments, for no damn good reason except that he wanted to spend time with his wife. Cole went downstairs, picked up his keys, and left the house.

Nora had been on edge ever since Cole mentioned the trip to Cozumel. Cole thought about what had happened between them, what had been happening between them as he drove toward Manhattan recalling an observation made by Bishop where Nora was concerned.

"A woman as beautiful as Nora has the whole world watching her. A woman as beautiful as your wife has a thousand men wanting her, Cole."

"What are you saying, Bishop?"

"Nothing, son. I'm an old-fashioned man, so I'm not saying anything. But I always know where my woman is, and what she's doing. But like I said, I'm old fashioned."

Bishop had said plenty. Until tonight, Cole's relationship with Nora had been back on track, and he couldn't have been happier. He thought she was happy, too. But Nora's snap change in attitude about Cole joining her on this trip stirred suspicion in him. He'd never had it before, because she'd never tripped on him this way before about something like this. The timing was the thing that got his attention. Nora came to him a day ago about a last-minute fashion shoot for Opulence. Cole told her that he might be able to adjust some things on his calendar to join her, and she goes off.

"So what the hell else is waiting for you in Cozumel," he muttered out loud, "besides taking pictures, Nora?"

Cole had never allowed himself to get jealous. Nora had traveled the world, she was stunning, and she was his. So what was this feeling he had all of a sudden eating away at his gut, warning him that she was bullshitting him?

MY HEART AND SOUL

He hadn't seen her in days and the last few times he called her, she was very short with him and rushed to get off. All the signs were there. Tauris had done something to piss her off. He had no idea what, but he knew some major damage control was needed and he had to step up his game in an uncharacteristically big way. So, he put on his best suit jacket, jeans, and shoes, got a haircut that day, and stopped at a floral shop on the way to Kristine's house.

"I've got a woman mad at me about something," he explained to the florist. "I don't know what it is, and I don't want to know, but I need to make up for whatever it is in a way that's over the top and too good to be true. What do you recommend?"

He showed up at her door with a dozen wild, plum roses, a smile, and an apology all made to order just for her.

Kristine answered the door wearing a pair of gray, over-sized sweats, socks, with her hair plaited down the back. She looked shocked to see him standing there, dressed to the nines.

"Tauris? What are you doing here?"

He shoved the flowers at her before she had a chance to slam the door on him. "Awww, sugah." He stepped inside. "You look good enough to eat, girl." He bent down and kissed her passionately on the lips.

She backed away and fussed uncomfortably with her hair. "I wish you'd have called. I could've put on some decent clothes, and did something with my hair."

He stood there smiling. "If I'da called, baby, it wouldn't be a surprise."

Naturally, she looked irritated, but even irritated looked good on her short, plump ass. Damn! He'd missed her. "I hope you haven't eaten. I'm taking you to dinner."

"Dinner?"

"Yeah," he cozied up next to her. "I have something special in mind."

Again, she stepped away. "No. I haven't eaten, but—I'm really not hungry, Tauris."

"No problem. You can watch me eat," he grinned. "Don't turn me down, Kris. I have missed you and it took a lot out of me to pull this together. The only reason I did was because of you, baby."

Kristine hesitated. Two days ago, she'd seen him with another woman, and now he stood here as if it never happened, looking good, smelling good, and desperate to do something special for her. Too many emotions filled her and clouded her judgment. "I'll have to change."

He protested and gently took hold of her hand. "No, you don't."

"Tauris!"

He led her to the door, picked up her purse and keys from the table next to it and shoved them in her arms. "You look beautiful, girl." He kissed the tip of her nose. "Got-damned beautiful."

They hurried out of the door, and climbed into his pickup truck that he'd had detailed earlier in the day just for her, and sped away. "I can't go anywhere looking like this," she exclaimed, taking down her braid, and then combing her fingers through her hair. "Tauris, please!"

He just smiled, then thirty minutes later, turned down a dirt road, following it until it ended at the top of a hill over-looking the city. Kristine sat stunned and confused by him, watching from inside the cab as he unfolded a small table and chairs and set them up in the bed of his truck. He flipped open a white tablecloth, lit candles, and set the table with two plates, silverware, glasses, then came around to the front of the truck, opened her door, and helped her out. He'd set up a stool in back for her to climb up in.

"I ain't much of a cook," he explained as he served food he'd bought at one of his favorite soul-food places in town, "but these folks do a hell of a job, if I do say so myself."

Tauris served fried fish, macaroni salad, greens, corn-bread, and black beans and rice, and then filled her glass with white wine and his with beer.

It was the most romantic moment she'd ever had.

He raised his glass in the air to toast. "I don't know what I've done, baby, but whatever it is, I'm sorry," he said passionately. "And if you can forgive me just for tonight, then I'm cool with that."

She was so overcome by his thoughtfulness, Kristine nearly cried.

"Don't do that." He saw it coming. "I'm not good with tears, Kristine. Just nod your head if you dig all this?"

She nodded. "I do." She tapped her glass to his and took a sip of wine.

After dinner, Tauris moved the table and chairs from the truck bed and put away the food. He pulled a blanket from inside the cab and the two of them sat, gazing down at the city. Kristine leaned back against him, letting him stroke her hair and kiss the side of her neck.

"I can't believe you did all this," she finally said. "It was beautiful."

He chuckled. "Yeah, well, don't you tell nobody," he teased. "I ain't the most romantic brotha in the world, but I have my moments if I try real hard."

"Your secret's safe with me," she promised.

"Besides, girl," he squeezed her. "I can say without a doubt that you are one special lady and definitely worth it."

"Am I?" she asked quietly.

"If I said it, I meant it."

Kristine sat quietly for a moment, before finally deciding to tell him what was on her mind. "And what about the woman I saw you with the other day, Tauris? How special is she?"

"What woman?"

"The one I saw you leaving your place with the other morning. I wanted to come by and surprise you with breakfast. It was the morning I called."

Tauris remembered that morning. Rayne had stopped by and spent the night. For the first time since he'd known Rayne, he'd promised himself that he'd keep his hands off of her, and he did. So why the hell did he feel so damn guilty?

"If I told you nothing happened, would you believe me?"

The way she looked at him pretty much answered that question. "She's a friend, Kristine," he explained. She looked like she didn't believe that, either. "Okay. She was more than a friend," he confessed.

Disappointment washed over her pretty face.

"She came by, but nothing happened."

"She just spent the night?"

Even Tauris could see how ridiculous his version sounded.

"And nothing happened."

It was pointless to elaborate, so he decided not to bother.

Kristine was on the verge of tears. "You know, I know we've never come out and said that we were a couple,

Tauris," she said softly. "I took it upon myself to believe that we were, so," she shrugged, "I'm jealous, and I'm hurt, and I'm disappointed."

"Nothing happened," he reiterated.

"I wish I could believe that."

"I'm telling you, Kristine. I have no reason to lie about it."

"She's someone you've been seeing?"

Damn! He didn't know what to make of this woman. Kristine was so damned controlled and proper. Any other sistah would've scratched his eyes out by now, but she sat there, with her hands folded in her lap, talking quietly and calmly like she was reciting from a script.

He cleared his throat. Tauris was at a loss. Should he tell the whole truth about his relationship with Rayne, or lie? What was there to lie about? He concluded the truth was the truth and there was nothing wrong with it from where he was sitting.

"We were seeing each other." He stressed the word "were." "We're not now." He blinked when he said that, because honestly, he really wasn't convinced that it was over with Rayne. Usually, he'd left that up to her. Since when had it become his call?

"What was she doing there?"

He shrugged. "She came by to talk," he lied.

"Should I back off, Tauris? If you care about this woman then maybe it would be best for me if I did."

"I don't want to hurt you, baby," he said desperately. He meant it. Rayne might've had him by the balls, but Kristine had him by something else, and he wasn't ready to let that go yet. "Look, nothing happened. She stopped by, and I fell asleep. The next morning I drove her home."

"You lied to me when I called."

"I had to," he blurted out. "If I'd have told you the truth, you wouldn't have believed me then, just like you don't believe me now."

"Do you love her?"

That shut him up. Of course, he loved her. He'd loved her since he first laid eyes on her. He couldn't imagine what it was like not to love Rayne, but their relationship had never been about love. It had been about . . . about trying to find a common ground between them and be able to meet in the middle. It was about him chasing and her running. Love had nothing to do with it.

"Take me home, Tauris," she said, deflated.

They didn't talk again the whole way home. But that didn't stop him from trying to find a way out of this and back into her good graces. For the first time Tauris was starting to realize how much she meant to him. If he didn't have a solution by the time they reached her front door, he might just lose her altogether. He finally made it to her house, but instead of pulling into the driveway, Tauris passed her house altogether, and decided to circle the block until he could come up with something to say that would convince her to give him just one more shot at this.

"What are you doing, Tauris?"

He glanced at her out of the corner of his eye. "Buying some time."

He'd passed her house for the third time when he decided to try his hand again at arguing his case.

"Okay, so I did love her," he started to explain. "I tried to love her, but it just didn't work out. I mean, I don't have to beg a woman to be with me. You understand?"

She stared at him like he was crazy.

"But maybe, I begged her," he reluctantly admitted. "I tried. I did the best I could. You know what I mean?"

Kristine was silent.

"Then I met you, and—. At first, I was like, nah, man. Don't go there because you have this other thing going on and you need to deal with that." Tauris sounded like a fool. He knew he did, and he hated himself for it, but he was desperate. And if the truth didn't set him free and get him through her front door tonight, then, hell, he'd just have to live with that. "But, I mean, I couldn't just not go there with you, Kristine. I, uh . . . you're gorgeous. And uh . . . you, uh . . . at some point, a brotha's got to know when to move on, and so that's what I decided to do. And there you were—are. And I'm like, well, damn! How could I resist, baby? I mean—I'm just a man. I'm not blind, and uh . . . you understand where I'm coming from?" Tauris had talked himself into a corner with no idea whatsoever how to get out of it. "I just want to see where this goes, baby girl. I'd like to think I know a good thing when I see it, and I really, really don't want to blow this."

He came around to her house for the fourth time.

"You need to stop this time, Tauris."

He took a deep breath and pulled up to her house. Without saying a word, Kristine opened her door and climbed out of his truck.

Tauris sat slumped in his seat, deflated and defeated. Obviously, he'd blown it.

She stopped short of closing the door. "You coming?"

He couldn't get out of that truck fast enough.

Tauris made slow love to her when they got back to the house. Kristine watched him as he slept, falling more in love with him by the moment. This was what she wanted more than anything. Not Lamar's filthy hands on her every time she turned around, but to make love to her man, and to lay next to him without feeling a shred of shame or regret. Tauris moaned and turned over on his side, then draped his long, muscular arm across her.

She turned to face him, and lightly kissed his lips. "I think I'm falling in love with you, Tauris," she whispered soft enough not to wake him up.

But Tauris heard her and smiled. "Good," he muttered. "Now, take your ass to sleep."

WHEN YOU'RE NOT STRONG

"You hanging on too long, Rayne. Life keeps moving and you keep standing still. When you gonna get tired of that?" Bear's wife, Mavis, was almost as big as he was. His "high-yella" woman stood nearly as tall as her husband, and weighed almost as much as he did, too. Bear was a gentle creature most of the time, except when he drank. He'd never hurt Mavis or Rayne, but he could be like a steam-roller with anybody else. Mavis was the one to call when Bear got out of hand. She was Beauty that tamed the savage Beast, even if it meant punching him in the jaw.

She wasn't one to hold her tongue, either. Whatever Mavis thought was highly likely to come out of her mouth if she felt so inclined. Rayne had stopped by for some of Bear's famous barbecue, and some of Mavis's motherly or big-sisterly advice, whether she wanted it or not.

"I ain't hanging on to anything, Mavis," Rayne responded, exasperated. The last thing she wanted was a lecture from Mavis, but Rayne knew better than to walk away before Mavis was finished saying what she had to say. Mavis cared about her, which was the excuse she used every time she fussed at Rayne about something in her life that she disagreed with.

"You hanging on to the past, and now you hanging on to Cash Dummy Man. It don't make a lick of sense for you to even be talking to that fool, Rayne. He ain't nothing but trouble, a drug addict, and he's biding his time trying to make you one again, too." Mavis wiped down the counters in the kitchen.

"I'm already an addict, Mavis. That hasn't changed."

Mavis pointed a wet dish towel at her. "Keep getting smart with me," she warned. "And since that's the case, then you really have no business being in the same town with the man. All he knows is trouble."

"I know, Mavis. Look, it's not like I've been seeing him on a regular basis. We met for coffee. That's it."

"That's too much." Mavis shook her head, braids swished across her shoulders.

"I know, Mavis," she said, defeated. "I know."

Mavis sat her heavy frame down at the table next to Rayne. "You need to find you a good man, Rayne, honey," Mavis said compassionately. "Get married again, girl, have some kids."

Right on cue, two of Mavis's bad-ass kids ran circles around the table where they were sitting, chasing each other and hollering at the top of their lungs, something along the lines of "Give it back!" and "I'm going to flush it!" and then finally, "I'm gonna kill you!" as they disappeared as quickly as they'd come in.

"Or get a dog," Mavis quickly added.

Rayne couldn't help but laugh.

"I'm just saying that you are a beautiful woman, you're sweet, got so much to offer, and you deserve someone who can be there for you in a way that J. T. never—"

"Mavis, don't." Mavis wasn't a fan of J. T.'s.

"He wasn't a saint, Rayne," Mavis continued. "Everybody knows that but you."

"I never said he was, so let's not talk about J. T."

"He sold you out for dope, Rayne."

Rayne rubbed her forehead. "We both did."

"As long as you know that he wasn't the hero you try to make him out to be."

Rayne swallowed hard, before answering. "Heroes are overrated, Mavis."

Time helped to make the memory of J. T. an afterthought. Mavis and Bear always seemed to bring him up in conversation but that was because they needed someone to blame for Rayne's transgressions. Rayne's recollection of her husband was an intoxicating brew of good and bad, and in those moments when she did let herself reflect on him, she preferred to focus on the good. And there were plenty of good memories of their marriage.

"My daddy used to call me his blue-black berry," Rayne confessed to J. T. not long after she met him. "I think he thought it would make me feel better since I was the darkest one on the block. It didn't."

J. T. reached out and touched her face. "I think he was bragging on you, sweetheart," he said tenderly. "I think he was boasting to everybody around that his darlin' girl was the prettiest thing he'd ever laid eyes on."

"A skinny dark-skinned girl with a big behind ain't pretty, J. T. Just ask somebody."

He threw his head back and laughed. "Damn, girl! Can't you see or are you blind?" He gazed deeply into her eyes and smiled radiantly at her. "You are the most gorgeous thing I've ever laid eyes on, Rayne Bow. I've traveled all around the world—at least twice—and I have seen some breathtaking sights, but not one of them took my breath away like the first time I saw you singing in that choir at Mount Si-nai Baptist. You made me want to get baptized all over again, girl."

She blushed.

"And I found myself shouting a few hallelujahs sitting in that congregation, but not for Jesus. I sent my praises up to the Lord for his good taste for making you."

"You need to stop." She rolled her eyes.

J. T.'s expression changed. "I mean every word," he said sincerely. "You are entirely too good for me, baby. I've known that since the first time I took you out, and you will always be too good for me. But I'm a greedy, selfish man, and I will take all I can get of you, for as long as I'm able."

Rayne blinked, and he'd left her speechless.

They'd been married less than a year when that conversation took place, and she'd just started singing in his band. Women fell all over themselves to get to J. T., and he knew he could have any one of them if he just reached out his hand.

"Before you came along, I was another kind of man, sweetheart, and I had pussy coming out of my ears," he laughed. "The only puddin' I'm craving now is yours." He winked, then licked his lips. "Can't get enough of that sticky, sweet stuff you got, girl. I swear I can't."

J. T. loved her in unnatural, overwhelming ways and Mavis had no idea of what he had meant to her.

"I always thought you deserved better than J. T., Rayne," Mavis said to her before she left. "He wasn't good enough, girl. But that's just me."

Mavis was entitled to her opinion like everyone else.

EBB AND FLOW

On the day she left, Cole made a call to Nora's agent, Cassandra. "Cassandra," he said, staring out of the window of his hotel room. "It's Cole. How are you?"

"Euphoric, Cole, darling," she said, in her usual exaggerated way of talking. "To what do I owe the honor of this phone call from the husband of one of my favorite clients?"

"You know me, Cassandra. I only have the best of intentions where Nora is concerned."

She laughed pleasantly. "Of course, you do. Which was why I warned her that if she didn't marry you, I certainly would've."

Cole grimaced at the thought. Cassandra was old enough to be his mother. She'd worshipped the sun to a critical fault and looked like a piece of dried apricot fruit on two legs.

"I want to surprise her, Cassandra," he went on to explain. "She left for that Cozumel shoot early this morning, and I thought I'd do the chivalrous thing, and show up at her hotel room with flowers, chocolates, champagne, and a big-ass chocolate kiss right on the lips."

Cassandra hesitated before responding. "And what do you need from me, darling?"

"Well, I need to know the name of the hotel she's staying in. She was in such a rush to get out of here for this thing, she failed to leave that information with her assistant, Lisa, and poor me, her dear old husband feels a tad bit uneasy, not knowing where his lovely wife is."

Cole could hear Cassandra flipping through papers. Usually, the woman was on the ball. She knew Nora's schedule better than her assistant knew her schedule.

"I thought it was a bit odd, too, that she didn't take Lisa along with her," he added. "She usually drags that poor girl with her everywhere she goes," he chuckled.

"Cole," Cassandra finally said, her luxurious tone all but gone. "I'll have to get back to you, dear. I'll call you."

She hung up before he had a chance to say good-bye.

He'd had his people call down to Cozumel, to all of the high-end hotels in the area looking for Nora, but they all came up empty as well. Of course, she could've been registered under another name. She did that sometimes for discretion sake. But he knew the names she'd used in the past and none of them showed up as being registered, either. And, of course, Nora hadn't returned any of his messages he'd left on her cell phone.

Cole loved that woman, but his devotion to her and this marriage were sadly growing thin. Nora was moody and volatile, and her behavior always seemed to keep him feeling off-balanced. He hated the thought of losing her, but even more than that, he was beginning to find himself hating the thought of riding this roller coaster of a marriage, too. Cole was getting older. There were other things he wanted to accomplish in life, like spitting out some kids and doling out all of his attention on them for a change, instead of this self-absorbed lifestyle he and Nora had created for themselves.

"We've got plenty of time for children, Cole." She looked downright uncomfortable every time he broached the subject. "Right now, it's just us, baby. We're free to do whatever we want, when we want. Having kids will change that, and I'm not ready for that change to come yet."

Other celebrities had kids, and they did just fine. Pack up the diapers, toys and nannies, and they could go anywhere in the world. Nora was full of excuses, and he was getting impatient.

She'd started that last argument on purpose. He realized that after he'd calmed down. She didn't want him tagging along with her on that trip, and she took the low road, and pissed him off to the point that she knew he'd leave and she could hop her ass on that plane without the pressure of him looming over her.

This marriage was bullshit, and it had been for a long time. Nora played along with it when it suited her, and then she spat on it and kicked it when she wanted nothing to do with it.

Cole might not ever find out what was really going on in Cozumel, but maybe he didn't need to, maybe he didn't really want to know. He knew one thing, though. He was getting tired of trying to hold on to a woman who didn't want to be held on to. If she found it so hard to be married to him, which was becoming painfully more obvious by the day, then maybe Cole needed to move on.

Nora whimpered. Her eyes rolled back in her head. She tasted sweat on her lips. Taylor had her wrists bound, and he dragged her naked body across the floor of the living room to the open sliding glass panel that faced the beach. He shoved her down on her back against the cold tile, spread her thighs, and pushed himself mercilessly inside her.

"Is this what you want, bitch?" he growled. "Is this what you've been begging me for all fuckin' day?"

"Yes!" She met his thrust with hers, gasping every time they met in the middle. Taylor wasn't as thick as Cole, but he was long. "Harder!" she said, breathless.

Taylor pounded against her so hard, the pain shot through her legs down to her toes.

Just as abruptly, he pulled out.

"No!" she squirmed. "Taylor!"

He stood over her and laughed. Then, Taylor stepped over her, and went outside on the deck, and stood naked, staring out to the sea.

"Finish!" she commanded. "Taylor!"

"Crawl," he said over his shoulder. "Crawl to me, Nora, on your hands and knees."

Nora did as she was told and crawled across the wooden deck on all fours making her way to him. She rubbed against his leg like a cat. "I need you to finish what you started, Taylor. Please."

Taylor grabbed her by her wrists and pulled her behind him over to the chaise, where he sat. He positioned her above him. "Fuck me, Nora!" he commanded.

She lowered herself down on top of him. Taylor gripped her face with one hand, and nearly gagged her with his tongue. Nora bucked wildly on top of him, drunk on the sensation of her flesh still stinging from his abuse earlier. She threw her head back, and savored the slaps he landed on her ass. The sun burned her back, the ocean lapped against the shore, and moments later, Nora exploded all over this man. But that was only the beginning. She'd just arrived this morning, and Nora knew that by the time it was over, she'd be a bruised and battered mess, but she'd be satisfied.

SET IT OFF

Rhonda felt like a fool in that black silk gown she'd spent all that money on to wear for Lamar. He was downstairs in his study, pretending to be working. He didn't want anything to do with her, hadn't in years. Tonight she'd bought wine, made a romantic dinner, put on this gown and a new perfume. She lit candles and played soft music to help set the mood. A woman should be able to seduce her husband without needing permission, she thought sadly, filling her glass again. Lamar wolfed down his food and made it plain and clear that he wasn't interested.

"I've got work to do, Rhonda," he said gruffly, pulling away from her.

She finished half the bottle of wine by herself. Alcohol gave her courage to face the truth and to face him. Rhonda went down to his office and stood outside that door, realizing that she was about to confront some things about her husband, her marriage, and herself—things that she had been reluctant to come to terms with. But it was time, it was past the time, to get to the core of her disappointment and heartache.

She saw no reason to knock, and Rhonda slowly opened the door finding Lamar slumped back in his chair behind his desk, staring at the computer screen that wasn't even on.

He didn't move when she came in. Rhonda sat down on the leather sofa across the room from his desk, pulling her robe closed around her, and shuddered. Whatever it was that was missing between them left her feeling so cold, and half full.

"It's been months, Lamar," she said quietly. "Do you realize that?"

Lamar never took his eyes off his computer screen. He never budged. He didn't say a word.

"I don't know what else to do," she shrugged weakly. "I've tried to be patient, but it hasn't been easy."

He wouldn't even look at her.

Tears flooded her eyes. "Thirty years is a long time to be together," her voice cracked. "It's easy to lose interest and desire for someone after thirty years, but I can assure you of one thing," she swallowed, "my desire for my husband hasn't changed, even after all that time."

Lamar lowered his head, and rubbed his tired eyes.

"Obviously," she continued, "you can't say the same." Rhonda waited for a response, but none ever came, and she knew that her worst fears were being realized. "Who is she, Lamar?" she asked, calmly.

He thought he would be better prepared when this day came. Lamar had rehearsed his speech over and over again, until he had it memorized and so rationalized that no one could question his motives or the events that had taken place over time.

"I love her," he finally said, relieved to be able to say it out loud. Lamar looked into Rhonda's eyes, and watched her heart break in that very moment, but it was too late to take it back now. He had crossed that line with his wife. There was no turning back now. "I love her, Rhonda."

Rhonda's lips quivered. All of her pride wilted from her shoulders, and her marriage of thirty years was suddenly over. The only question left to be answered weighed heavy on her tongue. "Who is she?" she whispered.

Rhonda had knocked on this door, and Lamar was too tired to leave it unanswered. He needed to confess. Lord, the weight on him was so heavy.

"Answer me, Lamar," she said more sternly. A woman's intuition is seldom wrong. She might fight it, or try ignoring it, but very seldom is it wrong. Rhonda felt sick to her stomach, and she struggled to find that one moment in their lives when she knew that her suspicions had proven to be true. Nothing concrete came into view, but snippets of moments—a look, a touch, a word, a hug that lingered a second too long . . . . Individually, they meant nothing, but together, they painted one complete picture, and it was ugly. "Tell me her name."

He took a deep breath. "You know it, Rhonda. You know who she is."

Hot tears streamed down her cheeks, as she stared intently back at her husband. "Kristine," she whispered, trembling.

Lamar turned shamefully away from his wife, and gazed back to his computer screen.

Rhonda forced herself to stand. Her knees grew weaker with each step she took toward him. "Have you slept with her?" she asked, determined to know the whole truth, and not just his fantasy.

Lamar backed his chair away from his desk and stood up, too. "Rhonda," was all he could say, staring helplessly back at her.

"Did you sleep with her?" she said, gritting her teeth.

She wasn't about to let him off the hook so easily. Lamar would rather choke on his answer than give it to her, but she needed to hear him say it. She needed to hear him confess it to her face. "Tell me, Lamar! I need to hear you say it!"

"Yes," he told her. He'd been so proud knowing he'd been intimate with Kristine. In silence, he'd been cocky and thrown it in Rhonda's face, without ever having to make the confession to her out loud, but here and now, Lamar's guilt weighed heavily enough on him to buckle his knees, his shame was almost too much to bear. "I made love to her, Rhonda," he said carefully.

Repulsion overwhelmed her and Rhonda had to force herself to take her next breath. The man standing across the room from her was a stranger. Dear God! How could she have been married to him for so long, and not known what kind of man he really was?

"Get out of my house," she said slowly.

Lamar looked helpless.

"I want you gone," her voice trembled. "Because—I can't stand the sight of you anymore, Lamar, and I want you gone."

YO PUSHER MAN

Horse wasn't the sedative it had once been for him. The high wasn't strong enough anymore to overshadow the pain, and he stewed in a odd combination of euphoria and agony.

"I ain't doing so good, sugar." Sometimes, Cash just felt bad. Bad enough to die, or to wish he was dead. A man as sick as him needed to see a doctor, but he didn't have insurance. More important, he didn't have the desire to be helped anymore. One doctor told him his liver was failing and that if he didn't stop using, if he didn't get a transplant, he'd die. Cash Money Man had lived and died a thousand times already, so what the hell was the big deal if he did it one more time?

He dialed her number because it was the only one he could call. Today was hard, but he didn't need to use being sick as an excuse to want to see her.

"I can't do anything for you, Cash," she told him over the phone. "Call an ambulance."

She was cold to him, hard and indifferent, but it was all right. He couldn't hold it against her. Connections like the one they had were permanent, whether she wanted it to be or not. Cash, Rayne, and J. T. shared the highs and lows of life that most people had no idea existed. They'd shared shit that could scare the hell out of people or make them green with envy. The chains of memory bound her to him, and he knew she'd come, if for no other reason than empathy.

Rayne sat next to him on the sofa and pressed a cool compress to his head. She'd appeared out of nowhere, and she smelled so good. "Hey," Cash said, breathless. Waves of pain surged through his gut, his chest, hell, even his toes. His death was going to be ugly, but he'd always known that. He'd done too much shit in his life for it to go any other way. "When'd you get here?"

"I've been here an hour, fool," she said, sounding sexy as sexy could be. "You so fucked up you don't remember answering the door?"

He chuckled. "Nah, ma'am. That's 'cause you didn't come in through the door. Heaven dropped you here with me."

"Shit, Cash. Heaven's got better taste than that. You need a doctor."

"I've got you."

Big, beautiful dark eyes peered at him. "You don't have me or anybody else." She almost sounded as if she felt sorry for him. "You are sick and if you need help—"

"Shhhh," he pressed his finger to his lips. "Sit still, girl," he inhaled deeply, "and let me just take you all in."

How could she ignore a call from a dying man? Common sense told her that she should have, but sentiment overruled common sense and on impulse, she ignored the warning bells going off in her head. Cash didn't have anyone, and it could've just as easily been her in his position. It could've been Rayne.

Pain threatened to split him in two, and Cash cringed. "Hand me that joint, sugar," he waved his hand at the half-smoked joint on the coffee table. "Light it up for me."

"What?" Rayne shuddered, and looked at him like he'd lost his mind. She hadn't been this close to heroin since the night J. T. died. She hadn't touched it, looked at it, she hardly even said the word anymore. And he was so far gone that he really believed she should pick up that joint laced with the shit, and light it.

He coiled again, and grunted. "Light it up for me, baby," he said desperately. He whimpered in agony. "Come on, Rayne. Come on, now."

"No," she said anxiously. Rayne wiped her sweaty palms on her jeans. Temptation. Lord, Jesus! Her body had memories she'd been trying to put behind her, instincts, needs, desires that she felt in every pore on her body. "I got to go, Cash," she told him. Rayne stood up and walked away from him.

"Don't!" He reached out for her. "Rayne! Please," he

pleaded, holding out a weak, quivering arm to her. "I just need you to light it up for me."

That shit gotchu good, Rayne. It gotchu and it don't let go. Don't be dumb and think it ever will.

There was nothing like it, being high and away from your own skin. There's nothing like chasing that dragon and catching him. Her skin crawled thinking about it. Her mouth was dry all of a sudden. Her heart beat fast like a small animal was in her chest.

"Just light it for me, Rayne."

She wanted to. She wanted to light it, and to inhale and taste it and feel it burn in her blood, her head, her heart.

Bishop's voice haunted her: *"Junkies only fool themselves into thinking they're clean. Junkies are just one high away from the truth of who they are. You are what you are, Rayne. You are an addict and that's all you'll ever be."*

Something primitive took over and drowned out the sound of reason. Rayne inhaled deeply, then closed her eyes and savored her shame, disgust, and relief of not having to fight, even for just a moment.

God! What had she done!

AIN'T NO SUNSHINE

Lamar sat slumped on the edge of the bed of the cheap motel room he'd rented. He stopped at the first one he saw and settled in, not having the energy to drive another mile.

He felt his age. Lamar felt ridiculous and lost. The liberation he thought the truth would bring him only bogged down on him in conviction and guilt. The way Rhonda looked at him stabbed him deep in the chest and finally brought to light the lies he'd convinced himself were true. He'd never made love to Kristine until she was sixteen, but he'd begun seducing her long before that day, long before she was old enough to understand or protest.

Foul memories berated him.

"Give Uncle a kiss, baby girl," he told the seven-year-old child. Lamar pointed to his cheek and waited for her lips to get close enough, and then he turned his head, and let her sweet mouth fall on his, quickly, when the two of them were alone. Confusion washed over her small face, but he laughed heartily to calm her worries and soon she laughed, too.

"Come sit on Uncle Lamar's lap, baby girl." Eleven-year-old Kristine protested quietly that she was too big to sit on his lap, but he insisted, and she politely did as she was told. His hand rested on her thigh. She squeezed her knees shut, and he laughed, and embraced her firmly against his chest, then kissed her lightly on her neck.

Lamar was the affectionate and caring uncle, her father's best friend, who loved this child even more than he loved his own. Fragile, sweet, more beautiful than anything he'd ever laid eyes on, he ignored warnings in him that he was crossing the line. And they were easier to ignore than to acknowledge.

"You asleep yet, little girl?" Bishop never trusted her alone with anyone but Lamar and Rhonda when he was out of town. She was precious to them all, and Rhonda had gone so far as to set aside one of the bedrooms just for Kristine, decorated in pink and white with butterflies and daisies.

She pretended to sleep, but he knew better, seeing her small chest rise and fall much too quickly to be asleep. He never understood where his feelings for her came from or why they were so strong. Lamar had known other little girls, but none of them had stirred feelings in him the way she had.

He sat on the side of her bed and gently smoothed his hand over her hair. "Sweet dreams, baby girl," he'd whisper and leave. One night though, he lingered, leaned down to her, and pressed his mouth to hers. It was just a kiss, nothing vile or disgusting. His lips to hers, but he was in no hurry to break the seal. Kristine opened her green eyes and stared wide-eyed at him as he slowly backed away. She was fourteen.

Lamar let out a painful sob at the image, not quite a scream, but a horrible sound coming from the darkest part of him. He'd been drinking since before he checked into his room, but all the alcohol in the world couldn't erase the kind of man he was. And it couldn't erase Kristine from him, either. He loved her, and she wasn't a child anymore. He never forced himself on Kristine. He never made her do anything she didn't want to do. She came to him willingly and of her own accord.

"You're my first, Lamar. Isn't that terrible? You could be my father."

"But I'm not your father, Kristine. I'm not even your actual uncle. I'm just a man who loves you more than you'll ever know."

"Is that what you call it?" she asked, confused.

Her callous disregard for his feelings was understandable, but hurtful. There was nothing he wouldn't do for her. All she had to do was ask. That's all she ever had to do.

He dialed her number again, only to get her voice mail.

"It's me again," he said gruffly. "Just talk to me, Kris. Please talk to me, baby."

His groin ached thinking about the last time they were together. Lamar rubbed himself, and then fell backward on the bed, staring up at the popcorn ceiling above him. He slipped his hand down the front of his pants and rubbed himself until he became rigid. Kristine hovered over him, her hair wild on her head, beautiful eyes gazing down at him as she ran her tongue seductively across her full lips. Rolling her round hips in full circles, she pulled every drop of emotion he had for her from him. Dark nipples danced inches from his lips, and Lamar flicked his tongue like a snake, grazing each of them until they swelled before his eyes like magic. The warm, sticky essence of Kristine seeped from between her thighs, glazing his balls, soaking the sheets beneath him. She bucked, and he knew he was gone. He cupped her hips, and held her in place, thrusting madly inside her until he collapsed underneath her, drunk from her.

Lamar passed out with his limp penis still in his hand.

TRAIL OF TEARS

"Yes," Mavis said anxiously into the phone. "R-a-y-n-e, Rayne Fitzgerald. Has anyone by that name been admitted recently?" She'd been on the phone with nearly every hospital within a twenty-mile radius asking if Rayne had been admitted. Mavis sat at her kitchen table, checking phone numbers out of the phone book as she called. Rayne hadn't been arrested, either. Mavis and Bear were beside themselves. They hadn't heard from Rayne in days. She'd missed rehearsals and even a gig they were scheduled to perform last night. This just wasn't like her.

Bear grabbed his keys off the kitchen counter and kissed Mavis's cheek. "I'll call you if I find out anything."

"You call me even if you don't," she called after him.

Bear drove for hours, stopping at all the places he'd known her to hang out: coffee shops, parks, even boutiques where a man like him would never set foot unless it was a life-or-death situation. Nobody had seen her, and the longer he looked, the more persistently his gut started to convince him that Cash had something to do with her being gone. He had one more place to look, and if she wasn't there, then he knew he needed to start to hunt down Cash's funky ass.

Tauris was on his way out when Bear knocked on the door. The two men barely knew each other except for an occasional nod or "whassup, man" every now and then in passing. Rayne had asked Bear to drop her off here a couple of times after rehearsal, which was how he knew where to find him. The big man filled the doorway, and for a second, Tauris recalled some strategic tips when it came to fighting somebody bigger than you: duck, don't let him catch you, and if you can find them, kick him in the nuts, then run like hell. He'd never kick another man in the balls unless his life depended on it.

"Hey, man," Bear's voice bellowed from the center of the earth and he wasn't even talking loud.

"Whassup?"

"You seen Rayne around?"

He shook his head. "Nah, man." Bear looked worried, and all of a sudden, so was Tauris. "What's going on?"

Bear leaned against the doorway and rubbed his tired eyes. "We ain't seen or heard from her in days, man," he explained wearily. "She ain't been to rehearsal, been missing shows. She ain't answering her cell phone, home phone, or her door, and that ain't like her."

"You think something happened?"

He shrugged. "Mavis, my wife, has been calling all the

hospitals, she even called the police, but Rayne ain't no-where to be found. I was hoping you'd heard from her. I'm about out of options, man."

Tauris shook his head. "Bear, man, I ain't talked to her in awhile. You think she might have gone back home—back to Florida?"

"Nah, she wouldn't do that. Ain't shit for her back there. She ain't close to her people like that."

Tauris thought about where she could be that maybe Bear hadn't looked. For someone with a raggedy-ass car, Rayne got around. She'd even taken him to a few places he didn't know existed and he'd lived here most of his life. "What about Zady's in McLean? You check out there?"

"What's Zady's?"

"I don't, man. I don't think she'd be there."

"Well, what is it, Tauris, man?"

"It's a spa. One of those fancy places with massages, facials, and shit like that. She loves that place. Had me take her there a few times."

"Get your shit, man. Let's bounce."

"I'm sorry, Bear—I'm on my way out. I got someplace to be in twenty minutes."

"Yeah, well, call her up—tell her you're sorry, but some-thing's come up. Take care of your business. I'll wait."

"Man, that place is probably closed by now, or at least it will be by the time we get there."

Bear didn't say another word, because he didn't need to.

• • •

Bear crossed DC from Maryland, driving along I-395, taking Exit 10-C, and eventually merging onto George Washington Parkway, northbound, crossing into Virginia. "I kept telling her dumb ass to stay away from that fool." Bear shook his head, frustrated. "Cash ain't about shit. Ain't never been about shit, but dope, and somewhere along the line, she got it twisted that he was her so-called friend. Her homeboy from Florida."

"Is he the one who got her hooked on drugs?"

Bear didn't answer right away. The truth always hurt him more than a rat turd like Cash ever could. "Her man got her on it."

Tauris was floored. "Her husband? He got her hooked on that shit?"

Bear nodded. "He was hooked on it long before he met her, but called himself kicking it. I knew better, though. Hell, everybody who knew him knew better. He'd kicked that shit a hundred times before, but never for long."

"She know?"

"Not at first. And you couldn't tell her shit, either. Believe me, I tried. I told her, he on that shit, girl. It's got a hold of him tight like a vise. You need to let him go, and take your ass back to Gainesville."

"She didn't want to hear it." Tauris knew how stubborn Rayne could be. He'd seen it plenty of times, firsthand.

"Man, he had that chick so sprung, if he'd told her the sky was falling she'd have believed it."

"Sometimes, she talks about him like he's Jesus, man. Like no other man on Earth can be the man he was to her."

"He was good people when he was clean, T," Bear said sadly. "He was my friend. Me and him had been playing together for years, and when he was clean—"

"Yeah, well, his ass was full of shit from the way it sounds, getting her into that mess. If he cared about her, he'd have left her alone."

"He cared. In the beginning he'd have killed or died for her without batting an eye."

"But he cared more about horse."

"He came running when she called his name. Dope was his first lady. Rayne did what she could to maintain second place."

"And here I always thought she had her shit so together," Tauris said irritably.

"After she got clean, she did," Bear retorted. "Don't get it twisted, bro. 'Cause I don't think either one of us could've pulled up the way she did from the bottom to the top, and lived to tell it. I'm talking truth. Rayne lived in the gutter—almost literally. And after J. T. died, she crawled out on all fours, and made a comeback like I ain't never seen before. If I got to have a 'shero' other than my wife, Rayne's it. Believe that."

"Then why is she hanging tough with this Cash dude? Sounds like she's asking for trouble."

"She is," he said, matter-of-factly. "But I think it's the drug addict in her that's drawn to him. She thinks she exorcised that demon, but deep down inside, she knows better. And the junkie in her smells smack, and it's making her mouth water and her veins itch. Cash reeks of that shit."

The two men rode quietly for several miles, each lost in his own thoughts. Bear was worried about his friend, and he struggled inside himself, pushing back against conclusions he didn't want to reach.

Tauris saw her in a different light than the woman he'd thought she was. Rayne had been the prize in the Cracker Jack box since he'd known her, and he'd bent over backward to win a place in her heart that her old man left behind when he died, but she could never see fit to let Tauris in.

By the time they made it to Zady's, one of the employees was just locking up. Yes, she knew Rayne Fitzgerald. She was one of their regulars with standing appointments the first and third Tuesdays of the month. But no, she hadn't seen her and, in fact, she'd missed her last appointment, which was something she never did.

It's amazing how quickly things can fall back into place, and how easily. Like any good pusher, Cash kept the shit coming, and like any good dope addict, Rayne soaked it up like a sponge. She'd started to leave so many times, but by the time she made it to the door, she'd stop and think about what was waiting for her on the other side of it. Regret. Sorrow. Abhorrence. Failure. She had shattered every hope she ever had for herself, and there was no one out there who she could stand to face again.

Bishop's voice rang through the fog she was in: *"I can help you, Rayne. I can help you, but you've got to get out of my way and let me. You've got to do exactly as I say. I can be strong enough for both of us, sweetheart, but you've got to let me."*

"Why do you care so much, Bishop?"

"That's what I do, Rayne. I care and I care harder than most."

Rayne felt herself start to cry over her own disappointing failure. If Bishop was alive, she wouldn't be here. She wouldn't be in this room with Cash because that old man had been her strength, her conscience, her conviction.

"Sit down, Rayne Bow," Cash's voice lured her back to the couch and next to him. She watched him freebase to perfection, with skill and ease.

"You look like shit," she told him.

"Shit is as shit does," he responded, filling a needle, then expertly finding a vein in her arm, until she drifted away again, back into a world void of anything that might've mattered to her before she walked through his door.

You should have stayed away from him, Rayne. Maybe it was angels telling her that. Maybe it was her voice, or Bishop's. But in any case, by the time she'd heard it, and heeded it, it was already too late.

THE QUEEN AND SOUL

"I didn't mean to do that," Nora said quietly over the phone the day she returned from Cozumel. He'd been staying at the Manhattan apartment, but had come home eventually. It was an uneasy truce at best, though, and Nora knew that if she didn't do something, if she didn't at least try to change her impulsive, over-the-top behavior, Cole would leave her. He never said it, but she saw it in his eyes, a dull disinterest in her, and when he did look at her, it was almost as if he didn't even see her anymore. She couldn't live without Cole. She prayed she wouldn't have to. "I know I need help, Cole," she explained humbly to him. Cole stood in the doorway of the bathroom, freshly showered with a towel wrapped low on his waist. "I was thinking that maybe we could go to a marriage counselor or something."

He didn't say a word, which made her even more nervous.

"I'll do anything, baby," she pleaded quietly. Nora stood up and slowly approached him. She stood in front of him, and pressed her palms against his chest. "Whatever it takes,

Cole," she tried to smile. "I love you, and I don't want to lose you."

He shook his head. "Sounds like a broken record, Nora."

Dinner tonight was her idea. He'd reluctantly agreed to it, but he'd agreed, and that was all that mattered. The two of them rode quietly in the back of the limousine, each in his and her respective corner, staring out of the windows. Nora donned a black Missoni keyhole tunic minidress, and a pair of sexy Dior crisscross sling-back pumps that made her long, shapely legs appear even longer. Cole looked too handsome for his own good in a dark Armani three-button suit, and a crisp white shirt opened at the collar.

She'd made reservations at Georgia Brown's, his favorite spot, located on Wisconsin Avenue, near Georgetown Park. Cole might've been raised in the city, but his heart and soul were born deep in the South, in a small Louisiana town called Opelousas, just northwest of Lafayette. He spent summers with his grandparents there when he was a kid, and to listen to him talk, there was no greater place on the planet. He'd taken Nora there once when they were dating, and she made a silent promise to God, that as long as she lived, she'd never set foot in that town again. Creole food was his favorite, and if she wanted to make amends with her husband in even the slightest way,

Nora knew that some red beans and rice was a good place to start.

Nora and Cole had traveled all over the world, they'd dined in some of the finest restaurants in existence, but even she had to admit, there was no place like this place. As recognizable as the two of them were, especially Cole, after winning the title for the second time, this was one of the few places they could come to, where they were just regular people, who'd come in to enjoy a nice meal and some good music. The staff had been alerted that they were coming, and a small romantic table in the back of the room had been reserved for them. Other than a few shouts of, "Way to go, champ," the evening was pretty quiet. Nora ordered baked jumbo shrimp stuffed with backfin crab, served with Creole cocktail sauce and red beans and rice, while Cole ordered his usual pork chops stuffed with sautéed apples and onions and, of course, red beans and rice.

The food was fabulous, the music was great, and Nora optimistically savored the slow thaw between them.

Nora reached across the table and held his hand. Despite the muscles and wicked uppercuts, Cole was a gentle man. If roles were reversed, she should've been the one in the ring knocking people out instead of him. "I really am sorry about my behavior, Cole," she said tenderly. "I don't know what got into me, baby. Stress, I guess. They called that shoot at the last minute, and you know I'm terrible when things happen like that."

Every word coming out of her mouth sounded rehearsed, and Cole didn't believe any of it. He wasn't in the mood for another fight with his wife, though. Not tonight. Not any night. He'd all but made up his mind that their marriage was over. Part of him actually enjoyed seeing her squirm as she wondered what that look in his eyes meant. Just like he wondered where all of this tenderness was coming from all of a sudden.

"Anyway," she smiled nervously. "I'm just glad to be home, baby. And if you still want to get away for a few days together, well—"

Cole pulled back his hand. "No," he said, calmly. "I'm not going to have time."

LOVE ME TENDER

It had been more than a week since anyone had last seen or heard from Rayne. Tauris had done his share of searching for her, too, but it was as if she'd just disappeared off of the face of the earth.

"Tauris, are you even listening to me?" Kristine asked. The two of them strolled hand in hand across the lawn of the Washington Monument.

He looked dumbfounded at her. "I'm sorry, baby. What did you say?"

"I said that the last time I was out here was back when I was a kid. Daddy brought us here to watch the fireworks one Fourth of July. And why don't you tell me what's on your mind because it's obvious something is. That's what I said."

Tauris walked over to one of the benches near a museum and sat down. Kristine sat down next to him. He wore a solemn expression to match his mood. "A friend of mine is, uh . . . missing, I guess you could say. I'm kinda worried."

Of course, he had to be careful what he said and how he said it. After all, he was talking to one woman in his life about another woman in his life, and this conversation could get tricky if he wasn't careful. But Rayne was someone he cared about, just like he cared about Kristine. His feelings were slowly changing, morphing into something he hadn't expected, but that didn't mean he had turned them off.

What if she was dead or, worse, using again? What if old dude, Cash, had her locked up somewhere? Bear's wife Mavis had filed a missing person's report, but being black and an adult meant that the media wasn't exactly going to flash her picture on the evening news, or put it on the front page of the *Post*. Tauris was scared.

"Who is it?" Kristine asked, concerned.

He took a deep breath and then said her name. "Her name is Rayne Fitzgerald. She sings in clubs and has a CD out. Was on her way to signing with a major record label," he said quietly.

"Was she the one I saw you with that morning?"

Tauris looked at her, and then nodded. "Yeah."

She sat back and gazed over the lawn.

"Rayne's got some issues she's been dealing with," he continued. "I just hope she—I hope she's all right. . . ."

"I can tell that you care a lot about this woman."

Tauris didn't miss the hint of jealousy in her tone, but he decided to ignore it. He wasn't in the mood today to play "Who do you love more, me or her?"

"She's a friend, so yeah. I care about her," he said, trying not to sound defensive.

"Are you still seeing her, Tauris?"

"Kristine—" he said, exasperated.

"Are you?"

"Would I sit up here telling you about her missing if I were still seeing her?" he asked, irritably. Why the hell did he even bother bringing Rayne up?

"I don't know," she snapped. "Would you?"

"She's a friend of mine."

"A friend you had or have a relationship with, Tauris. Which is it?"

"That's over, Kris. Been over."

"Has it? Then why are you so worried about her?"

He stared back appalled. "Because the woman is a friend of mine. I do care what happens to her, just like I'd care about what happened to anybody I considered a friend. She could be anywhere. She could be in trouble. Why the hell don't you get that?"

"Because you were sleeping with her, Tauris," she said angrily. "She's not just your friend if you were sleeping with her."

"You're killing me, Kristine," he muttered, and then sighed.

"I just need to know where I stand with you," she said gravely.

Tauris didn't have the interest or energy to even give her an answer. If she didn't know by now, then obviously he was spinning his wheels. Rayne had a place in his heart, and she always would have, regardless of what happened between them. Tauris was falling for Kristine. He might even be willing to go so far as to say he loved her under the right circumstances. However, at this moment, he had to confess to himself that he wasn't completely over Rayne, but he was trying to get over her. And he wasn't completely in love with Kristine, but he was trying to get there, too.

He stood up to leave. "Let's go," he said quietly. "I need to get you home."

Kristine didn't know what else to say. And she certainly didn't know what else to do. Tauris still had feelings for this Rayne woman, and it seemed no matter how hard she tried she just couldn't win him over completely. Kristine desperately wanted to be the only woman in his life, but the ties he had to Rayne were stronger than Kristine's desire to make him hers.

She expected him to take her to her house, but Tauris surprised her and headed in the direction of his own.

"I thought you were taking me home?" she said to him.

He didn't say a word.

Back at his place, they lay stretched out on his sofa, with Kristine on top, resting her head on his chest. Tauris held on to the remote like it was an extension of his arm, flipping through channels, and staring with disinterest at the television.

The best defense in a case like this was a good offense, and a good offense meant not saying another word to Kristine about Rayne, or friendship, or relationships, or any damn thing. He made a silent vow to just grunt the rest of the day, if she did decide to have a conversation. Some things were basic, though. Hold a woman. Kiss her every now and then. Make her feel wanted by keeping her close. Don't mention another woman's name unless it's her mother's. And no matter how hard she tries, under no circumstances, should he even think about going toe to toe with her in an argument.

PHOENIX RISING

"The Orianne lingerie line is only six months late, Neville, not six years late." Nora's main investor was backing out and she had spent the last hour on the phone with him trying to convince him not to take his money and run. She paced frantically back and forth in her office, while her assistant tried frantically to get her temperamental French designer on the phone. "I'm waiting on Basile," she explained. "Yes! He's an asshole, but he's brilliant, and if— Neville, please! I'm good for it! You know me! Fine! Then I'll fucking fire Basile's ass and hire someone new, but it's going to take time to— Gotdammit, Neville! Neville? Neville?" She turned angrily to her assistant. "Is he on the line?"

"No, Nora," the young woman said, shakily. "He isn't answering his cell, his home, or his office phones."

Nora threw her cell phone across the room, smashing it into the wall and shattering it into a thousand pieces. "Fuck!" She spun on her heels back to the trembling assistant. "You stay on that fucking phone until you get him. Do you hear me?" she said, clenching her teeth. "Or it's your ass."

• • •

Cole had a car pick him up from the airport. He was exhausted, having taken the red-eye from Los Angeles after doing a stint on the *Tonight Show*. He'd have stayed if he didn't have a fund-raiser to attend back in DC later that evening.

Sometimes, his life was a whirlwind and he had a hard time keeping up. Cole wanted to box professionally ever since he watched a tape of the Sugar Ray Leonard and Roberto Duran bout in New Orleans from November 25, 1980. Sugar took it this time, and Cole watched in awe how the mastery of skills took over and ended up being no match for brute strength. Duran was a brawler, but Sugar was an artist, pure and simple.

Early in his career, Cole boxed because he loved it, but a love like that takes its toll on a man, and he was getting tired. The passion he'd once felt for the sport was growing thin, and more and more, he was beginning to see himself in a light that didn't suit him despite thinking, when he was younger, that it would.

Cole wasn't a superstar or a celebrity. He played along because he was expected to. Nora was much better at this game than he was, and there were times when he wished he could just stand back and let her do her thing, while he waited patiently in the shadows.

He had a few hours before he had to start getting ready

for the evening's event, and Cole hoped he'd be able to catch a few winks. Otherwise, he wouldn't be worth a damn.

"Back up off me, Nora!" Cole's deep voice shook the walls as he walked away from her, before he'd do something he regretted. Nora tailed hot on his heels behind him. What he'd hoped would be a quiet afternoon at home had quickly turned into a trek into a war zone, ready and waiting for him as soon as he closed the front door behind him.

"You ought to know me better than that, Cole. I don't back off until I good and damn well feel like it, and baby, I'm just getting my ass started!" She pushed the back of his head with her index finger.

Cole stopped and started to turn around, but thought better of it. He was tired, irritable, and she was digging in for an all-out knock-down, drag-out, full-fledged brawl. She hadn't changed. Nora had put on a damn good show, though. He slowly turned to face her.

"Is this what you call doing 'whatever it takes,' Nora?" he asked bitterly. "Is this what you call working on our marriage?"

Her eyes blazed angry, hateful vibes. Nora was in a zone that no amount of reason or even love could bring her back from. "You are such a bitch, Cole," she said, maliciously. Nora stood toe to toe with him, her hand on her hip. "Mr.

Fuckin' Champion of the World," she sneered. "You whine, Cole. You whine like a little girl, and it's getting on my fuckin' nerves."

Cole glared at her, his jaws tensing in anger. He turned and started to walk away again, but Nora was relentless and followed him. "Who the hell do you think we are, Cole? You want some shit that's perfect, and sweet, and fine all the damn time like some gotdamned fantasy?"

He stopped abruptly and turned quickly. "I want a marriage to a woman who's not a fuckin' lunatic, Nora!" he blasted her. "I fight in the ring! I don't need to ball up my fists here!"

"You wanna hit me, Cole?" she dared him. Nora was close enough for the tip of her nose to touch his. "Is that what you want?" She suddenly stepped back far enough to put both hands on his chest and push him. Cole barely budged as he defiantly stood his ground. Nora pushed again. "Hit me, mothafucka!"

He turned to walk away again, and Nora pushed the back of his head with her hand. "Fuckin' bitch!" she growled.

He knew he should've kept walking, but instinct and anger took over, and Cole spun around fast, grabbed her by the neck with one hand, and shoved her backward into the wall behind her. "Keep your gotdammed hands off me, Nora, or I swear—"

A burst of pain sent shock waves through his entire body, causing him to double over and buckle down on his knees to the floor. Nora had kneed him in the groin. She stood over him, taunting him, cursing at the top of her lungs, hurling insults at him fast like jabs from a left hand. Rage welled up inside him like lava, and he grabbed her by the front of her dress, pulled her down on the floor facing him, and forced her onto her knees, too.

"Let go of me, mothafucka!" She struggled to get away, scratching and pounding on the fist holding her in place, but Cole was too strong for her.

As the pain in his groin slowly began to subside, he took deep breaths, and grabbed a handful of her hair and pulled her head back. Cole was blinded by the kind of rage he'd never felt before, not even in the ring or in the worst fights he'd had with Nora. The strain of her head being pulled back put pressure on her vocal cords and Nora's full, angry voice sounded flat. "Let me go, Cole," she struggled to say. He was in his own zone now, thoroughly fed up, and pushed to limits he didn't even know he had. Cole couldn't hear her. He watched her mouth move, he saw the helplessness fill her eyes, but he couldn't let her go. He pulled her backward, folding her long legs underneath her, as he pinned her back onto the floor at his knees.

Nora struggled to straighten her legs out from under her, hoping to gain some leverage in a better position. The veins in his neck swelled and Cole held her there, staring down at her like a madman. For the first time in a long time, Nora was afraid of him. His muscles bowed, his breathing slow and deliberate, his strength paralyzing. She was helpless, and it turned her on in a way she never thought possible.

"Cole," she mouthed, reaching up with one arm, and pressing her hand against the side of his rugged face. Nora burned hot between her thighs, and spread her legs wide enough to signal him that she wanted him inside her. She pulled his face slowly to hers, opened her mouth, and drew him in with her tongue. Cole's grasp on her loosened, and Nora unzipped his pants and grabbed his rigid dick with her hand, squeezing it until cum oozed from the tip. She rolled over on her side, and filled her mouth with him. Cole still held a handful of her hair as he leaned back and watched Nora work magic on him with her mouth. He stopped her just short of releasing his orgasm, then dragged her over to the staircase, pushed her facedown on the stairs, raised her skirt, ripped off her lace thong with his hands, then rammed into her from behind, thrusting as hard and deep as he could, knowing he was hurting her, but ignoring her painful cries. He knew better than to stop. Nora met his thrusts with hers, as if he couldn't possibly ever hurt her enough. She yelled and convulsed violently when she came, and so did he.

When it was over, she lay exhausted and satisfied, bare ass up on their staircase. Cole stood behind her, zipped his pants, and saw the stunned face of Nora's young assistant, staring at the two of them, with her mouth hanging open. Cole stepped over Nora, then went upstairs, packed a few things, then brushed past her on his way out as she sat listless on the stairs.

"Cole," she called after him.

He closed the door behind him, and never looked back.

SISTAH

Courage had to be summoned from somewhere, even if it had to come from the dirt under the soles of her feet. Rayne had lost track of time since she'd walked into Cash's place. Had she been gone days? Weeks? Months, maybe? Or maybe, she'd never left, and even after J. T. died, she'd been holed up with Cash, sticking needles into each other, nodding in and out of consciousness and she dreamed everything and everyone in between.

"It's hard to say," she whispered to herself, unaware of the reaction from the person sitting next to her on the train, who got up and moved away.

Rayne wrapped her arms around herself, and smoothed her hand over her hair. She knew she looked bad. That shit always made her look so—

She fumbled through her purse looking for her cell phone. Of course, it was dead. Rayne had left her place without her charger. She hadn't meant to be gone—

"—so long." She completed her thought out loud, fighting back tears of frustration and disappointment. Rayne had no idea where she was going. Her thoughts tumbled against each other in her head, and things that should've made sense, didn't. Decisions that should've come easily, didn't.

Bear. Of course, he'd fuss, and Mavis would be so upset with her. She sobbed quietly. Of course, they would be upset, and Rayne couldn't take seeing the looks of disapproval on their faces. She'd have called if her phone worked, though. They were worried about her. She knew that even without talking to them. Her damn phone was dead and she—she couldn't call like she needed to.

Mavis and Bear lived so far away, though. Rayne's skin crawled, like it was covered with a million tiny spiders, and she knew she couldn't make it to their place. There was no way.

The overwhelming feeling of starting over engulfed her. Rayne had fallen too far down the rabbit hole, and voided years from her life—good years, straight years—only to end up back at the beginning of a long, long race. She was out of breath, and exhausted, and not so sure she'd be able to catch up this time. Hopelessness was strangling. You didn't just go cold turkey with heroin. You didn't just decide you wanted to quit and chew on some gum or stick a patch on your arm and call it a day. Heroin was a stubborn bitch, and she never gave up. God! She never left you alone, and she never felt sorry for you. She was too damn needy, and high maintenance, and relentless.

"Wonder where T. Diggs is," she said, quietly to herself. Rayne stared out of the window, trying to figure out what time it was, what day it was. Could he be home? She should call, but— Maybe she could find a pay phone and call. His place wasn't as far away as Bear's, and he could give her a ride to— Damn! To Bear's house? She should've called Anna, her intervention counselor. Anna was the first person she should've called when Cash offered her that smoke. Rayne pounded the palm of her hand against her head. "Stupid!" she muttered, startling passengers. She should've called Anna even before she went to his place, because Anna was cool, and she'd have told her not to go. She'd have come picked up Rayne and the two of them would've gone to Zady's, and gotten their fingers and toes done, and Rayne would've been so enamored with her toes that she'd have forgotten all about Cash and his dope.

"I gotchu back, Rayne Bow," his voice came from far away, but she knew he was closer than she wanted him to be. "I'm an evil man, girl," he laughed bitterly. Rayne opened her eyes long enough to see him topple to the floor at her feet and lay there like he was dead, but she knew he wasn't. Cash cried. "I gotchu back, Rayne Bow," his voice trailed off. "Didn't matter how. Didn't matter—"

She had no idea how long he laid there, but however long it was, it was too long, and Cash wasn't getting up. She stepped over him on her way out. Rayne couldn't hide or run away from herself. She nudged him in the thigh with the toe of her boot. "Get up, Cash," she told him. Cash's empty eyes fixed on the wall across from him. Rayne cried out, then stifled her cries with her hand. A man had died again. And she had lived again. "Get out!" she heard the sound of her own voice, and obeyed. Rayne gathered her things, hoping she had the presence of mind to leave no trace of herself in that room, and finally she stumbled out the door, and left him there to rot in what he loved even more than he said he loved her.

"I gotta go, baby." The sun wasn't even up yet, but he was on his way to a job in Gaithersburg, Maryland. Kristine lay sleeping on her stomach, with the sheet covering her from the waist down. The rest of her was beautifully naked. Tauris slid the sheet down low enough to kiss one cheek of her behind, then tenderly covered it back up. She moaned, and barely stirred. "I'll call you later," he whispered in her ear, then kissed her lips.

She was becoming a habit he found himself digging. The day just went by easier with her in it. Tauris hadn't felt this good over a woman in awhile, and he was starting to feel pretty possessive about it. If she wasn't at his place, he was at hers and he was cool with that.

Tauris was a typical man. Kristine sipped on the coffee she'd made when she got up, and sat on his sofa, studying the lack of character and style in his place. The place looked like he'd barely just moved in, or was on his way out. No pictures hung on the walls, or curtains covered the windows, not even an area rug over the hardwood floors. He told her once that he actually owned several places. He rented out two, and kept this one for himself. His bed was comfortable, though, she smirked. Or maybe it was just him in it next to her that made it comfortable.

The knock on the door startled her. It was early. She glanced at the clock on the wall and it wasn't even nine o'clock yet. Kristine wore one of his T-shirts, and a pair of his socks, but that was all she had on. She initially didn't want to answer, but whoever it was, was pretty persistent. She looked out of the peephole and saw a woman standing there. Kristine cracked open the door, careful to leave on the chain.

"Yes?"

The woman looked awful, with dark circles under her eyes, spit crusted in the corners of her mouth, her locks matted, and tied back away from her face.

She stared wide-eyed at Kristine. "Tauris?" she muttered, nervously. The woman turned to look at the other houses on either side of this one. "I must have the wrong— Is he—?" She pursed her lips together. "I'm trying to find T. Diggs."

It took a moment, but suddenly, Kristine recognized this woman. But no . . . it couldn't be her.

"Tauris?" Kristine repeated.

Rayne scratched one arm, and shifted her weight from one foot to the other. "Is he here? He is, isn't he?" Rayne pleaded with her eyes for Kristine to tell her the answer she needed to hear most. She needed Tauris. Fuck the fact that he had a bitch in here with him. That didn't matter. She needed him more than she ever needed anybody in her life. "Tell him it's Rayne," she said desperately.

"But he's—"

"Just tell him I'm here, gotdammit!" she shouted, causing Kristine to jump. "I'm sorry," Rayne started crying again. "I'm sorry, lady." She tried to calm herself. Going off on the woman wasn't going to get her anywhere. "Please," she lowered her voice. "I'm sick, and I need to . . . I need him to take me to—"

"He's not here, Miss," the woman responded. "Do you need to go to a hospital?"

Rayne stared at her helplessly. "No," she whispered. Tears escaped and streamed down her cheeks. "I need to go to a treatment center."

Rayne didn't know this woman, but she appreciated her kindness. The woman might've told Rayne what her name was but she didn't remember, and she knew she'd probably never remember because she'd probably never see her again. The woman drove Rayne to a treatment center in the city, and went so far as to walk inside with her and even made sure she got checked in.

Rayne didn't remember saying good-bye, or thank you. But the woman called out to her before they took her to a room. "Take care."

WHEN THE BLUES

CATCH UP

TO YOU

ON A CLEAR DAY

"So, you've got rape fantasies," Cole said, irritably. "Is that it?"

Nora sat across from him in his hotel room at the Ritz-Carlton in the city. She'd practically begged him to see her. Reluctantly, he agreed, but Cole made it clear that he wasn't even thinking about coming home to her.

She ran her fingers through her hair, frustrated. "That's not what it is."

Cole sipped on bourbon and paced around the room, unable to look at her, or to touch her. "Then why don't you tell me what the hell *it* is, Nora, because I just don't understand. You want me to beat your ass, then you want me to fuck you. I'm sorry, baby, but that's some shit I just don't get."

"I don't, either," she muttered. "But, there's something about you and me getting angry at each other, fighting, and then, making love."

He looked shocked. "Making love? Is that what you call it?"

Nora tried not to look offended. "You're my husband, Cole. Of course, we make love."

"That shit we did the other night wasn't making love, baby. It was barbaric."

"Why? Because it was passionate, and emotional, and spontaneous?"

He couldn't believe what he was hearing. "Is that how you saw it?"

"Yes," she responded softly. "It was raw emotion, Cole. It was exciting to me, and to you, too. Don't try and deny it, because I know it was. I saw it in your eyes, and felt it inside me. You loved it as much as I did." She dared him to deny it.

This time, it was Cole who looked offended. "You think what you want to think, Nora." He took a drink from his glass. "That's not lovemaking to me. And I don't get off on calling my woman names or slapping her around before we get down to business on the staircase in front of the help."

"So, I'm the freak. Is that how you see it?"

Cole paced back and forth before finally responding. "I just want to know where this is coming from. I mean, have you always been like this? Is this the kind of relationship you want from me?"

Nora had to choose her words carefully. Yes, she wanted to say, but in all honesty she had no way to answer his questions without possibly hurting him and widening that divide they already had between them.

"I can't help or change who I am," she responded.

Cole waited for her to elaborate, but Nora was reluctant. "What the hell does that mean?"

"It means that I like rough sex, Cole," she admitted. "I get off on the pain and even the degradation. When you get angry, I get excited, but—you never get angry, baby. Not with me, and never on your own."

Cole stared intensely at her. "So you get off on getting me riled up? You do that shit on purpose."

She could see the hurt in his eyes. "Yes," she whispered. Confession was good for the soul, they say, but not necessarily all that great for a strained marriage.

"Then I'm the fool, Nora, because I let you."

Nora could feel him slipping away from her with each passing moment. She loved Cole more than he could ever know, but it was this single point of contention between them that threatened to tear apart their marriage.

"Why do you love him so much if he can't satisfy you in bed, Nora?" Taylor had the nerve to ask her once.

"Because he satisfies me in every other way," she told him.

"You're not a fool, baby," she said, getting up from the sofa and approaching him. "Cole, I don't know why I'm this way, but I know that you mean the world to me, baby, and the thought of losing you is too much for me."

Cole stared coldly at her. "So, if it's not me giving you what you need in the sack, Nora, who is it?"

His accusation caught her off guard. "What? What are you talking about?"

"I'm talking Cozumel," he said coolly. "There was no photo shoot, and I couldn't find you registered in any hotel down there."

"I told you, I stayed at a friend's villa," she said hurriedly. "What would make you think there was anyone else, Cole?" Nora sounded hurt.

"Obviously, you haven't been getting your jollies with me, baby. If I'm not knocking you around or slamming you into a wall enough, according to what I'm getting here, you're not getting yours from me." He shrugged. "So, naturally, I'm assuming there's someone else giving you what you need."

Nora studied him, and concluded that Cole was grasping for straws. He didn't know about Taylor. How could he? He was speculating, and as long as that's all it was, Nora still had a chance to run damage control.

"The photo shoot was last minute, Cole," she swallowed. Tears filled her eyes for effect. "If you don't believe me, call my publicist at Opulence. I'll give you her number."

"Cassandra didn't know anything about any photo shoot," he challenged.

"Well, Cassandra doesn't know everything."

"Fine. I'll take that phone number before you leave."

Nora was good at covering her bases. Someone would answer that number, claiming to be that publicist, and she'd confirm Nora's version of the story. Cole wasn't getting away from her that easily. Taylor gave good sex, but he wasn't worth losing her husband.

"No problem," she said.

Silence loomed between them for several minutes.

"I can't give you what you need, Nora," Cole finally said.

"I'm not that man you're looking for," he shrugged. "I fight in the ring, baby, not in my own house. I shouldn't have to. You want it rough, and that's not who I am. You want me to take it, and I want you to hand it over to me willingly, lovingly. You want me to degrade you and that's not how a man treats his queen, in my eyes. Our marriage is missing a link, Nora, an important one, and sweetheart, we both have to face the fact that it can't work like this."

Nora stared at him in disbelief. Cole was wrong. He was dead wrong if he believed they couldn't get through this. "We said we'd try counseling, Cole," her voice trembled. "We can find someone who can help us to get through this."

"You think so," he said dryly. "I'm not convinced."

"Why? Why won't you even try?"

"Try to do what? Come to some middle ground on this thing? What? Maybe I only slap you around occasionally, and you agree to come like a maniac when I'm not putting my dick up your ass?"

"You're being ridiculous, Cole!"

"No, Nora, I'm being realistic. Because one of these days, you might push the wrong button and I might lose my damn mind and hurt you in a way that destroys me. I came too fuckin' close to that the last time and I'm not risking crossing that line again."

"But you didn't cross the line, baby!"

"But I could! I could, Nora, and that scares me as much as you get off on it!"

"I can't lose you," she sobbed. "I won't, Cole. Please, baby. Please." Nora went to him and wrapped her arms around him. Cole shrugged away, but she held on to him.

"Cole, please! Let's at least try, baby. Let's talk to someone and get help. Maybe there's a solution. Maybe we can get some answers, honey." Nora kissed him, and Cole surprised her and let her. "I love you. And I know how much you love me. But before we throw all of that away, we need to try at least one more time to get through this."

"I don't know, Nora," he said, disappointedly.

"You do know." She wiped away her tears. "You know that you want our marriage to work, and that you don't want to lose me, either. You know that much, Cole."

Cole couldn't argue with that.

"We need to both swallow our pride and ask for help, baby," Nora forced a smile. "You wouldn't give up on a fight in the ring, Cole." Nora kissed him again. "Don't give up on us."

Nora drove home somewhat satisfied, and at least hopeful. Cole had agreed to counseling, but he hadn't agreed to move back home. But that was fine. Nora hadn't completely lost the war—a small battle maybe, but not the war.

THE MIDNIGHT HOUR

Rhonda saw Kristine with new eyes after Lamar's confession. The young woman sitting across from her in Kristine's parlor was so far removed from the child she'd helped raise. Rhonda felt like they were meeting for the first time.

Kristine had offered her a customary cup of tea, but Rhonda refused. Her stomach couldn't handle tea, or anything else for that matter. She needed Kristine's version of the truth. Rhonda needed to know what kind of people these were in her life, people whom she'd loved so much.

There was no easy way to ask the question so as Kristine settled down in the chair across from her, Rhonda just opened her mouth, and let the questions come. "Are you having an affair with my husband, Kristine?" Her voice trembled, but her gaze fixed on Kristine, unwavering. Rhonda leaned forward on the sofa, straining to see or hear any sort of reaction that might give a sign to the truth, regardless of what that girl said.

Color slowly washed from Kristine's face. "What do you mean, Auntie?" she answered stoically.

She might as well have shouted yes from the rooftops, as far as Rhonda was concerned. But Rhonda braced herself for Kristine's denials.

"You know what I mean," she said, a little annoyed. Common sense told her that her resentment was misdirected, but she couldn't help what common sense thought. Resentment was all around her like smoke, and she was choking on it. "Have you had sex with Lamar?" Rhonda nearly choked on the word sex.

"We— he—," she stammered.

Rhonda sighed deeply, then leaned back on the sofa at this near confession. Kristine seemed to shrink under the weight of Rhonda's glare.

"He's always been affectionate, Auntie," she said, composing herself and hoping to create a different version of reality. Kristine shrugged casually. "He and I have always been close. That's all."

"That's not all," Rhonda responded softly. "You tell me the truth," she threatened. "You tell me what the two of you have been doing."

"We didn't do anything!" Kristine exclaimed. "What makes you think—"

"*He* makes me think it!" Rhonda shouted. "I want you to tell me the truth! Did you sleep with my husband? And don't you lie to me, girl! I mean it! You tell me the truth, Kristine!"

Tears filled Kristine's eyes. "What do you want me to say?"

"Tell me when!" Rhonda shouted. "When was the first time? When was the last time! How long have you been having sex with Lamar?"

There was no name for the kind of turmoil churning inside her. Rhonda was a bloody mess on the inside, destroyed and devastated by her husband and what he'd done with this girl—woman.

Her bloodshot eyes drilled conviction into Kristine. Lamar had confessed as much, but she needed Kristine to openly confirm what she already knew.

Kristine grimaced. "Auntie—" she started to protest.

"It is true, isn't it?"

Rhonda was never supposed to know. Kristine had stopped seeing Lamar. She had a new man in her life now whom she loved and was looking forward to spending her future with. Rhonda was never supposed to find out.

"Yes," she whispered.

Rhonda moved quickly, crossing the room in seconds, crying uncontrollably, whipping Kristine across her face with both hands open and slapping. Kristine curled up in a ball to protect herself as best she could, and let Rhonda beat herself to exhaustion. Eventually, Rhonda collapsed on the floor, shaking her head in disgust, mumbling to herself. "I can't believe— Why?" she wailed. "Oh, dear Jesus! Why?"

It was a miracle Rhonda was able to drive herself home. She didn't remember getting from Kristine's house to hers.

It was as if someone lifted her up and placed her down here in her bedroom. She rocked slowly in her chair in front of the window in her bedroom, numb and lost over the farce that had been her life.

Kristine never cried out, or told Rhonda to stop hitting her. Not that it would've mattered because she wouldn't have stopped anyway.

Lamar was the worst kind of man, and she loathed herself for not seeing it in him. He'd been a kind of a monster, able to manipulate the girl on some level that she'd been too naive or ignorant to know better.

Rhonda choked back sobs, feeling victimized by her own failures and by the failures of everyone surrounding that girl who was supposed to protect her and teach her right from wrong. Bishop. Kristine's mother. Rhonda. And Lamar. Especially Lamar.

"Your wife came by, Lamar," Kristine said over the phone. Her voice was cold, like stone, void of emotion.

"I need to see you," he pleaded. "Let me come by and—"

"No," she cut him off.

"Please, Kristine," he pleaded. "Let me come by, Kristine. I promise I won't touch you, sweetheart. I just need to talk."

"You told her?" she cried.

He hesitated before responding. "Yes. I did, Kris. It was almost as if she knew."

"You're an idiot." She didn't give him a chance to respond. Kristine hung up, and then turned off the ringer on the phone.

Her face burned red from where Rhonda hit her, but she'd deserved it. She scrubbed herself raw in the shower before going to bed. The filth of Lamar would never wash off of her. She crawled into bed, then saw the face of her phone flash, revealing Tauris's number. "Hello?" she answered quickly.

"Hey, sweets!" he said jovially. "Whatchu up to?"

She hadn't told him about that woman, Rayne, who'd come to his door—the crackhead. Maybe she should've, but—

"I haven't been feeling well," she cleared her throat.

"Well, maybe I need to stop by and take your temperature?" he teased.

"Not tonight, Tauris," she replied solemnly. "I'm going to try and get some sleep."

"All right, baby," he said, disappointed. "I'll stop by tomorrow and check on you."

"See you tomorrow, then."

MAMA AND PAPA BEAR

Calling Bear and Mavis took almost as much courage as checking into the treatment center. But Rayne was glad to see them, despite the fact that they both were pissed as hell. Bear walked in, cut his eyes at her, and then planted his big self in front of the only window in the room, blocking every ray of sunshine from filtering in. Mavis sat in the only chair in the room, across from Rayne, who sat cross-legged on the bed. Her locks had been washed, oiled, and tightened, the dark circles underneath her eyes were gone, and without any makeup, Rayne looked like a young girl, far removed from the strung-out mess that had been admitted nearly a week ago. But the experience of what she'd been through, despite the fact that she couldn't remember all of it, lingered in her eyes, the experience permanently etching itself somewhere deep inside her. Mavis prudishly held on to her purse and avoided eye contact, a sure sign that one wrong word from Rayne and she would use that purse as a weapon to take her ass down.

They were the closest thing she'd ever had to family up here, and she knew that despite it all, they loved her.

"They got you back on that methadone like before?" Mavis asked, almost too politely.

Rayne shook her head. "I'm on buprenorphine this time."

Mavis was obviously at a loss for any good words to say, but Rayne had to give her credit for trying. "How's that working for you?"

Rayne shrugged. "It's supposed to be less addictive than methadone, and make for an easier transition from heroin. I'm not throwing up as much as I was, though, so that's good—I guess."

Bear grunted and just shook his head.

"You say something, baby?" Mavis asked, trying to get him to step up to the plate and not leave her alone with the task of having to interact like civilized human beings with this woman.

"Yeah, baby," Rayne smarted off, annoyed by these two trying to act like anything but the two people she loved, more than anybody in the world.

Mavis shot her an angry look.

Rayne smiled for the first time in weeks. She'd hit a nerve, and it showed.

"You fall off the gotdamned wagon." His deep voice echoed from across the room, sounding the way God would probably sound if He were mad. "Could've OD'd, died, been hooked on that shit all over again for the rest of your life, and all you care about is throwing up?"

Rayne looked at Mavis, half expecting her to come to

her defense, but, she didn't. Instead, good old Mavis just looked at her for the first time since she'd come into that room.

"That's the Big Bad Bear I know and love," Rayne shot back, sarcastically.

"If you don't shut up I'm going to hit you in the mouth with my purse," Mavis threatened, clutching her purse so tight her knuckles grew pale.

A soft spot warmed in Rayne's heart, and it felt good to be back in their good graces.

"We were worried sick about you," Mavis said, clenching her teeth. Muscles in her jaw flexed. "You had no business running around after that cockroach, Rayne. We told you that, and you should've known better."

"You could smell that shit on him," Bear added, "and your dumb ass was drawn to it like a fly to shit." He turned, stuffed his massive hands in his pockets, and looked at her like he was her daddy instead of her music director. "I thought you was smarter than that."

Rayne stared at him tenderly. "I thought I was, too, Bear."

"They found him dead," Mavis added. "Don't know if it was the drugs, his heart or what—but I say he just rotted like he deserved to rot. And if you're not careful, Rayne, you will end up just like him—or J. T." Her lips quivered and Mavis fumbled through her purse until she found a tissue. "If anything were to happen to you—"

Rayne was touched that Mavis and Bear cared so much,

and the last thing she wanted to do was to hurt them. She reached over to start to hug Mavis.

"Back up!" Mavis demanded. "Don't you put your hands on me, or I swear—"

Rayne reluctantly backed away, but as soon as she did, Mavis came over to the bed, and gathered her up in her arms. "We're going to get through this just like we did the last time," she said, consoling Rayne. Rayne squeezed her tightly in response. "Me and Big Bear are here for you. You know that. Right?"

Rayne nodded. "Oh, yes. Mavis," she said sincerely. "I know it better than I know my own name, girl."

Bear stood across the room, clearing his throat. He never cried on the outside. Bear was too much of a bad-ass to do that. But he cried like a baby inside. "Maybe you should come stay with us for a few days after you get out of here," he suggested.

Rayne and Mavis broke their embrace, looked at him, then back to each other, and laughed. "Not with all them bad kids you got running around the house," Rayne blurted out.

"Girl," Mavis chimed in. "They'll drive you to drink."

Bear shifted uncomfortably, obviously not finding the humor at all. "I was just saying—"

Rayne got up from the bed, walked over to him, and stood right in front of him, tilting her head back to get a good look at him. "I know what you're saying, Papa Bear," she said lovingly. "And I adore you for it."

• • •

When it was time to leave, Rayne walked them to the door. "Call Tauris," Bear told her before leaving. "He's been asking about you, worried."

"He's good people," Mavis added, and winked. "Seems like a good man."

Drug addicts lived twelve steps at a time. Tauris was a good man, but she wasn't ready for him yet. Nobody felt as sorry about that as she did, though. There was a time when he'd have walked across fire to get to her, but he hadn't been that enticed by her in a long time, and with good reason. Good love is hard to find, but before she could find it in anybody, even in him, she had to find it within herself first.

"Ms. Fitzgerald," the desk clerk called to her as she was passing by on her way back to her room. She handed Rayne a slip of paper. "A Miss Fontaine called. She asked you to call her back."

Kristine Fontaine. Rayne didn't know any Kristine Fontaine, so she dismissed the note, and stuffed it into the pocket of her robe.

FORBIDDEN FRUIT

"Don't hang up." The last time Taylor had seen Nora, she was crawling on her hands and knees, begging him to fuck her. Too much time had passed and he was starting to miss her in his own sardonic way.

"Where are you?" she demanded to know.

"I'm in the Big Apple, lovely lady." Taylor's tone was always laced with sarcasm, so if he ever was serious, she'd never believe it. "You should stop by for a visit. I'm beside myself, fidgeting over you."

"I can't."

"Can't, or won't?"

"I can't."

But she wanted to. However, Nora had too much at stake to give in to her desires now, and at the moment, impulse was a convenience she couldn't afford.

"Where's 'The Hammer'?" he asked, dousing sarcasm all over Cole's nickname.

Instinct warned her to hang up, but temptation kept her talking. "He's not here right now."

"Out of town?" he probed.

"None of your business, Taylor," she said irritably.

"Trouble in paradise." He said it as if he knew.

"I'm hanging up."

"Don't, Nora," his tone softened. "I flew out here hoping to spend some time with you, even a single night."

"Don't tell me that." Nora rolled her eyes.

"Even if it's the truth?"

"Even if it is, you know that's not how we operate," she said. "The whole world is watching constantly, Taylor. We can't afford to be careless."

"I would never dream of being careless, but I am the kind of man that goes after what I want, and right now, I want you. You want me, too. Say it."

"Fuck you, Taylor."

"I'm long and hard right now, Nora, but I only have eyes for you, darling. You know that."

"I'm hanging up."

"Cole leaves you hungry, Nora, and when you get hungry you come running to me. Wouldn't it make a hell of a lot more sense to walk away from what doesn't satisfy you and walk right into the arms of what does?"

"What? What the hell are you talking about, Taylor? Are you suggesting that you and I have an actual relationship?" She laughed. "Since when have we ever been anything but a good romp to each other?"

Taylor wasn't amused. "I know your triggers, love, and you know mine. If that isn't a match made in heaven, then what is?"

"My marriage is, Taylor."

"You sound ridiculous."

"Well, ridiculous or not, I love Cole. I can't say I feel the same way about you. Sorry."

"But you need me, and that trumps love any day."

"Maybe in your world."

"Is he there?"

"I told you that's none of your business."

"According to the tabloids, if you bother reading that trash—Houston, we have a problem. Now, I'm not one to believe everything I read, but as you know, just like anybody in this business knows, eighty percent of the shit they write is the truth."

"What the hell ever."

"Okay, seventy percent, but those are some pretty good odds, and from what I've read, the part about you and Mr. Hammer has a seventy to seventy-five percent chance of being pretty accurate, and if that's the case, then I see opportunity here."

"You can't be serious," she laughed again. "You want to move in on Cole's turf?"

"I want Cole's woman to be my own. There. I said it, and I don't care who knows it."

"Well, Cole's woman doesn't want you, Taylor."

"Cole's woman craves my dick almost as much as she's bored to tears by his. I am the cure to what ails you, Nora," he said smugly. "And as long as you and I are alive in this world, you'll be drawn to me like a magnet."

• • •

It was late when the phone rang. It was Taylor again. "Open the gate," he told her.

Nora's knees felt weak, and she hated herself for it. "Go back to Los Angeles, Taylor," she said feebly.

"In the morning, love," he said. "Now, open the gate and let me in."

She was putty in his hands, and Taylor did whatever he wanted with her until the sun came up. Nora savored every minute and every drop of their sexual tryst, appreciating every ache and pain her body suffered at his hands. He'd tied her up, spanked her ass and thighs hard with his belt, and forced himself into every orifice on her body, until she begged him to stop. But Taylor was good. It took more than a little begging to make him stop.

Nora lay curled up on her bed, exhausted and shuddering from the remnants of her last orgasm.

Taylor kissed her gently on the lips. "When are you going to figure it out, Nora?" he said, tenderly. "Cole isn't the man for you. He never has been."

She cried herself to sleep after Taylor left, loathing herself for not being stronger and resisting him—and regretting that he might just be right.

MAKES ME SING LA-DEE-DA

Bear had been the one to tell Tauris that Rayne was back, fresh out of rehab, and back at her own place. For whatever reason, she wasn't answering his calls, but Tauris thought that he'd have a better chance of seeing her if he knocked on the door. Lo and behold, she opened it and let him in. Rayne greeted him with a welcoming smile, despite herself.

"Well, I'll be damned," she exclaimed halfheartedly. "Looka here . . . looka here."

There was no denying the effect that woman still had on him, and probably would always have over him. Tauris stopped trying to make sense of it a long time ago, and just accepted it for what it was. He wrapped her in his arms, and the two of them stood in her doorway, swaying in a tender embrace.

"I'm pissed at you in so many ways, I can't even count them," he told her, kissing the top of her head.

Rayne sighed. "Get in line, man. You can stand behind me."

She poured them both coffees, and they sat on her sofa, with Rayne's head resting on his shoulder.

"You gonna be all right?" Tauris asked, concerned. "You kick the habit again?"

"I don't know if I'll ever truly kick it, T. Diggs," she spoke quietly. "I'll definitely have to do a better job of avoiding it, though."

"Yeah, well, I ain't going to fuss. I'm just glad to know you're okay."

Rayne raised her head and smiled at him. He was such a handsome man, and he had a good heart, too. "Tell me something, Tauris, what is it that you see in me? I never understood it, but there were times when I always thought you cared too much, and I never could figure it out."

Tauris shifted uncomfortably, unprepared for such a deep question from the woman. "I don't know, Rayne," he responded, dumbfounded. She stared tenderly at him. "Hell," he started to confess, "what don't I see in you? You're gorgeous, sexy, real. And you got a knack for straight-arming a brotha, making me want you that much more. But I came to terms a long time ago that I was never going to have you because you would never let me."

Tears glistened in her eyes. "How many times do I have to tell you that you are now and have always been too good for me?"

He grinned. "That's probably true. I just put up with your luscious ass because I felt sorry for you."

Rayne laughed. "Pity love. Ain't nothing wrong with that."

"Pity or not, it's real, though, baby girl. Believe that."

"But, you've got yourself someone new. Am I right?" Of course, she knew the answer and, of course, she was disappointed.

"I must, since I'm not running around sniffing after you anymore."

"Yeah, well, those were the good old days." Rayne squeezed his arm. "That's what I get for not paying attention."

"You paid attention, sweetheart. You just weren't feeling a brotha like that. No harm. No foul."

"Oh, there was plenty harm, T. Diggs, and my behavior was plenty foul, too. I messed up with you, and I'm sorry."

"I love you, Rayne. Maybe I always will. Maybe this feeling will pass and someone else will come along who appreciates it. Maybe someone already has," he finished quietly, thinking of Kristine. "But because I love you, I can back off and let you have some space to do what you need to do to get yourself together. And that's all I'm going to say, because I feel like I sound like Oprah Winfrey."

Of course, she couldn't help but to laugh, and feel genuinely touched by his conversation because the bottom line was, Tauris was right.

"That's some serious truth-talk," she said quietly.

Tauris held up his fist for some dap. "Give me some on that, sistah-woman."

Rayne moved his hand out of the way and leaned in and kissed him. If she'd learned anything these last few weeks it was that life was way too short to spend it living in the past, and that a good man was hard to come by, and most of all, that she was really glad that he was here.

"Will you do something for me?" she whispered.

"What's that?" Tauris smiled.

"Promise me that you won't give up on me yet, Tauris. I know I've been hard on you, but I know a good thing when I see it, and I see it all over you. I can't give me to you all messed up like this. You deserve so much better, but just leave the door open a little bit. I promise, one day soon, I'll come knocking."

The flavor of Rayne lingered on his lips for the rest of the day. He'd waited a long time to get any kind of a promise out of her, and today she came with it, and all he could do was shake his head. He'd just gotten comfortable with where he stood with Rayne, but leave it up to her to shake his ass up all over again. Tauris knew better than to think he would ever be able to completely close the door on that woman. As much as he knew he should, he had a weakness for her that was as strong as any addiction.

Kristine crossed his mind. Tauris sighed, and pulled into his driveway.

CAN'T STOP, WON'T STOP

"I don't want Rhonda, and you don't want me, Kristine." Lamar sat at her dining room table, staring desperately at her.

He'd begged and pleaded for her to see him, just once, so that he could explain why he'd told his wife about them. Reluctantly, Kristine agreed, in the hopes that she could finally get him to understand that she had moved on, and had no plans of ever being with him intimately again.

"What am I supposed to do?" he asked her. "I've lost everything."

He looked like he hadn't shaved in days, and like he'd been wearing that same suit for just as long. Half-moon circles cradled his eyes.

"I don't know what you need to do, Lamar." She was so sick of this man, calling her at all hours of the day and night, pounding on her door. He was like a nightmare, obsessed and desperate for her to continue on with their relationship. "But you need to leave me alone."

He shook his head. "I can't. Baby, I can't do that."

"You could if I were any other woman, Lamar," she

snapped. "The fixation you have with me has nothing to do with me, now. Can't you see that? You want that young girl who needed you because she didn't have anyone else, but that's not me anymore. I have someone. I love someone and it's not you."

She'd hurt him, but she needed to. If that's what it took to get him to see reason, then she would hurt him all day long if she had to.

"I've given up everything for you! Every damn thing that mattered to me!"

"You didn't do it for me! You did it for yourself, Lamar! It's not my fault that you stopped loving Rhonda!"

"If not yours, then whose?" he asked maliciously.

"I'm not going to sit here and let you blame me for that," she said gravely. "Whatever feelings you did or didn't have for your wife, are not my fault."

"I loved you, Kris! I loved you and that cost me what love I had for Rhonda!"

"That's bull and you know it! Maybe I was the excuse, but I never loved you like that, Lamar! I never told you I did! Not once."

"Then what was I to you? Just some dick because Daddy wouldn't let you out to find one on your on?"

Before she realized it, she'd slapped him. Lamar stared back, glassy-eyed at her. "I hit a nerve, sweetheart?"

"I was sixteen years old," she said, clenching her teeth, and pointing her finger in his face.

"You knew what you were doing," he said venomously.

"So did you, and if you loved me the way everyone thought you loved me, then you would've stopped it right then and there, Lamar." Her hand trembled. "You wanted me long before that. We both know you did. So, what does that make you?"

Lamar slumped back in his seat. "That's not what I am," he said weakly.

How many times had he pushed that thought out of his mind, afraid that there was some truth to it?

"You had sons, Lamar." Kristine wasn't about to let up. "If you'd have had daughters, would you have done to them what you did to me?"

Lamar broke down crying all of a sudden. Kristine watched this man crumble right in front of her eyes, and she knew she'd gone too far.

She waited quietly, while he composed himself. Lamar couldn't bring himself to even look at her. He was a shell of the man he'd once been, confident and sure that she belonged with him and that someday, he could find the happiness that had eluded him for so many years, hidden away in her arms. Kristine had no idea the depths to which he truly loved her. He realized today that she never would.

"There's nothing I wouldn't have done for you," he said quietly. "All you had to do was ask, sweetheart, and I'd have given you the world."

"Then I'm asking, Lamar," she pleaded. "Leave me alone. If you really do care about me, you'll leave me alone."

It was late, and he was the only one in the office. Lamar felt like scraps of himself were scattered in the wind, and it would take a miracle to put him back together again.

DREAM LOVERS

Nora and Cole had met three times now with Dr. Burton, one of the top marriage counselors in the country, and this was the first session that truly brought them to the main issue of dissention between them. Sex.

Dr. Burton insisted on a casual environment. He sat in a well-worn leather chair, Cole sat on the floor, and Nora lay stretched out on the sofa as if she were lounging at home.

"Since I was fourteen," she explained. "I have lived my life here." Nora stretched her arm straight up in the air above her. "You're beautiful, Nora. We're flying off to Milan in the morning, Nora. You have a photo shoot in Spain this afternoon, Nora. Do you really like that Zac Posen 'Alexia' handbag, Nora? Here. Take two. Eventually, it all becomes numbing," she admitted. "Eventually nothing is as exciting as it once was, because it's just my life, Dr. Burton. My mother was a model, and before I experienced this world in my own life, I lived it in hers. Do you know how hard it is for me to get excited—truly excited about anything?"

"Cole," Dr. Burton addressed him. "Have you known this about your wife?"

Cole shook his head. "Not to that extent, no. I just thought . . . I mean to me, it's all exciting. I came from the 'hood—I came from nothing, and I worked my ass off to get to where I am. I'm enjoying every last piece of fruit of my labor, including being married to this gorgeous woman, and every day I thank God for what we have. It never dawned on me that she—you—were bored by it all, Nora."

"Desensitivity can bring about some destructive behavior," Dr. Burton explained. "I think it gives us a better understanding of where the temper comes into play, Nora. Don't you agree?" He directed his question to both of them.

"So, what?" Cole interjected. "Because Nora's bored, I need to beat her ass as foreplay for the next fifty years?"

Dr. Burton laughed.

"Why not?" Nora blurted out. Both men stared perplexed at her. "I don't mean it like that," she quickly corrected herself. "But I've been racking my brain to try and figure out a way to enjoy normal sex, Cole." Nora sat up. "I've been trying so hard to be this docile, little sex kitten you seem to want me to be."

"That's not what I want," he protested. "I want it passionate, too, hot and heavy—sweaty . . . I don't want you to just lay there."

"It's the violence he's concerned about, Nora," the doctor spoke up. "Am I right, Cole?"

"I don't want to hit her. I don't want to be pushed to the point where I might seriously hurt my wife. Why am I wrong for that?" He looked to Nora for the answer.

"You're not going to hurt me, Cole," she said flippantly.

Cole suddenly became angry. "See, that's what I'm talking about. You either think I'm a pussy or that I have no limits, and either one is a grave mistake to make, Nora," he warned. "You grew up spoiled and I grew up in the streets. I channel my anger in boxing, and I learned to do that at a very young age because if I hadn't, I'd have either ended up dead or in prison. When I hit, it's to hurt a man. The last thing I want to do is to turn that energy loose on my wife, and if we can't reach some kind of agreement, then—"

"That's why you're here, Cole," Dr. Burton quickly intervened, dousing water on the argument before it got too far out of control. "I don't think Nora wants you to kill her," he said, trying to make light of the situation. It worked, and both Nora and Cole seemed to relax a bit. "Just give her that hot, sweaty, bruising sex that excites her and—undoubtedly—you, too."

"What are we going to do about our anniversary?" she asked him, riding down the private elevator as they left the doctor's office. Keeping their marital woes out of the limelight of the press had been difficult, but both of them had worked hard to maintain appearances. "Lawrence, the guy we hired to plan the event, has been calling frantically to finalize the details, and I need to know what to tell him."

Cole shrugged. "I don't know. If we want to keep the

press out of our business, I guess we need to do what we can to make them think everything's cool."

Nora wanted to reach out to him, to hold him, to kiss him—but she knew better. Cole's indifference to her physically felt crueler than any blow landed between them. "I'll call him today, then," she said. "He's probably going to want to talk to both of us about some of the details, though."

The elevator doors opened to the garage, and Cole pulled his keys from his pocket. "Well, if he does, call me." He started to turn to head toward his car parked on the other side of the garage away from hers, when he quickly grazed her cheek with a kiss.

She wanted him to come home. Nora needed to make love to her man. His scent lingered in the air where she stood, and Nora's pride blew away in the breeze. "Cole!" she called out. He stopped and turned. "Can't you just— come home?" she pleaded. "I miss you, baby."

There was nothing in the world he would've loved more than to go home with his wife. For a while, things between them would be cool, and then, without warning, they'd turn on a dime, and he'd be fucking her in the ass on the lawn, tasting blood in his mouth from a blow from her, watching the bruises burn red underneath her skin. The image made him hard, but it saddened him, too. What the hell was wrong with them that sex like that was good sex?

He smiled. "Sure wish I could," he said, before leaving.

Nora watched him leave and a part of her knew that her marriage was hanging on by a thread.

CLOSE TO THE EDGE

Rayne Fitzgerald hadn't returned any of her calls. For all Kristine knew, the woman had left that rehab clinic, and gone back to the rock she crawled out from under, high on crack or alcohol, or whatever it was she poisoned her body with. She had no idea why she wanted to talk to that woman, except to find out what he saw in her. It was an obsession Kristine couldn't get past.

She was torn over him. Kristine had been looking to Tauris to be the answer to the question of her happiness. And she'd given him her whole heart and soul without hesitation or question. He still hadn't said he loved her. "I care about you too, Kris," was the best she'd ever been able to pull from him, and as much as it hurt, she assured herself that if she were just patient enough, one day he'd surprise her and say the words she wanted to hear most.

Tauris made love to her like he meant it. She lay back, staring across the dark room, reliving the tender moments between them. "He made love to me," she muttered quietly, with conviction. What better memories did she have than that? He was still in love with Rayne, and knowing that abhorred her. He never openly discussed Rayne, but Kristine suspected that he was still seeing her, or that he at least wanted to.

Kristine had never been so in love, and never longed for anything so much in her life than for him to love her, too, and she knew that if she walked away, another woman would win the prize of Tauris Diggs. As angry as she was with him, as much as he'd hurt her, the thought of letting him go just wasn't an option she could live with.

"Kris," Tauris said into her voice mail. "Baby, I'm sorry about tonight. I got caught up in something, and ... I should've called. I'm sorry. I'll make it up to you. I promise."

She listened to his message, disappointed. Jealousy warned her that he was spending time with Rayne, but her heart wanted to believe that he really did "get caught up in something."

SING-SONG

Nora and Cole worked the room like the superstars that they were, mingling together and separately. No one in the world would've ever suspected that there were problems between them. A private party of two hundred closest friends attended the event in the ballroom of their estate. Nora looked stunning in a pastel-colored, floral, floor-length sundress, while Cole wore jeans and his typical white, button-down shirt, with the sleeves rolled up to his elbows.

The room was filled with fragrant Oriental "Stargazer" lilies, Nora's favorite, and lit with elegant candles. A casual buffet of exotic foods spread across a table the length of one wall of the room, and the champagne flowed freely. At the center of it all, was a life-size slide presentation of the attractive couple photographed together from the time the media first caught wind of them, to their marriage, to more recent photos of them in a photo shoot in Barbados.

He'd been living in a hotel room for the last month, but it felt good being here. Nora looked like something he'd dreamed up, and all night long, he could hardly keep his eyes off of her. "If you ain't careful, Cole, man," one of his trainers said to him jokingly, "people are going to start to think you got it bad for that chick."

Nora found his gaze from across the room and held it. He lifted his glass to her in a toast. "Well, they'd probably be right," he confirmed.

Nora glided across the floor to where Cole was, and kissed him lightly on the lips. "Hey, handsome," she smiled. "Who are you here with?"

This coy come-on from his estranged wife definitely aroused him. "I'm here with this fine babe who looks good enough to eat right about now." His eyes traveled up and down the length of her.

Nora pressed her finger to his lips. "Shhhh . . . rumor has it that our marriage is in trouble."

Cole took her hand in his. "Not tonight it isn't."

You're my heat . . .
Love me now or I'll go crazy

Rayne Fitzgerald's gritty, but sensual voice singing Chaka Khan's song filtered nicely through the room, complementing the laid-back, intimate vibe of the celebration. Nora and Cole swayed subtly back and forth to the melody. Rayne was a local R&B singer that came highly recommended by a friend of Cole's at All Talk Records.

"I want you home," Nora whispered seductively in his

ear. "We belong together, Cole." Her long lashes brushed against his cheek. "You know it just like I do."

Cole pressed his rigid penis between his wife's thighs. "See what you do to me, girl?" He grinned.

Nora chuckled. "You're making Momma proud, son. Say you'll stay tonight."

He wrapped his arm around her waist. "No uppercuts, right hooks, or body punches," he joked.

Nora laughed. "Not even a playful slap on the ass."

Cole nodded. "Then hell, yeah, I'm staying."

That night, Cole pushed and pulled luxuriously in and out of his wife's body, savoring every stroke like it was his last. He had no idea it was possible to miss a woman as much as he'd missed her. The nectar of Nora was intoxicating, filling his nostrils each time he inhaled. He had lapped up the juices of his woman with his tongue before plunging into her. Cole took his time, drawing out every minute, hoping to make their lovemaking last until sunrise.

Cole was in his element. Nora had to imagine hers.

"Beat it up!" Nora commanded him in her mind. *"Deeper, dammit! Deeper! Hit bottom, Cole! Fuck the hell out of me!"*

LET YOU SEE MY WHAAA?

Work was kicking his ass. Tauris had more jobs than he could handle even with the extra help, and he'd spent all day interviewing and writing up proposals to try and keep up with the demand. Tauris was tired and irritable, and in no mood for the silent treatment he was getting from Kristine.

"What's wrong?"

"Nothing."

That was the extent of their conversation for the last two hours over dinner, and frankly, he was getting sick of asking. She'd asked him to be honest, and that's exactly what he'd done. That was the thing about women, though. Whenever they asked a man to be honest about something, the smartest thing he could do would be to lie.

On the drive home, Kristine stared out the window the whole time. He pulled up into her driveway, and turned off the radio. She started to get out of the truck, but stopped when she realized he hadn't budged. "Aren't you coming inside?"

"Nah. I'm gonna head on home."

All evening, he'd had to sit through attitude, and he wasn't in the mood to take it inside.

"I was hoping you would." She did that thing with her eyes, that needful, expectant lash-batting thing. Whatever the official term for that technique was, it usually worked.

She had barely spoken to him all night, so Tauris was clueless as to why she'd want him to come inside. They went into the family room, and Kristine turned on the television. "Would you like a beer?" she asked sweetly.

"Sure, baby." Tauris sat down and flipped through channels.

Several minutes had passed when Tauris realized he could hear voices coming from another part of the house. He hadn't heard anyone knock or ring the doorbell.

". . . the police!"

Kristine sounded like something was wrong. He hurried out to see what was going on. That creepy-ass uncle of hers was standing in the parlor, looking like some bum off the streets.

"You won't return my calls, so what do you expect?"

"What's going on here?" Tauris interrupted what looked like a bad situation to him.

The man stared hard at Tauris.

"Kris?" Tauris asked, coming up behind her. "Everything cool?"

Kristine didn't answer right away.

"We've got business to discuss," the man said, tightening his jaw. "And it ain't got shit to do with you."

Tauris stepped between Kristine and this uncle of hers and dared him to put his ass out of the room. "I got business here tonight, man," Tauris warned. "And I think whatever business you have here, can wait for another time."

Tauris towered over Lamar by a foot, and easily outweighed him. He assumed that uncle was no fool and was smart enough to leave without incident.

"Do you know what you're doing to me?" Lamar looked as if he were about to break down. He looked at Tauris. "Do you have any idea what the fuck she's doing to me?"

"Just go, Lamar!" she shouted, standing behind Tauris.

"To what?" Lamar yelled. "Ain't a damn thing out there for me to go to!" The man wept bitterly and Tauris just hoped the fool didn't have a gun or something on him. Scenes like this usually led to somebody getting shot, and the man looked unstable enough to do something crazy.

"Why don't you go home?" Tauris told him, trying to remain cool and to keep this fool from losing his. He could've easily picked him up and tossed him out the front door, but who knows what he was likely to do after that.

Lamar ignored Tauris and fixed his sights on Kristine. Lord! Look at how far gone he was over this woman. Everything about the two of them screamed wrong, and in Lamar's head he knew that, but he was lost and trapped in a web of guilt and lies and denial and love. He'd lost his mind and, in that moment, he realized it and felt like such a fool.

The look of disgust on her face cut him in two. She didn't respect him. Kristine certainly wasn't in love with him, and he had nothing in the world to lose anymore. Lamar pulled the loaded nine millimeter out of his pocket and waved it in the air.

"Fuck you, Kristine," he said, apathetically, then pointed the gun to his temple.

Tauris was on him before he had a chance to pull the trigger. The gun went off but it was pointed in the air when it did, releasing the bullet through the ceiling. He yanked the gun from the man's hand, then pushed him into the wall. Lamar slowly slid down to the floor, crying like a baby.

"Call the police," Tauris demanded.

The cops showed up in minutes, and after being told what happened, the two watched them take Lamar away.

Kristine was all shaken up, and begged him to stay the night. That was the last thing Tauris felt like doing, but reluctantly, he agreed. They didn't make love, but he held her in his arms.

"What the hell is up with that fool, Kristine?" he asked quietly in the dark.

Kristine traced her fingers lightly over the scattered hairs on his chest. She'd wanted to keep Lamar as far away from Tauris as possible, because just his presence was threatening enough to ruin everything between them. Tauris knew enough about her relationship with Lamar, but he didn't need to know the details. "I can't get him to leave me 'alone," she admitted. "He's crazy, Tauris, and I don't know what to do."

"He either needs a good psychiatrist, or a good ass-whooping. I see him around here again, I might have to take care of that ass-whooping part."

"I've got a realtor who is looking for buyers for the house," she explained. "I'm just going to have to leave and go where he can't find me. I think that's the only way I'm going to get rid of him."

"You shouldn't have to sell your house for that."

"I want to sell it. I've been wanting to sell it. Lamar just really makes me want to hurry up and get it sold."

Between this mess with Lamar and the uneasiness she was feeling over Tauris and Rayne, Kristine was starting to feel as if her life were unraveling before her eyes. Lamar's obsession was beginning to scare her, and she felt like Tauris might be pulling away from her for Rayne.

Kristine replayed the conversation she and Tauris had had earlier over and over again in her mind until she drifted off to sleep.

"Have you found Rayne, Tauris?" *she'd asked, not telling him that she'd actually seen her.*

"Yeah," *he admitted, reluctantly.* *"She's all right. Had a rough time of it, but she's cool."*

"Are you seeing her again? Be honest."

He shifted uncomfortably in his seat. "I'm there for her the same way I'd be there for anybody I care about, Kristine."

It was a last-ditch effort on his part to salvage the mess he'd made of the conversation. Tauris had taken words she'd dreamed of hearing him say someday, and turned them into cheap imitations of a dream, and she resented him for it.

"I don't want to lose you, Kris," he whispered to her before he dozed off to sleep. "I haven't done as good a job as I should've with you, but I swear I'll make it right."

She hoped he'd keep that promise, one way or another.

DARK SIDE OF THE MOON

"Clean and straight for a month now," Anna boasted on Rayne's behalf. "I'm proud of you, girl." Anna's long wavy hair hung luxuriously down to her waist. Rayne had agreed to meet with her at the treatment center once a week since her relapse, and quite honestly, she looked forward to each and every one of them.

"Do I get a gold star?" Rayne asked sarcastically, but Anna could see that she was very proud of herself.

"Next time you come in, I'll have it waiting for you," she smiled. "I'm proud of you," she added quickly. "I want you to know that."

"I do," Rayne nodded introspectively. "And thanks, Anna. I'd like to think I'm a tad bit smarter now than I was before and no more hanging out with former friends slash drug addicts."

Anna nodded. "Brain over brawn, girl . . . I always put my money on brains. Did Cash ever tell you why he came back? I mean, why he really came back?"

"I don't think he knew," she said sadly. "Kind of like a salmon swimming upstream just to lay eggs and die." She sort of chuckled. "He said he wanted me, but maybe he just wanted me to see him die. Sounds twisted, but maybe he wanted me to see that that part of my life was completely over by him dying."

Anna frowned.

"I don't know, girl. I have to try and give up making sense of it because it might never make sense."

"Maybe it's not supposed to."

"Maybe not. Everybody is dead except for me. Each time, Anna, I was a hit away from being dead, too—but I'm still standing." Rayne shrugged. "In so many ways, I've loathed myself for being alive, and I've blamed myself and buried myself right next to J. T. I've spent the last four years walking around like a zombie, touching but not feeling anything or anyone."

"That's no way to live, Rayne."

Rayne smiled at her. "Yeah. I can see that."

"So," Anna grinned, "what do you want out of this life?"

"It's okay for me to want something from it now—isn't it?" she asked, hopeful.

"The sky's the limit."

Rayne held out her hand and started counting on her fingers. "Well, first I want to get this record deal, win about a dozen Grammys, make millions, and buy myself a couple of mansions. Eventually, I want a man of my very own." She sounded giddy. "Real love, girl. The kind that tickles your stomach when he says your name."

"I know that's right!" Anna laughed. "Got anybody in mind?" she winked.

If she didn't know better, Rayne felt like she'd almost managed to blush. "I might have." She sounded like a teenager, thinking of Tauris, who happened to have been the only man she was sort of seeing at the moment, but he wasn't a bad choice.

"Oh, and I want a car. I'm sick and tired of this roadkill I drive that only works when it feels like it. I'm thinking Mercedes."

Anna walked her to the entrance after their meeting was over. "You wanna go back to just calling me when you need me?" Anna asked, satisfied that Rayne was over the hard part of her recovery.

Rayne shook her head. "I like meeting every week. You're my friend, Anna, and I need to keep in touch with my friend."

Anna put her arm around Rayne's shoulder. "Cool. But from now on, let's get together and go someplace good to eat. You like Peruvian chicken and rice?"

"Love it!"

On Rayne's way out, the receptionist stopped her. "Ms. Fitzgerald? I have some messages here for you."

"Messages?" Rayne took the stack of handwritten notes from her and flipped through them. They were all from the same person. "Kristine Fontaine," she muttered. "I don't know anybody by that name."

"She says she knows you and that it's urgent that you return her call. She's been pretty persistent, going so far as to ask me for your personal number and address, but of course, I told her I couldn't give out that information."

"Thanks." Rayne smiled, and left.

Kristine almost didn't recognize Rayne when she walked into the restaurant. The woman looked like another person altogether. Long onyx-black locks hung past her shoulders, her flawless dark-chocolate complexion glowed, and deep-rich penetrating eyes stared searching as she approached Kristine waving her down.

"I'm Rayne," she introduced herself as she sat down. "I can't believe I don't remember you."

Kristine had told her over the phone that she had been the one to give Rayne a ride to the treatment facility. "That's okay," Kristine said hurriedly.

"No," Rayne frowned. "No, it's not okay. I was so messed up—but thank you. Thank you so much for helping me," she said earnestly. "Fontaine? I knew someone else with that last name. An older man. Bishop was his first name. Bishop Fontaine."

Kristine was stunned. "He was my father. How did you know him?"

Rayne smiled. "I met him when my husband passed away." She stared at Kristine and slowly watched as the resemblance started to materialize. "Bishop was good people. He helped me during a really rough time in my life. It broke my heart when he died."

She couldn't imagine her father having anything to do with a woman like her. Kristine's father could be such a cold and judgmental man in a way that didn't come across as obvious, but growing up in the same household with him, and hearing some of the things he'd say about people to her mother, she knew a side of him that most people never thought existed.

"His passing broke a lot of hearts," she said quietly. *Except hers.*

Kristine had come here prepared to hate this woman, but Rayne wasn't anything like she thought she'd be. Polished and sophisticated, she was a woman with issues, but obviously, she was working hard to overcome them, and for that, Kristine had nothing but admiration for her.

"I'm glad to see you're doing better," Kristine said sincerely. "I can only imagine what it must've been like."

"Don't even try to imagine it," Rayne gently warned her. "And please, please don't feel sorry for me," she added. "We all have burdens to bear. Mine just happens to be heroin."

The waiter came over to the table. Rayne ordered a diet cola, and Kristine ordered a cup of coffee. "Are you hungry?" Kristine asked. "I ate earlier, but if you're hungry—"

"No, girl. I'm good." Rayne smiled.

Awkward silence loomed between them. Kristine had expected to meet an unruly, lewd woman, defensive and ready to fight for her man. Rayne didn't come across as that kind of woman at all. Not that Kristine had been prepared to fight anyone. Her whole purpose for meeting Rayne was to find out the nature of her relationship with Tauris, but without coming straight out and asking her.

All of a sudden, a man came over to their table. "Excuse me," he said, unable to take his eyes off of Rayne. He reached out to shake her hand. "Ms. Fitzgerald?" he asked, looking downright starstruck.

"Yes," she said graciously.

"I thought that was you." The man leaned down and kissed her hand. "I hate to call myself this, because it's embarrassing, but it's the truth. I'm a huge fan, Ms. Fitzgerald. One of your biggest fans, to the point of being a damn groupie," he laughed, and so did Rayne.

"Well, ain't nothing wrong with that, baby. I'm flattered. Really."

"I'm sorry, Miss," he said, apologizing to Kristine. "I really didn't mean to interrupt, but," turning back to Rayne, "could you sign this napkin for me? Then I'll leave you and your friend to your meal."

"What's your name?"

"Franklin. I own an art gallery downtown, near the Sitting Room. That's where I first saw you perform."

"Okay," she nodded, staring into some of the most delicious-looking chocolate eyes she'd ever seen. "That was awhile ago, though. I sure hope you've been out to see us play since then?" she questioned playfully.

"Most definitely," he assured her. "Every chance I get."

Rayne signed his napkin, and just before leaving, the man kissed her hand again, and apologized again to Kristine, sitting dumbfounded as to what had just happened.

"Did I miss something?" she asked sheepishly. "Are you an actress or something?"

Rayne smiled modestly. "No. I sing."

Kristine had forgotten that Tauris had mentioned it to her. "Really?" She pretended to be surprised.

Rayne laughed. "I sing in clubs, locally. Every now and then I venture out—Chicago, Atlanta, sometimes Europe—but mostly I just perform around here."

Rayne downplayed it, but Kristine was still impressed. "I had no idea. I'm going to have to come out and hear you perform one of these days."

"You should," Rayne nodded. "We'll be playing at Davenport's in Georgetown this weekend. Come on down, and I'll buy you a drink."

"I think I will." Kristine couldn't help it—she liked the woman. "And maybe I'll bring a friend of mine."

"Please do. The more the merrier."

There was no easy way to do this. There was no right way to say it. There was no opportune time.

"I think you know my friend, Rayne."

Rayne stared back at her confused, and Kristine regretted having Tauris between her and someone she could possibly have genuinely liked.

"His name is Tauris," Kris said carefully. "Tauris Diggs."

Rayne's expression went blank, but her memory flashed briefly, recalling where she'd seen this woman before. "You were the one who answered the door," she said, conclusively. "That day . . . I went to Tauris's looking for help, and you answered the door."

Kristine nodded. "That was me."

Rayne didn't know what she felt. Disappointment didn't quite sum it up. Anger was nowhere to be found. Ambiguous was probably the best word she could find to describe what she felt. "Tauris is your man?"

"Yes," Kristine said with conviction, quietly preparing herself for the backlash she was sure was going to come.

"So, is that why you wanted to see me?" Rayne probed. "To make sure I knew that?"

Kristine pressed her bottom lip between her teeth, and looked as uncertain as a teenager. "Yes," she whispered, lowering her gaze.

"Fine," Rayne said. "Now I know."

Kristine stared bashfully at her, stunned by Rayne's lack of response. "What does that mean?"

"It means what it means. Don't try and read more into it than that. I assure you. I'm not that complicated."

"Are you going to stop seeing him?"

Rayne tilted her head to the side. "What makes you

think I'm still seeing him?" She used the word *still* to let Kristine know without a doubt that she and Tauris had been together.

"I don't know. I just—"

Oh, this girl had it bad for that man. Rayne could see it oozing out of her, and she remembered being just like her when she and J. T. were together. It was that sick love, the kind that made you blind to yourself, and invisible to him, because like air, he just took for granted that it would always be there.

"Has he told you about me and him?"

"Yes," she said. "A little."

"I care about him. He cares about me."

Kristine found the courage to look Rayne in the eyes. "I love him, and I don't want to lose him," she said bravely.

"He's not spare change, Kristine, and you don't have a hole big enough in your pocket for him to fall through. If he truly cares about you and wants you in his life, then he ain't going nowhere. Tauris is loyal if he ain't nothing else."

Kristine sighed, and rubbed her forehead in frustration. "I know this may not make sense to you."

"It doesn't."

"I've never met anyone like Tauris, before. He makes me happier than I've ever been, and all I want is for us to be together."

"Oh, Tauris is one of a kind all right." She tried hard to hide her sarcasm, and thankfully this woman was too far gone in the essence of T. Diggs to notice.

"We spend a lot of time together," Kristine continued. "And I know he cares about me just by the things he does, and says, and—I know you probably think I'm a fool."

Been there, done that, Rayne thought. After all, who was she to judge? Besides, T. Diggs had some serious game. But despite it all, he really was good people. Like everybody else, though, he had his imperfections, too. This girl loved him—that much was obvious—and he must've felt something for her, too. Rayne had noticed the change in him.

"I'd do anything for him." Kristine had tears in her eyes. Rayne really did feel for the woman.

"You want me to back off?" Of course, she knew the answer to the question. Rayne just asked it for the hell of it.

"I do," she pleaded with her eyes. "He and I just need a chance to make this work," she reasoned. "I know it won't be easy with you still in the picture."

Rayne raised her eyebrows. "Don't you think you should be talking to him about all of this?"

Kristine waved her hand in the air. "I've tried, but he sulks whenever I bring it up."

"Are you just bringing it up, or are you whining about it? Complaining? Pouting. You know how some of us women do," she smirked.

"I know you know what it feels like to be in love."

"I do," she said thoughtfully.

"Tauris is my first love, Rayne."

Stop the presses! Like she never would've guessed.

"I just want a chance to make this work."

Kristine was unique, for lack of a better word, and Rayne wondered if Tauris knew just how unique this sistah truly was. Maybe she should tell him. Maybe, she should just stay out of it and let him figure it out for himself. It was times like this when she wondered if the rest of the world wasn't shooting up, too.

Kristine composed herself, and sat up straight in her seat. "I just wanted to tell you how I felt, Rayne, and to clear up any misunderstandings that might've been between us."

"No misunderstanding here, girl."

"I love him, Rayne. I wanted you to know how much. In a way, I saved your life." Kristine stared intently at Rayne. "I would think you could do this one thing for me to return the favor. Leave him alone. Please?"

Rayne gathered her purse to leave. "I can't make you any promises, sistah, but I can give you a word of advice. If I were you, I'd start an open dialogue with my man and I'd make sure he knew good and damn well where I was coming from. Since I'm sure he has no idea that you and I have met, I'd start by coming clean on that one, because if you don't, and it ever comes up in conversation, I will. Honesty is a damn good policy, I always say, and I'd start being honest now, if I were you, long before you manage to get T. Diggs walking down that aisle or whatever."

DO YOU TAKE THIS WOMAN . . .

Cole was comfortable again. He and Nora had been attending marriage counseling regularly, and more and more, he found himself at home sleeping in his own bed, instead of the one in his hotel room. He and Nora were like teenagers dating. He'd come by with a pizza and a six-pack, and the two of them sat on the floor of the media room, eating and watching horror movies in between kissing, rolling around on the floor wrestling, and exploring body parts.

"When's the last time we had this much fun with our clothes on?" she asked, giggling like a girl.

Cole rolled her over on her back, and buried his head under her sweatshirt and nibbled on her belly. "It's been a while," he said, sounding muffled.

"You wanna sleep over?" Nora asked playfully.

Cole nodded underneath her shirt. When he emerged, he looked like a kid. "You wanna get married?" he teased.

Nora put her finger to her chin. "Ummmm . . . sure!" she squealed.

He really was her best friend. There was nobody else she liked being around more than him. Cole brought her back to Earth to that humbling place where she was just a woman and he was just a man and that was all that mattered. They'd both put their schedules on hold to focus on mending their marriage. The disconnect between them was sex, but Nora had come to terms with the fact a long time ago that Cole wasn't interested in what turned her on sexually.

"I can't get with that, Nora," he told her time and time again in counseling.

Despite the fact that she knew it turned him on, too. Not the violence, but the sheer spontaneity and raw passion of it did turn him on. Cole was afraid of losing control. What he couldn't seem to grasp, and what didn't make sense to her, either, was the fact that that's exactly what she wanted him to do.

"If I lose it, and I hurt you, Nora, I could do some serious damage that could cost both of us. Why can't you see that?"

She had a blind spot to it. It was inconceivable that he could ever hurt her like that. But was it a fantasy? Was that what she wanted? Deep down, did she want him to go too far?

Nora decided that the best way to handle this, and to keep her marriage together, was to put a bandage on a broken leg, and to get her satisfaction the way she'd been getting it for months: outside of her marriage. She still saw Taylor because he had just as much to lose as she did if word got out about their affair and she knew that their encounters would never go beyond the bedroom. And he knew her. He knew how to get her off, and with Taylor she could push the limits just far enough to be dangerous. The fact that one of his women walked in on them only made Nora hotter.

Lately, Taylor had been pushing the envelope to new thrilling heights, suggesting that they should invite a guest into their trysts and have a threesome. Of course, the thought excited her. She'd never done it before, but it wasn't like she hadn't thought about it. Except in photo shoots for high-end fashion magazines, Nora had never touched another woman, but she was more than willing to give it a try, or better yet, invite another man into the mix.

Cole pulled down her sweatpants, and buried his face between her thighs, flicking his tongue in and out of her moist folds. Nora raised her knees to her chest, and held his head in place. She wished he'd bite it, the way Taylor did. Cole loved her too much for that.

"I don't like hurting you, baby," he'd say. "Let me make love to you."

She moaned and bucked on cue, but in all honesty, her orgasm came and went, almost unnoticed by her. When he sat up and smiled at her, proud of his efforts, she feigned an expression of satisfaction and gratitude that inflated his ego even more.

Nora wanted him to ram his big cock in her ass, but Cole would ease it in gradually—slow, steady, easy—and bore her to tears with his lovemaking. She hated herself right this second. Nora hated the fact that she couldn't be happy with her man, making love to her man, the way most women dreamed.

He balanced over her, and pumped in and out of her a couple of times before pulling out altogether. Cole leaned down and kissed her. "Let's take a shower." He helped her up off the floor and Nora followed him upstairs to their bathroom.

Nora stripped down to the skin first, racing Cole to get into the steam shower first. Truth be told—he let her win. "What's that, baby?" he asked, trailing behind her, noticing some kind of bruising on her behind, and hips. Cole caught her from behind and examined her more intently.

"What?" she asked impatiently, looking over her shoulder trying to see what he was talking about.

"Are those—" The playfulness faded from his face. "Bite marks."

Nora suddenly felt flush, and pure shock washed over her.

"How'd you get bite marks on the ass, Nora?" he asked harshly. Cole was no CSI agent, but points of bruising around her pelvic area looked an awful lot like somebody had pressed his fingers into her. He hadn't noticed them earlier in the media room because except for the light emanating from the screen, it had been dark.

Nora's brain flipped through excuses like she'd flip through pages of a magazine, but for the life of her, she couldn't find a way to explain away teeth marks on her ass. "I—I don't—I—"

He'd been hit upside the head a few times during his career, but Cole wasn't so thick he couldn't figure it out. He stared disappointedly and angrily at his wife, shook his head, and turned and walked away.

Nora chased after him. "Cole, please!"

"Please what?" he shouted angrily. "Fuck, Nora! We're supposed to be working on this," he waved his hand between the two of them. "And you're out there fucking around? And the mothafucka's gotta bite you to get you off? You're a gotdamned lunatic!"

Nora's own anger and resentment surfaced quickly in retaliation. "Why? Because I want a man to do more than sweat and moan on top of me?"

"I make love to you!"

"You make love to your damn self, Cole, because you sure as hell ain't doing shit for me!"

She resented it as soon as she'd said it, but there was no denying the truth. She'd tried it, and look at where it had gotten her.

He looked so wounded, but not enough to go down without a fight. "You skanky ass, ho," he said, maliciously. "I've been wasting my time, and giving you way too much credit."

Nora's hand came out of nowhere and landed hard against the side of his face. Cole clenched his jaw, and held his fists rigid at his side. "You can't handle what I've got, bitch!" she sneered. "So I found somebody who could, Cole. And he fucks my ass dizzy, just the way I like it." He turned and kept walking, grabbing his shirt on the way out of the bedroom.

Nora pushed him harder. "What? You can't take hearing it, Cole? Huh? I like it hard, and I like it deep and rough and that's how he gives it to me!"

"Fine!" he yelled over his shoulder. "Then you keep getting it from him like that, Nora, because I'm through!"

This time, he meant it. Nora knew deep down into the depths of her soul that he was leaving her for good this time, and suddenly, she had nothing left to lose.

"I don't have to lie and tell him it was good when it wasn't!" she berated him. "You think you get me off, Cole?" Nora picked up a framed picture of the two of them and threw it at his back. "Nobody gives it to me the way he does!" she cried bitterly. "Fuckin' you doesn't even come close, Cole! I'd be better off fucking a gotdamn corpse!"

Cole's worst nightmare came true in a flash, and before he could stop himself, his fist landed squarely against Nora's jaw, sending her airborne across the room, and landing unconscious into the wall. She slid down it like a limp doll, and if he hadn't killed her, Cole knew he'd come close.

He was taken away in handcuffs. Nora was loaded in an ambulance and taken to the hospital. True to the nature of superstardom, Cole was met at the precinct by the paparazzi, and Nora had her share at the hospital. Her jaw had been broken, and she had a concussion, but Nora would recover. Cole was charged with domestic violence, and released on bail. The World Boxing Federation held an investigation of its own and unanimously voted to strip him of his title.

Nora's and Cole's business was splattered all over the television, in newspapers, and in magazines. Taylor watched mesmerized as the media tore away at their lives like piranha with their bloated speculations and analyses, spewing their idiotic theories on how the pressures of stardom can drive even the best marriages to destruction.

Nora had been like a caged animal with Cole, pacing back and forth, seeking her freedom and escape. She never wanted to admit it, not even to herself, but Taylor had reached that conclusion a long time ago. Well, now she was free, and eventually, he knew that she'd find her way to him, and of course, he'd be waiting, to welcome her home.

THINKIN' BOUT YOU

Tonight was all about the rhythms and the blues, and Rayne had to feel sexy when she sang the blues. She wore her tightest jeans, her sexiest tank top, her highest heels. Her freshly washed and twisted locks hung long past bare shoulders. The blues was about being real, being natural, so she'd left the makeup on her vanity, except for her favorite Mac lip gloss that shimmered in the low light of the room.

She paid tribute to the greats tonight: Aretha, Betty Wright, Millie Jackson, Mavis Staples. Rayne was neck-deep into singing her sultry rendition of Bettye LaVette's version of "Thinkin' Bout You" when she spotted him, coming into the club and taking a seat in the back of the room.

I hope you can feel me too, baby . . .
So we can sleep with Orion in the middle of the winter

Rayne couldn't remember his name to save her life, but she realized when she saw him that she'd been anticipating him ever since he first introduced himself, and all because she had changed her mind and decided to look forward to life for a change, instead of being convicted by it.

"Why you so happy all of a sudden?" Bear had asked a few days ago, during rehearsal.

"Why you gotta say it like that?" She furrowed her brow.

"I'm just asking. In all the years we've been playing together, yo ass ain't never been on time to rehearsal, and now you ain't cussed nobody out, rolled yo eyes, yo neck, threw a temper tantrum—nothing. What's up?"

Leave it to Papa Bear to put things into perspective. "Damn. Have I really been that bad?"

In unison, the whole band responded, "Yeah."

Rayne couldn't pinpoint the moment her outlook changed. One morning she woke up, and noticed the sun shining, birds chirping, that she'd lost ten pounds and could finally fit into those two-hundred-dollar jeans she'd splurged on like a fool but refused to return even though they were too small.

Cash was gone. And when he died, so did her loathing for him. It took her going to hell and back to figure it out, though. Rayne had played the blame game for so long that she'd forgotten how to pick up and move on. She'd been stuck in a deathtrap of drugs, hopelessness, and love for a man who wasn't even capable of loving himself, let alone anyone else.

The thing was, she hadn't died. In fact, she was standing on this stage, singing some good music, looking fine, with another day ahead of her to do something new. It had taken her too damn long to start over, but now that she finally had, she figured she might just start with old boy sitting in the back of the room with the pretty eyes, bobbing his head to the rhythms of Rayne Fitzgerald.

He looked absolutely stunned when she weeded her way through the crowd to where he was sitting with his friends. One of them quickly pulled a chair over for her. "I was hoping to see you again." She turned on her Southern charm full force. Was it her imagination or was he blushing?

He ordered her a club soda and lime. "I told you, I don't miss a show if I can help it."

"Thank you," she said graciously.

Right at that moment, she thought of T. Diggs and of how broken up he'd be if he walked in and saw her sitting and grinning at any other man but him. Tauris meant the world to her, but it was time to move on to new things. And this seat right here, next to this handsome fool, was as good a place to start as any.

"I told you, Ms. Fitzgerald," he grinned. "I'm a huge fan."

Rayne smiled appreciatively, and winked. "So am I, sweetheart. So am I."

THAT FUNKY STUFF

Kristine had made a fool of herself with Rayne Fitzgerald. When it was all said and done, the woman probably thought she was a blithering idiot over Tauris. But the meeting hadn't been a total bust. Kristine had spent most of her life lurking in the shadows, keeping her true feelings pent up inside her, or expressing them in despicable ways like she'd done with Lamar.

Rayne obviously wasn't that kind of woman. She said what she felt and didn't bother apologizing for it. If she truly wanted to break free from her old ways, Kristine needed to work harder to fix what had been broken on the inside with the same conviction she'd put toward her outward appearance.

She spent days going over their conversation in her mind, meditating on the woman and the qualities about her that Kristine found mesmerizing. Despite whatever issues she might've had, Rayne radiated with the kind of confidence and self-assurance that Kristine had never been able to find inside herself. Rayne was the kind of woman who had no qualms with telling a man exactly what was on her mind, without worrying about hurting his feelings or scaring him off.

Kristine realized that she'd been tiptoeing around Tauris the same way she'd tiptoed around her father, and maybe even Lamar on some level, afraid to stir the pot, to cause too much of an uproar, and to accept that they knew best, and she'd do well to just be quiet. She'd grown tired of keeping quiet.

Tauris stared at her like she'd lost her mind. "I don't believe this shit! You telling me that Rayne came to my house and you never said nothing?" He was pissed. "You took her to the hospital, and you never told me, when you knew we were all worried about her?" Tauris paced back and forth in her living room, shaking his head. "Damn, Kristine! Why would you do some shit like that? Why didn't you tell me?"

She knew he'd be angry. But seeing him now, she was angry, too. "She's fine now, Tauris. I don't understand why you're so upset." Kristine struggled to maintain her composure.

"That's not the point! The point is, back then, you knew where she was. All you had to do was say something."

She studied him for more than just anger over her not telling him about Rayne. She studied him, listening for something in his tone, looking for an expression in his eyes that told her that Rayne was more to him than just a good friend.

He took a couple of deep breaths to help calm himself

down. "You saw her again?" He looked at her. "The two of you talked the other day."

"Yes," she said softly, averting her gaze.

"About what, Kristine?"

She couldn't bring herself to look at him. "We just talked, Tauris."

"About me," he concluded.

Kristine put away her embarrassment and looked him in the eyes. "Yes."

Tauris shook his head, and sighed. "What the hell is wrong with you," he asked, exasperated. "I told you Rayne and I ain't nothing but friends. I'm seeing you, baby. Either I'm here or you're at my spot every free minute of my time. I didn't sign up for this, Kris. This jealous thing is really starting to mess with me, girl."

"Like it's not messing with me?" she blurted out. Kristine couldn't believe the gall of this man to sit here and act like he was the victim in all of this.

"You're sneaking around behind my back—"

She stood up and walked over to him. "Yeah, and you're straddling the fuckin' fence, Tauris!" Kristine pointed her finger hard in his chest.

Tauris was caught off-guard by her cussing. Kristine never cussed and when she did, it just didn't sound right. "What fence? I'm not straddling anything."

"Liar! You've got one foot in my house and the other in hers. Maybe not physically," she rationalized, "but you still care about her, and as more than just a friend."

"I'm not the one who brings up Rayne in our conversations, Kris. You are."

"Because she's always between us, Tauris."

He started to say something, but she interrupted him. "It's as much what you don't say about her as what you do say," she argued. "Rayne is on the tip of your tongue. You just go out of your way not to spit it out when you're with me."

He couldn't argue.

"You think I don't know?" she asked softly. "You think I can't tell how much you care for her?" She waited for him to say something.

Eventually, he did. "I care about you," he confessed.

"Yeah, and that's as good as it gets, isn't it?" she said wearily. "You care about me, but you love her. Isn't that it, Tauris? And no matter what I do, I'm beginning to think that's as good as it's ever going to get."

They stared at each other in uncomfortable silence for several minutes. Kristine hadn't been set free so that she could find someone who "cared" for her. She'd been pent up her whole life in a prison with no bars that nearly smothered the life out of her and forced her to find solace in the most unsavory places. She deserved better than to just be "cared" for.

"I love you, Tauris," her voice trembled. "But—I think I deserve more than you."

Being free of her father's rule meant so much more than just being able to wear a pair of tight jeans and high-heeled shoes. It meant more than just selling his house and finding a new place to live that she could call her own. She had the whole world at her feet now, and enough money to see every inch of it if that's what she wanted. And maybe it was time for her to take off from the confines of Woodbridge, Virginia, and see what other possibilities lay waiting for her to discover.

She cried after he left. But even a broken heart was a new experience to be savored, and she said a silent prayer, thanking God for it.

PRIVATE PARTY

"I don't blame you for not wanting to see me." Rhonda stood nervously in the doorway, hoping Kristine would at least listen to what she had to say. She'd behaved so terribly before, and Rhonda couldn't live with herself if she couldn't at least apologize to Kristine in person, and make her understand that she didn't mean to blame her for her husband's transgressions.

"Pardon the mess," Kristine told her, stepping aside to let her in. "I'm packing."

Rhonda sat across from Kristine, who sat on the sofa, putting books into a box.

"Are you putting those in storage?" Rhonda asked, smiling.

"For now."

Rhonda had been rehearsing what she'd say to Kristine if she got the chance to, but at the moment, she'd forgotten almost every word of her speech. "I am so sorry for my actions, Kristine," Rhonda said sincerely, searching her memory for those things she needed to say that mattered most. "I was so angry," she tried to explain. "You were young, and I realize that every last one of us, including your father, Kristine, let you down. Lamar—no man should've been allowed to get the opportunity to take advantage of you like that. He was my husband, and if anyone saw it, it should've been me," she quivered. "In retrospect"—Rhonda's voice grew quiet—"and I hate that I can admit this, but there were signs, and . . . I excused them. I ignored them because I couldn't stand the thought that my suspicions could be right. There were times when I saw the way he looked at you, but I dismissed them, thinking I was being silly. There were other things, too—I was angry and I took that anger out on you because it was easier than punishing myself. I didn't know how to do that, Kris. And I wanted to. I wanted to take your suffering, sweetheart, and make it my own, but I couldn't do that and I behaved terribly." She looked nervously at Kristine. "I don't expect you to now, but one day, I hope you can forgive me."

"The police took Lamar away," Kristine finally told her, still busy packing. "He had a gun, and he was going to shoot himself."

"I know. Lamar is a sick man, Kristine."

There were things that Kristine needed to say to Rhonda, too. She thought for a moment, and then finally looked the woman in the eyes. "I'm sorry, too, for what happened, Rhonda. I had a part in it, just like Lamar."

"But you were young, Kristine."

"I'm not so young, Rhonda," Kristine said confidently. "You all have it in your minds that I'm a helpless little girl who can't fend for herself, but that's not true. What's really sad is that all of you had me almost believing it, too. I was old enough to know better with Lamar, Rhonda, and I hurt you and that's something I never meant to do. You've been like a mother to me, and I'll always love you for that, but none of us is the same anymore. I think Daddy took a piece of all of us with him when he died."

Regret washed over Rhonda. "It's a shame."

Kristine smiled. "No, it's not. Not to me. When they buried him, they buried that helpless little girl you all thought I was, right along with him, and I'm glad they did."

Rhonda tried to smile, too. "I see you sold the house."

Kristine sighed. "Finally."

"Where will you go?"

"I don't know," she shrugged. "I'll be staying in a hotel until I decide."

"Will you call me, once you get settled?" Rhonda asked, hopeful.

Kristine saw no reason to pacify this woman. Rhonda was nothing to her now. She wasn't her aunt, and she wasn't even her friend. "I don't know, Rhonda. Probably not."

Rhonda drove away, thinking that Kristine had the right idea. Lamar had always said that house was too big for just the two of them; well, it was certainly too big for just Rhonda. Grandchildren or no grandchildren, she liked the idea of having a smaller place, a new one where she could plant some new memories.

DOWN FOR THE COUNT

Cole pleaded guilty to the charges of assault and domestic violence against his wife. Nora had insisted on attending his sentencing. Accompanied by her private nurse, she sat in the courtroom, horrified as she heard the judge's sentence, despite the note given to him by her lawyer with her confession that Nora had hit Cole first, and that she'd provoked him.

"You are a professional boxer, Mr. Burkette," the judge spoke solemnly. "Despite your wife's confessions as to her role in all of this, for a man like you to use his fists against anyone outside of the ring is no different than a professional hit man shooting a passerby on the street. Your hands are weapons, sir, and because of that, I have no choice but to hand down a sentence of three years in a federal facility."

Nora sobbed out loud, despite the wires locking her jaw in place. Cole stood rigid, unemotional, fully accepting the consequences of his actions and ready to get down to the business of serving his time. He never even looked in her direction when they took him away. "I'm sorry, Cole," she shouted through clenched teeth. "I'm so sorry!"

• • •

Back home, Nora insisted that she be left alone. How many times had he warned her that she was playing a dangerous game? Cole loved her in a way that she didn't deserve to be loved, and because of her, he'd paid the ultimate price and lost absolutely everything he'd worked for all of his life. In her mind's eye, all she could see was that little boy, growing up in the streets of South Philly, working so hard not to end up in prison or dead. Cole fought his way out of that dismal future the only way he knew how, and the irony was almost too much for her to bear.

Days after his sentencing, Nora was served with divorce papers, and a letter from her husband.

I can do this time, standing on my head, but we both know, I shouldn't have to. In any event, I can't blame anyone but myself, Nora. My temper has always been my Achilles' heel, that one thing I was most afraid of in myself, and to control it, I overcompensated for it, limiting myself to taking out my frustrations in the ring instead of on anyone else. I made money being angry, and for the next few years, I've set my sights on getting out of the business of boxing and focusing my time and attention on something more positive. In a strange way, I believe that God is using this situation to make that happen for me, and while I'm here, I'm going to work hard to find the good in the bad.

Bishop once told me that to love a beautiful woman is a dangerous thing. "You can love her so much, that you miss seeing the truth about her, or you'll drive yourself crazy worrying over who else is surely loving her." That old man was right on both counts.

I am not, nor have I ever been the man you needed. I realize that now, and I know that if I'm ever to have any peace, I need to let go and move on. People are crazy when they think that love is enough. There's nothing further from the truth than that, and you and I are both witnesses to that end. I have loved you beyond what was right. And I may never stop loving you. But you bring out the worst in me, Nora. And I can't live like that.

Whatever it is you're looking for, I truly hope you never find it, because I'm afraid of what will happen to you if you do. You walk on the edge of disaster, and the next man to come into your life might be more willing to exploit that weakness in you, Nora, and hurt you in ways I always hoped I wouldn't. For the next three years, I'll have nothing better to do than

to exorcise my demons. I pray that you can exorcise yours, and one day find happiness.

Cole

The death of a marriage is like mourning the death of a
loved one. She was empty without Cole. Nora signed the
papers, and then put them on her desk for her assistant to
mail out the next day. A part of her wanted to respond to
his letter, but she knew she'd never hear from him again.
And there was nothing she could say anyway that would
make a difference. She'd done what no man in his last
thirty professional fights could do. She'd knocked out the
champ without even trying.

LIVING MY LIFE LIKE IT'S GOLDEN

"Would you look at what the cat dragged in," Rayne said sarcastically, sitting next to Tauris at the bar.

He laughed. "I tried to stay away, but you know that's damn near impossible."

"You still sweating me?" she asked teasingly.

"And what if I am?"

"What are you doing here, T. Diggs? For real?"

He had no idea. Tauris was on his way home, but decided that's not where he wanted to be. If he and Kristine were on speaking terms, he'd have no doubt ended up at her place. He landed here because he knew Rayne would be here, and hell, he just wanted to see her. It had been a while.

He turned to check her out. "You look good."

"So what else is new?"

"How've you been?"

"Oh, I've been cool. I'm flying out to L.A. next week to start working on my brand-new CD with my brand-new label," she bragged.

"Damn! Really?" He grinned.

"You are looking at the newest recording star at All Talk Records, son," she said proudly. "So, don't be surprised if you look up one day and see my ass at the MTV Music Awards sitting next to Beyoncé and Jay-Z in the front row!"

"Well, go on with your bad ass," he raised his fist for some dap. "Just don't forget the little people on your way up."

"Don't worry," she nudged her shoulder against his. "I'm always going to remember who my real friends are. Maybe when I get paid, I'll send for you and you can come out to Cali and we can get our party on." She snapped her fingers and bounced up and down in her seat.

"We can do that," Tauris nodded. "And maybe, you'll be ready to be my girlfriend when I get there."

She laughed. "You still on that? I thought you had a woman. Short and sweet and dripping all over your ass like honey. She tell you how she and I met?"

He grimaced. "Yeah. That's some bullshit."

Rayne shrugged. "Maybe, but I can't say I blame her for keeping it on the low."

"Yeah, whatever," he said dryly.

"Oh, so you're pissed at her now? Why? Because she's sneaking around her man trying to get the competition to back off?" she said sarcastically.

"Something like that."

"Speaking as a woman, T. Diggs, even though I'm not the same kind of woman that she is. I mean, she's a tad bit creepier than your girl, but, we still have that XX chromosome thing in common, and honestly, I ain't mad at her. She has it bad for you, and I could appreciate that. Love can make a woman do some crazy shit, and she was crazy enough to call me up, buy me a drink and ask me politely to back the hell up off of you so that she could have a clear shot to do right by you. Now, that's some deep shit."

"It was dumb."

"No, you're dumb. I don't know much about her overly possessive ass, but I know she seemed genuine about how she felt about you. And she wasn't bad on the eyes, either. Had nice tits. I'm not a man, but you can't help but to see them, and they weren't bad."

He looked at her like she was crazy.

Rayne shrugged. "Most women can appreciate a set of nice tits, especially when they're real. Trust me. I don't swing that way. You know better."

He sighed. "I do. And you're right. She's got some very nice tits," he admitted. "Yours ain't bad, either. A little on the small side, but you never heard me complaining."

Rayne laughed. "Gee, thanks."

"Too bad you weren't feeling me deep down in your heart, though."

"I cared more than I let on," she said tenderly.

"Yeah, right."

"For real," she exclaimed. "I cared more about you than I knew what to do with, cowboy."

He cringed when she called him that.

"But you never loved me."

"Maybe not like she does."

He thought for a moment. "Yeah, she digs a brotha."

"Besides, it was never you I couldn't love, T. Diggs. It was me. Honestly, if we'd met up some other time, who knows. We might've ended up walking down the aisle together, living in a house out in McLean or Silver Spring or something, raising kids. Who knows?" Rayne took his hand in hers. "Look, all I'm saying is, don't treat her the way I treated you, because I promise you, you'll end up regretting it."

"Hey, baby." Franklin walked up beside her and kissed her cheek. "You ready?"

Rayne smiled at the man, and then turned to Tauris. "Tauris. This is Franklin. Frank, this is T. Diggs. An old friend of mine."

Franklin extended his hand for Tauris to shake, which he did reluctantly.

"Frank's taking me to a showing at his gallery. Some new artist from Sierra Leone," she said excitedly. "You know me," she beamed. "I love me some art."

"Wonderful," Tauris replied dryly.

"Can you please give me a minute, Frank?" she asked sweetly.

Frank left the two of them alone.

"I see it didn't take you nearly as long to pick up the pieces this time," he said bitterly.

"Because I've learned my lesson." She rested her hand on his arm. "Life moves too fast for you to hang on to the past too long. I wasted a lot of time, and missed out on some opportunities that might've made me a happier woman, T. Diggs. But I figured it out." She smiled, and kissed his cheek. "I hope you do, too.

Rayne turned to leave. "You think about what I said, Tauris. Don't make the same mistake I did. I think she deserves better than that. Do the right thing, or leave it alone. You hear me?"

Rayne left him sitting there alone. And somewhere out there, Kristine was sitting alone just like him.

THE TROUBLE I'VE SEEN

He didn't even look like her husband. Lamar had asked to see her after they released him from the hospital from his suicide attempt. After thirty years of marriage, she felt that she could at least give him a few minutes of her time. He'd lost weight. Lamar, a man who once prided himself on his appearance, showed up at the front door wearing faded jeans, a T-shirt, and sneakers. His once neatly trimmed hair and beard had grown out and the gray grew rampant, making him look so much older than he used to.

"Thank you for seeing me, Rhonda," he said hoarsely, as she let him in.

The two of them were like strangers now, awkward with each other, and uncomfortable. Lamar scanned the formal living room, amazed by how white it was. He'd insisted on it being that way, despite Rhonda's protests about having kids and how the dirt would show up. But he never allowed the children in this room when they were younger. This was a meeting place, a place for grown people to congregate and socialize. Kristine had been allowed in here, though. Not often, and only when the two of them were alone. Making her feel special had always been his driving force. He'd had to come to terms with that and it wasn't easy.

"How are you feeling?" Rhonda asked politely.

Half moons hung under his eyes, and the pride, and even arrogance that had once been Lamar, were both gone.

"I have been—thinking," he spoke slowly, carefully.

"Where are you staying?"

"I've got a room," was his only response.

The two of them sat in the quiet, reflective space of time, waiting for the conversation to develop at its own pace.

"Your lawyer has been calling," she told him. "He believes he has someone who is interested in buying the business."

Lamar nodded approvingly. "Good. Good. Then, he'll have to get in contact with Kristine and her lawyer to discuss her options for her half of F and B." An anxious, desperate look flashed in his eyes when he mentioned her name, but he blinked it away just as quickly.

"I think we should talk about our divorce, Lamar," Rhonda said calmly. "I don't want to drag it out any longer than necessary."

"I agree," he said, clearing his throat. "Just let me know what you want, and— I'm not going to hurt you any more than I already have, Rhonda."

The whole time he'd been sitting in the room, Lamar hadn't looked at her. He sat across the room, leaning away from her, his gaze fixed on a porcelain figurine of a married couple, embracing. They'd gotten it as a gift one year from Bishop.

"What are you going to do, Lamar?" Rhonda asked, genuinely concerned. Lamar looked so lost and so far gone, she worried if he'd ever get back to being the man he once was. Somehow, she didn't think that was possible.

He shrugged. "I'm not sure," he said, matter-of-factly. For the first time since he'd arrived, he faced her and forced a smile. "I'm not the man I used to be, but then . . . maybe that's a good thing."

"Maybe with your doctor's help— I'm sure things will get better for you in time," she did her best to reassure him. No one was more surprised than she was by her sympathy for this man. Rhonda couldn't help herself. He looked like he needed encouragement.

"I took advantage of that girl, Rhonda," he admittedly quietly. He couldn't stop the anger and repulsion surging through him, and that's what he struggled with most of all. "I'm sorry. But it's something I have to face and admit, especially to myself."

"Why her?" she asked. "Why, Lamar? Help me to understand this! Please!"

"I can't tell you! How can I tell you when I don't even know myself?" He stood up and paced the living room like an animal in a cage. He gathered his memories and tried to put them in place so that he could try and make sense of his behavior. "Kristine was so quiet," he went on to explain.

"She was a lonely girl, afraid of disappointing Bishop, and she needed—me," he nearly choked on the word. "She needed someone to hold her, and to tell her that everything was going to be fine."

"She had her father!"

"Her father was as dead on the inside as one of those corpses in the funeral home, Rhonda! When he looked at that girl, all he saw was his dead wife and what he'd lost."

"So you let that be your excuse for seducing her?" Her face twisted in confusion.

"I loved her!" He pounded on his chest. "I never touched her the way you might think. I held her, kissed her, rocked her."

"You seduced her, Lamar." Rhonda bolted to her feet. "She was a child and you seduced her like she was a grown woman!"

"I never meant to," he said meekly.

"You crossed the line with her, and by the time she was a teenager, that girl was so confused she didn't know whether she was coming or going!"

"Yes," he admitted. Lamar collapsed back down in the chair he'd been sitting in, exhausted and overwhelmed by the truth of what he'd done to her.

"How long did the relationship between the two of you go on?" Rhonda's voice trembled. "I need to know."

He stifled a sob, and Lamar shrank shamefully right before her eyes. "For years, Rhonda, until around the time she started seeing someone else."

Rhonda's knees buckled, forcing her to find a safe place on the sofa. "That long?" she whispered in dismay. "Oh my God!" she gasped. "Lamar."

"Until he came along, she hadn't been with anybody else but me."

Rhonda was numb. "You bastard."

He nodded. "That's what I am, Rhonda. That's exactly what I am."

Coming face to face with the reality of what he'd done had been almost too much for Lamar. Confessing his sins was cleansing in some ways, but in others, it just brought all of his dirt to the surface, leaving him no choice but to swim in it. He had taken that young girl's innocence and, through the years, molded it to fit him perfectly. Was it any wonder that she was so willing to make love to him when she was old enough to be curious about it? He thought back to that day, when she was sixteen and ready.

"I will never be able to forgive myself for what I've done to her," he admitted to Rhonda before he left. "And I'll never trust myself around her again."

"That's fine, Lamar," she said, unemotionally. "Because I'll never forgive you or trust you, either."

WHEN THE SMOKE CLEARS

He pulled up in front of her house, just as she was leaving. Kristine had booked a room in a hotel in DC. The movers had spent all day putting most of the things in storage. All she had with her were a few pieces of luggage.

He leaned to kiss her and then picked up her bags. "So, the way I see it, you can sleep on the left side of the bed, and I'll take the right. Since you're the female, I'll go ahead and do the chivalrous thing and use the spare bathroom. That way I don't have to deal with bumping into stockings, and panties, and bras hanging up all over the shower rod and shit."

"What do you think you're doing?" she asked, perplexed.

He dropped the bags and stared at her indignantly. "I'm getting my woman. What the hell do you think I'm doing?"

Kristine propped her hand on her hip. "Your woman? Since when?"

He sighed, stepped closer to her, and put his arms around her waist. "Since I came to my senses and realized that you are a dream come true, baby girl. And if I mess this up, then I need my ass kicked."

"Rayne didn't want you?" she dared to ask.

"See, why you gotta go there?"

"Is that what happened?"

"No," he confessed. "She didn't. And that's cool, because she made me take a long hard look at myself and you."

"Me?"

"She thinks you're kind of out there."

"I am not!"

"You're just sweet, baby. And Rayne don't know nothing about that."

"So you want me because you're on the rebound? That's not good, Tauris."

"I want you because I love you, Kristine," he said, gazing into her beautiful green eyes. "I love you and I want you and if you don't take me back, I'm probably going to do something drastic."

"Like what?"

"Hell, I don't know. Um . . . I'll get down on my knees." Tauris got down on his knees. "I'll beg you to take me back, and to be mine, and to give me a second chance to be the man I know I can be for you. I'll cry, baby. You want me to cry?"

She couldn't help but to laugh. "No, Tauris."

"Look, we can do this. We can make it work. I want to make it work."

"I've already got a room booked. And I've got a trip

planned to Bermuda. I'm not sure I want to be with you anymore, Tauris," she had tears in her eyes, but she meant it. She meant every word. "I mean, maybe I'm the one who deserves better. Maybe I can do better than you. Maybe, I just want to jet-set and to date and sow my oats for a change."

"Aw, girl. Nobody knows better than me that you deserve so much more than you've gotten from me. But nobody knows better than me that I want to be the one to give it to you."

"I have a lot to think about."

He stood up, held her face in his hands, and kissed her softly. "You going to think in Bermuda?"

She nodded. "I guess."

"Then, maybe I can come with you and we can think together."

She laughed. "Oh really? How am I supposed to think about whether or not I want to be with you if you're there with me?"

"I swear I'll help you to make up your mind."

"You will, huh?"

"By the time we leave Bermuda, you'll know good and damn well how much you mean to me. Won't be a doubt in your mind, Kristine. Won't be a doubt in mine, either."